# BLUNT FORCE KINDNESS

## CLAYTON LINDEMUTH

BLUNT FORCE KINDNESS
Clayton Lindemuth
Hardgrave Enterprises LLC
SAINT CHARLES, MISSOURI

BLUNT FORCE KINDNESS/Clayton Lindemuth

**ISBN:** 979-8630985194

# WE 'PRECIATE YA:

**Gail Lambert:** *Your editing and insight made this a much better book. Thank you for your dedication!*

**Kathryn Pynch:** *Your work and vision made Red Meat Lit Street Team happen. I appreciate you.*

**Dubhghlas Kraus, Sam Donoho, Ruth Gordon:** *I (we) couldn't keep up without your help! Thank you!*

**Victor Shultz:** *Your ideas for Stinky Joe and Chicago Mags made this book better and helped me flesh out the next... Thanks!*

*Dedicated to Joel Montgomery*

THE KINGDOM OF HEAVEN SUFFERS VIOLENCE, AND VIOLENT MEN TAKE IT BY FORCE.

MATTHEW 11:12

# CHAPTER ONE

HEARTBURN LIKE I ATE SIX CABBAGE HEARTS.

Fast rolling chunks of late-spring, black blizzard sky above. Glenwood Springs ahead. We grab a few hundred mile every couple day.

Two hour back some teenybopper dipshit hit the brakes in a Corolla and me sliding at him on ice, I jam the tranny in reverse and gun it. Tranny call bullshit. She start slipping in the lower three. Fourth is okay and fifth just fine. Like a fool I race the storm up the mountain. Pissed in a big mouth Mountain Dew and Tat did too. Last twenty mile I can't hardly enjoy the scenery for all the transmission stink.

Exactly when's a man get a say about who he carry on his back? Last six months I got twelve hours peace... the day I left Tat in the mountain lair. But she track me down with Cinder, gimme a Jeep, stuck chains on my feet and wrist. Now I got to break free.

My mind is torment.

They's north of a hundred million places to camp 'tween Flag and Denver. Had it in my mind I'd see the city so I can say I saw it then pass through and see something else.

All my life I said to myself when I got west I'd be there. Things'd be better. But dropping the old me in the new there didn't change shit for nobody—not when I took all the people I wanted to ditch. Including me. Top of that, people out west deceive as much as folk back east, but under the big sky it feel wronger. They got less excuse.

Nobody need to lie and cheat—only thing I can think is they keep they skills honed in case they ever move back east.

Most times Tat and Corazon talk in Spanish and I don't pretend to listen. It's when they yammer in English that aggravates. After I learned Mae was my daughter, part of me felt robbed I wasn't the one to raise her. Listening to Tat and Corazon, I'm glad.

I had a girl—and knew it early enough to have a hand in raising her—I wouldn't let her disappear the way Corazon do. She keep her nose in a cell phone most time, always poking 'round the world. Moab, Utah. I fill the tank with gas and she say she be a while in the bathroom. Not feeling good. Maybe I might should park in the shade and get some rest. See her trade a look with Tat and she go in the truck stop and back the hallway. She don't walk like a girl got a belly in phase with the moon. Tat get out the Jeep and walk the paved lot, must be a quarter mile to a lap. I tilt the seat and shut the eyes. After a good snooze the sun's low and prying the lids like a crow bar got leverage, and must be a half mile off Corazon run on the sidewalk headed for the Jeep. By now Tat's inside dozing too and I nudge her elbow. She perk up and look. Not a word. Corazon dodge behind a building and take an alley to the truck stop, see her through the glass at the corner. Next thing she come out the glass doors with her hands on her belly. Walking like her monthly hit her in the guts with a railroad tie.

Accourse I feel the juice. See the red. She got it in her eyes...

And some on her shirt, by the neck. More blood on her sleeve.

Corazon don't carry a gun. She prefer a blade.


Since we pass Grand Junction and start the hill up Glenwood Springs, I been gawking at the mountains and rocks, the river beside the interstate, railroad tracks weaving in and out... They call me to see how I measure up nekkid, my wits and grits against the rocky unknown.

In such a situation, as a man imagines the comfort of solitude and the crackle of his fire, his vision rarely includes two female teenage chatter boxes. 'Less it's time to slip in the sleeping bag and beat down an insurrection.

So I keep the gaze out the window. Green nubs peer out the branches like the whole land want to shiver off winter and stretch out under the sun. As flurries start to stick.

Corazon switch from English to Spanish but she forget her sullen look says words too. She's too young for sex but those men in Salt Lake took it anyhow; now she needs time to find her stance on things. She has plenty right to the nonsense in her head. I'll abide her. She can lay it down when she choose.

Any luck, I won't be there.

Trees flash by close but out a ways the eyes can grab aholt. Wind's picked up. Weather's called for storm the last fifteen hours since we broke camp in Utah. If we's about to get buried in snow I'd like supplies and a evergreen grove for cover. Figured once we hit Glenwood, I'd grab some staples and disappear on a hundred mile forest road. Stop when the tread won't grab. Sit out the storm joyful and lazy, since I got nowhere to go and nobody jabbing me with a stick.

I see them trees a-swaying in the breeze. I see the river burble and splash. They's fish. Elk and deer. All the world to disappear, and for a man knows how to still corn into cash, they's fields of gold right across the mountain.

Sometimes as the girls talk or even when they don't I drift. Hear the tinkle of a still as the fire catch hold. You don't ever hear it next the boiler, but fifteen feet off with the three-eights copper to ear, they's a quiet hiss while steam split into cool air and shine. Tat and Corazon get to running they voice boxes and I'm off someplace in the mountains, maybe looking from one peak to the next, lawless because the land don't give a shit about man's laws, and if a man succumb to nature, freedom dreams easy.

Nobody talks man's law but man.

Glenwood Springs sign on the right, fifteen mile ahead.

Snow stick to the sign.

Transmission stink and grind. Miles roll under. Tat's been looking at me three miles. Stinky Joe or Corazon, one farts in the back seat. No one says nothing. Tension is strong when a fart don't break it.

"We should steal a new car and keep going," Tat say.

"Ahead is Vail Pass. It's forty mile tall. Storm catches us there we'll never dig out. Nah. We grab a spot by the river and wait it out."

I get a strong whiff of burnt transmission fluid. Engine race while the speed fall. She about to give out. A couple mile from Glenwood I swing right. Road 134 got an exit.

Look in the rearview. Got a Ford truck right up on the bumper. I stop at the stop and cut right. Tach says five thousand RPM and we got maybe five mile an hour for the trouble. Smoke heavy enough to spread on toast. Tat check her mirror and punch the four-way flasher. Look back like she expect the truck'll pass. Don't know how she knew the blinker button.

Truck pull around.

I let out the clutch and shift up through 'til third grab enough to move us from the stop sign. Road 134 go under the highway then swings left and follow the river.

I lift off the gas. Jeep's done. Time to wipe her down and walk.

We drift 'til unpacked snow stop us under the bridge. Tat open the door and bang metal on concrete. She look out the window and back to me like I sweet talked the transmission into giving out where the concrete block her in.

Maybe Tat and Corazon ready to find a sunrise on they own.

"You gotta get out my side."

Engine's running and even in neutral the tranny grinds and pops. I kill the motor and pop my door. Smoke spill up from the ground. We under the bridge looking out on snowfall. Wipers flap but the glass is dry. Tiny sounds seem big.

We got a mess of junk in the back, tent, stove and the survival basics. Could use a month's supply of foodstuffs but without, we'll survive on game.

I'd a liked to get this vehicle hid but we got no choice.

"Tat, you girls get everything out the back and I'll wipe it down inside. We leave it here."

Stinky Joe perk up in the seat. Corazon point ahead.

"Look."

I twist back forward. The Ford that was on us and passed got reverse lights on, coming back.

Two inside. Driver got short hair.

"Shit. I forget my name."

"Alden," Tat say. "Alden Boone."

"Yeah. Alden Boone."

I reach under the seat and grab an FBI Glock. Don't care for the boxy feel but it shoots bullets and that's fine as water. Got one in the tube so I rest it on my leg with the barrel at the door. The man step out his truck while exhaust tumble out the muffler. Passenger look through the back window.

Man got Hitler hair and walks like his knees recall a horse. Eyebrows say lawman. Face is gray like his eyes, and for all his rigid stance he's got the backwards glow of a sick man—that look that goes in a happy room and all the smiles sizzle like water scorched off a skillet, and they's nothing left but dead conversation with a dead man. He walk like he see the end, but as he ain't ready to go, he keep his right hand perched a little high and his eyeballs steady on me.

"Alden fuckin' Boone," says I. "Alden. Ald'n." Name finally sits.

Stinky Joe growl.

"Me too, puppydog."

Gray man stand outside my window. Look back where traffic would come from. My guess—this road see maybe two car a week.

I roll down the glass.

"From that smoke I'd say you got trouble."

"Transmission."

He keep the demeanor level while his eyes jiggle here and there, checking out inside. Checking out everything. Cop for sure.

"Grand Junction's already half buried in snow." Man stare over the top of the Jeep like he can see it. "I have a feeling if we call a tow truck you'll still be here waiting when this weather system moves in for real."

"That what you call a storm? Weather system?"

He hold my look.

"I got supplies, Officer. Figger we'll wait out the storm other side the river there. Make the best of it."

He smile. Nod slow. Stoop for a better gander at Tat.

"Got your daughter along. Daughters."

"And Stinky Joe."

"Saw your plates. Coming from Arizona?"

"That's right."

"Where you headed?"

"Uphill." Smile. A thought I never fully cognized boils up. All these lawmen see the same liars and cheats everywhere. I see the red eyes and electric—cops gotta deal with the same, blind. So they always watch for the cheap shot.

"Camping. Taking in the sights. You know. Figger we'll find a spot in the woods here where it's low, then after the storm, cross Vail and maybe re-stock the kitchen in Denver. So I can say I bought groceries in Denver, is all."

He wince. "Will the transmission engage? Will the Jeep move?"

"I got the winch, but the gas mileage ain't so good."

He look ahead. A truck roars on the bridge above and the man's eyes fade like the heavy thinking don't leave much of his resources to do the standing with a heartbeat. Snow blast sideways but the air go calm in a second and the snow all come down straight again, heavier 'n before.

"You can't leave the Jeep here as a road hazard. I can tow you from under the bridge, but you can't park up there either, or at the boat launch. This road's so narrow we'll be a half mile before we find a place to pull over, and that'll be my driveway."

"You want me to park in your driveway."

"If you were planning on camping, you may as well sit the storm out at my place. I have a wife and kids so there's no room in the house. We'll have you to dinner, of course, and you can set up camp in the garage. It's heated and you'll have a bathroom. We'll get you towed into town when the storm breaks."

"I appreciate you—I do. But I'll go my own way."

"Listen." He lean. Look to the back seat. "I have no doubt you can handle anything this storm throws at you. But I bet your girls would rather be warm."

He use that cop voice, says, do as I fuckin' say.

I look at Tat. She hold her gaze steady into the falling snow. I bet a nickel she got her right hand on a Sig Sauer. Glance in the rearview. Corazon got her eyes down, most likely staring at the cell phone. Miracle of copper and transistors. Tubes and whatnot.

When we was on the highway traffic kept the snow blowed off, but here where the cars is less common they's two three inch already. I don't want this man's hospitality but the situation has its own truth and this lawman see it. Broke down Jeep. Avalanche on the way. Two girls with black hair and eyes and tight lips. What alarm bells he hear when I say no thanks? The girls is tough as nails but he don't know it. He'll ask questions. Then I'll kill him. It's best I do as he says, so maybe I don't got to.

"What's your name?"

"Jubal White."

"That's a damn happy name. Damn happy."

He look.

I keep his stare. "A day or two and we move on."

He nod.

No sparks. No red.

"Okay. Me and my girls appreciate the help."

He relax and let his right arm fall straight at his side. Says, "What's your name?"

"Alden Boone."

He keep his mouth flat but I get a spark. He ain't meant for playing cards.

"I'll be back, Alden Boone. Welcome to Colorado."

Jubal White tromp to his truck.

"There's someone with him," Tat say.

"A peedo," Corazon say.

"How you know?" says I.

She hold up the phone. "There's a website for sex criminals."

"Hunh?"

"So people know their neighbors." She press a button. Wait. Hold up the phone. "See this map? There's only two houses on this road. The next one is a peedo."

"What's his name?" Tat say.

"Dwain White."

"This man said his name is Jubal."

"He looks like a pervert," Tat say.

"A half dead cop *pre*-vert."

"Website says stat-chu-tory rape and probation. What's stat—"

"He poke a kid. She was willing but under age."

Corazon look out the window. Close the phone and slip it in her pocket.

"Stay here."

I get out and behind the door, tuck the Glock in my back so if it misfire I got a backup asshole.

Stinky Joe jump to the center and tumble in the driver seat. He leap out, study the plainclothes cop and trot the other way. Lift his leg at the first concrete bridge support. Share his thoughts.

Joe spent a week eating nonstop cheeseburgers—offered up in guilt and love—and after two week look alive and healthy agin. Though he don't talk as much as before and he won't lick my nose 'less I lick his first.

Done squirting, he lope to the cop messing around in the back seat of his crew cab truck. Sniffs legs and hurry 'round front, then down over the bank to the Colorado River. Tat lean forward in her seat with eyes that don't trust.

I close the Jeep door and Jubal enter his truck cab. Sky's already black enough the taillights brighten the snow. He drive in reverse and halt ten feet from the Jeep. I join him at the grill and he tethers Jeep to Ford with a olive drab green nylon strap.

"We got a half mile. I'll tow you close as I can get to the garage."

I climb back inside the Jeep and Jubal resume his truck.

Tat touch my shoulder. "We should drive away." Her hand flutter off like a bird.

"We should," says I.

"Stinky Joe," Corazon say.

"He can run. Do him good." I latch the door. Drop the window and stick my head out. "C'mon, Stinkydog."

Jubal open his door and look back. I wave. He ease forward. Nylon go taut and the Jeep roll from under the bridge. Turn left, pass a parking area by the river then he drive a half mile with the river on the right and Interstate 70 on the left. What vegetation I saw on the way up disappears and they's scant pine here nor there, and where the angles is too sharp for snow, they's red dirt and yellow tufts of grass. The road drifts right, cross a small bridge and now the railroad, highway and river is behind us. Red and white hills grow taller and closer but never get us fully swallowed. They's always a little sky.

We follow the Ford. Past the bend they's a lonesome tree bright with last fall's red and orange. Right next is another with green buds poking out.

This lawman's half mile is likely more ambitious than Stinky Joe's. I lower the window and encourage him. "C'mon, Stinkydog."

"I found a news story," Corazon say. "Dwain White was arrested for rape, but the charges were reduced to statutory rape because the girl was fourteen."

"How old he?"

"Twenty."

"Sound like more rape, not less."

"The story says he was represented by a lawyer from Denver."

"Bigshot."

"His father is a cop and the judge is corrupt."

"A news story say that?"

"A blog."

"A what?"

"Website."

"Who?"

"I don't know. The Internet."

"Ah. Maybe find a newspaper."

Steep slope on the left; to the right the land hits bottom and curve back up. On both sides and ahead the road look like a paved path through a labyrinth. Curves thisaway and that 'til I wonder what they had in mind. Road go nowhere. After a minute I spot the house.

Got yellow siding hung vertical with the wavy bottoms. Somebody thought that was a good idea. Off'n the right they's a garage same size as the house. Bay doors on the left, middle and right.

Jubal cut a wide circle and the Jeep point half back at the entrance. The Ford's brake lights flash.

A figure move behind a curtain in the house.

Garage door motors up.

Jubal step out his truck and I pop the door. Stinky Joe nose it open. Eyeballs me. Got no words for what I done. I scruff his head and climb out. Stoop to kiss and he bolts.

That's *fucking prick*, in dog speak.

I join Jubal at the grill.

Passenger from the Ford truck unlatch the door and stand beside it. Look thataway and this. Keep his face low where his hair can hide it. Thirty seconds he can't stand it no more. Comes back to stand next his old man and allow himself a long, steady look inside the Jeep... at Tat.

# CHAPTER TWO

BAER CREIGHTON SAT ON A NATURAL ROCK BENCH IN A NORTH Carolina cave, gagging, coughing, spitting, hacking.

"Vu like zis," the old man said.

"Holy *fuck*."

The old man snorted. "Try zis one."

Sitting in a tangle of half rotted blankets with a mixed breed dog at his side, he selected a Mason jar with no particular label but the pattern of rust on the lid. His veiny hands strained and the seal broke. The old man rested the ring and seal to the left of another, upside down. Each arm in motion, he took the jar from Baer's left hand while placing the new in his right.

"Tell me ze difference."

Creighton shook his head. Blinked three times. Inhaled and set his frame. Dry swallowed. Looked out the cave mouth to darkening forest. It was evening and he needed to find a new place to camp—now that he would live.

So what the hell was he doing drinking poison with a hundred year old German caveman?

Baer placed the glass rim to his lower lip and tipped until the fluid blazed a path to his stomach. He coughed and cool liquid splashed on his fingers. His throat was numb. As the second pull floated on the first, he closed his eyes. After a wave of distress, his soul lifted.

Mouth and throat seduced, Baer gulped. He brought down the jar and stared at the old man.

"What's that dog's name?"

"Rommel."

"Yours?"

"Günter."

"Baer."

Günter lifted his brow and nodded. "Good name. Your eyes, zey look better."

Baer looked away and then met the man's gaze.

Günter nodded at the jar. "What is ze difference?"

"Blueberry."

Günter grinned. "You drank two dollars."

"That pull was two bucks?"

Baer's mind swam. He wanted to laugh at the absurdity of a two dollar swallow of moonshine when the same currency could fill a five gallon gas can, but the old man's lever action Winchester leaned on the cave wall next to his squirrel gun, and somehow, after selling life insurance and turning wrenches on diesel truck engines, Baer's business sense told him this environment might be less forgiving than others he had seen.

Illuminated by a lantern and a few stray rays of evening sun from outside, Günter's eyes were white and clean and inside a cave, like any enclosure, if there was juice to be felt Baer would feel it strong.

The old man didn't lie. He wanted two dollars.

## CHAPTER THREE

HOUSE LOOK LIKE IT WAS MADE OUT FORTY DOLLARS' WORTH YELLOW paint.

Jubal lead inside the garage. First thing I spot gaskets, wrenches, belts on the walls and insulation about the garage door. Got four heat radiators suspended from the ceiling. Painted cement. Painted drywall. They's a red racing stripe four feet high, all the way around. Shiny tools bought new and polished after use. Two bays got cars and the third is empty.

That skinny boy of his—like to hide behind his hair—he empty the Jeep. He put the tent, three backpacks, a five gallon water jug and a hatchet just inside the garage door.

Tat watch. Glance at me and I don't know where the juice come from but the forearms tingle.

She seen a good sample of the world's evil. Stabbed men to death. Shot a dozen in the heart or head. This Longhair boy—only reason a twenty year old poke a fourteen is he's a pussy. Weak. Can't get a girl his own age and pees his sheets every night knowing he don't measure up to the world.

If I could catch Tat's eye we'd share a squint and roll—but she don't peel her look off him.

Jubal knock snow off his boots and step inside the garage. Under the fluorescents, his face got the pearly gray of polished cement. His stance is more shallow 'n when he walk back from the truck to offer help, when he was maybe puffing up for a fight.

"You can set up camp here," he say. "Grab some of that cardboard folded under the work bench so your sleeping bags aren't on the cement."

He eyeballs me studying a red car on jack stands.

"That's a '72 model," says he.

"It ain't a Nova."

"Mustang."

"Told ya."

He stand beside the hood and his face fall a little, like he wistful on a girl from forty year back. "Mach One," Jubal say. "All my life I wanted a '72 Mustang. Some guys swear by the '69, but the lines on the fastback always gave me shivers."

"Yeah, see. You talk a language I quit. All I see is bloodied up knuckles."

"It was supposed to be a project with my sons. Was gonna do a factory restore. Every last nut and bolt, straight up stock."

"You didn't finish. Waiting on tires."

He give a head shake with a quick frown. Car make the man susceptible.

"I found this one in Florida. I bought it off a little old lady, you know, like the song."

"Pasadena, Florida."

"Right. I didn't want to have to do a lot of body work, you know? All that dust is no good for the lungs. Then I get the car hauled back here and give it a good study and look at that quarter panel, up underneath. It's all chicken wire and putty."

I gape about the garage. Gotta be something else he want to talk about. If we was next my campfire I'd tell him silence is a virtue. But I can't muster the gumption—not in his garage with the storm outside, and his old lady cooking my supper.

I stoop and feel up under like he says. "All that rust wouldn't bother me. Like wrinkles on a pretty girl. You don't put her in a show but she's plenty fun to drive."

He nod like he don't hear, smile when he do. He look at Tat and Tat look at me.

"Anyhow, it didn't matter in the end," Jubal say. "Got the car and, you know."

"I know what?"

"Life."

"It's persnickety."

Jubal's low key and tired like a fella I knew after twenty years of the Lyme disease. "I called you a cop back there and you never fessed up."

"Where'd that come from?"

"You walk tight and hold your right hand a little high."

He look away. Back to my eyes. No red, no juice. He say, "How's that?"

"Coming back to the Jeep, when you pulled over to give us help. You was ready to pull a pistol."

He lift his coat, show leather. "I was."

"Thought so. Still on the force? State or local?"

He gives me a long study. "I'm on leave."

Red.

Shoulda kept my mouth shut—knew he was a cop without his say so. Me wanted in fifty states, every man or woman's a lawman whether they think it or not. Hint of trouble, folk'll snitch. They was no need to get this man's noodle curious—but now he got mine keen. Cop on leave? What'd he do?

"Guess I better mind my P's and Q's." Smile. Fake but he don't see it. "So a cop turns wrenches? How that happen?"

He shift on his feet like to start a waltz.

"Funny thing about being law enforcement," Jubal say. "You never take a day for granted. Even someplace as easy going as Glenwood Springs, with the highway going right through her belly, you never know what kind of people are driving through. Or what they're hauling."

"Heard it all my life."

He cock his head. "What?"

"They's no crooks here. Just the bad folk driving through." Grin big. "Giving you shit, is all."

"No, crooks are here too. They don't come from nowhere. They just stand up someday and chuck a mask at you. Anyhow I spent years nursing this idea that if I lived to retirement, I'd restore a seventy two fastback."

"You retire yet?"

"More or less."

He offer that same lie-smile. Tinge of electric. He ain't straight-up lying but he ain't shooting straight, like he don't even know his own truth.

Snow swirl into the open bay. Light outside drop two shades the last five minute. Can't see the sky for the mountain but I bet she's black. Conversation waste time good as anything else.

We'll settle here 'til the storm front dumps all the snow it cares, then if I'm not in jail somewhere 'cause this not-retired cop didn't figure me out, maybe I'll tell Tat and Corazon it's time we let our fates get on with what they had in mind, afore I stuck my nose in Tat's affairs. And saved her life.

Stinky Joe sniff a tuft of grass at the edge of the lot. Mark it yellow.

They ain't enough trees to fill a proper nightmare with bodies but what I did is all the time on my mind. All the men. They ain't even rotted to bone yet. Still got the meat. Still got they death faces. Some with black sockets 'cause the eyes is rotted. Eyes rot fast. I shut my lids and see 'em stiff-limbed like they was pinned ten feet high on the tree with a spike through the neck. Legs straight, arms straight. Faces twisted like they saw something give 'em pause at the end. They's one in this tree and two in that. Up high, down low. Look off through the dream woods and they's more bodies than trees, more arms and legs than leaves and limbs.

The men I sent forward.

Then at once those eye sockets glow red. Whole hundred and ten of 'em, or whatever I done plus the men I kill next. Hot spots all about the wood, in pairs and red enough to know in a just world someone else would've killed 'em first.

Or maybe that red says in a world with forgiveness, they'd still be out there telling lies.

When it was me and Fred cooking mash, we'd eat, shit and talk and that's all it was supposed to be about. I had a good woman—close enough for dreams, far enough I didn't see her. After twenty-what years, I knew what I knew. It was all good exercise. Convenient. Women is rotten as men and it was good I had one set aside I could pretend was different. Then all that evil come for me. I knew it was out there and I hunkered under a tarp in the woods so maybe it'd pass me by. I'd imagine my dream woman was pure as pink pussy and snuggle low but the spirit come across the woods and draw me out to do my evil and I never fought like I should.

"You said they's a toilet in here?"

"Back against the far wall. See that corner?"

"Uh-huh."

"Good?"

"Yep."

"So you all can get situated and let's see, quarter of four, let's say give it an hour and come to the house for dinner."

"Appreciate the hospitality."

Jubal close the garage door with a button on the wall and leave through a door on the house-side.

"You need any help or anything? Like with your tent?"

I spin.

Longhair's by the compressor with Tat.

Tat shake her head. Won't meet his eye. First I thought her look was contempt but her eyes dart quick and her lips seem ready to pull into a smile if he could only get a straight look from her.

Corazon walk to the bathroom in back and the boy finger combs a foot of sandy tangles from his eye. These two is having a moment like I ain't here. They's both shy and queer for it. It's what I knew before Tat rode me. I had no business with a girl her age. Truth is, these two is magnets and all they want is an excuse to strip away the world. Get to the point of living: a good raw screw that leaves 'em weak muscled and empty headed.

"—Yer name, boy?"

He jump. "Dwain."

"Run in the kitchen and help your mother."

He's already moving. Boy don't think to respond, just get busy doing what he told.

Tat don't move. Longhair Dwain don't look back neither but that make me think he's the sneaky sort.

They's lots to like about Tat. All those miles on the road I figured out you get both her best attributes by changing a couple letters.

Longhair Dwain go out the same side door as his daddy and I think on Stinky Joe. Follow Dwain outside. Joe's at the door looking his place inside. He slip by my legs.

Close the door with me outside.

Dwain's half to the house.

"She ain't the one for you, boy."

He snap back his head, turn away 'fore he see what he looking at. Tromping at the house, lift each foot high so he don't drag his sneakers through the snow. At the door he shoot a glance and duck inside.

I try to remember having my guts all tangled up for a girl, so I didn't know how to talk. Try to recall being young, like the world was set and I didn't have a rightful place in it.

Any boy wants a lay. But you got to look up to life and be hopeful to do right by a woman. Is why neither of us ought to lay with Tat.

Regardless they's so many layers of evil truth 'tween Glenwood Springs and 1970 I don't think I'll ever feel much kinship with Longhair Dwain.

Boy want to stick a girl, is all.

# CHAPTER FOUR

AFTER THROWING LARRY, RUTH AND BABY MAE OUT OF THE HOUSE HE grew up in, Baer wandered the woods with his backpack and hatchet, never more than a half dozen miles from Gleason. He needed to slip into town for supplies every few days and why walk more than necessary? Returning to his house—a place choked with memories of Ruth strutting like perky trash and Larry claiming her—was out of the question. Baer had forced them to leave and when he had the run to himself, couldn't tolerate being there.

Instead he stomped the woods and cast his hatchet at tree trunks. In the beginning he'd throw the hatchet and pick it up from where it bounced to the ground. Soon he had to pry it from the tree. Sometimes he walked for hours on end, not caring where his random pattern took him. Cast. Fetch. Select another tree. Throw. Fetch. His skill grew but instead of relieving the pressure, his anger cooked hotter. The action focused his fury and reinforced it. After ten thousand wagons crossed the rock, grooves steered the next ten thousand. Soon it wasn't enough to throw; he had to hurl the hatchet with all his might, until the muscles in his shoulder grew weary but his aim flawless. When his strength flagged, he added breathy curses to keep his physical rage apace his mental. As weariness sharpened into shoulder pain, he spoke full voice and at last shouted outrage at a forest that ignored him.

Except the red squirrels. The fearless bastards chattered back and always saw the hatchet coming.

After days of random motion he rested on a boulder and ground the blade against a flat lubricated with moss and mud. He worked the metal until dragging it across his arm removed the hair.

Baer meditated for hours about other ways a hatchet could prove handy. Some cultures employed them offing heads.

Which cultures?

North Carolina. Gleason culture. There's always a first.

She was back there right now, only a few miles away. Larry rented a place in town and Baer reconnoitered after getting word. He knew the location because Larry's high school buddy, Terence the Boner, grew up in the house across the street. Baer watched and learned when the neighbors rose in the morning and turned off the lights at night. Ruth would be in the apartment right now, a duplex with the other half unrented. She was there with milk swollen tits straining against her jelly-stained t-shirt, prancing about in her gym shorts, two sizes small. Probably screaming at the baby since Larry would be off at his apprentice job. The prick was taking night classes and working hard to leave Gleason behind him.

Busy building the sort of life Baer couldn't have because of the curse.

At first, knowing when someone was lying was groovy. He had a leg up. But in the end it turned out everyone lied all the time. Near every word produced red eyes and a shot of electric. When he was ten the curse was a tingle. His talent waxed as he matured into full blown sinewy manhood. He couldn't walk a street without feeling the lies going on inside the cars that drove by. It felt like heat from the sun. Radiation. Lies made his chest tight.

He'd look at town at night and the whole valley glowed pink.

Resting on a boulder he debated the simplest path to end it all. Should he climb a mountain and dive from an outcrop? Or create some primal justice for Ruth first? Return to her apartment in Gleason and remove her head? Wait for Larry and give him the same?

He Ain't Heavy.

Not missing his head.

Baer slid from his boulder squinting so hard he saw stars. It wasn't the world that was wrong. If everyone is one way and you're another—maybe, Baer, you're the problem.

He lifted his pack and hatchet, turned a circle. Oriented to the afternoon sun and the contours of the mountain, Baer set himself for a rocky outcrop with a perfect hundred-foot cliff. He walked with a slow gait, hatchet handle bumping his thigh. First time he'd holstered it through his belt.

What was that scent? Some kind of sweet smoke like burning leaves, but more pungent. Enticing like the aroma of seared beef or a woman's crotch. Mystical—the kind of scent that hooked the heart and pulled.

A smell like that didn't happen on its own. Nearing the top of the mountain he slipped his pack from his back and let it slide down his arm then knelt and placed it without sound on the leaves. Standing again, he extracted the hatchet from his belt and froze to the sound of male voices.

Baer crept from cover to cover, boulder to tree trunk. He stopped and listened but the voices ended. The smoke smell grew more powerful. He stepped to a dirt trail that led forward to the outcrop and back the other way, to Gleason. The voices were male. Subdued and childlike in their enthusiasm for thin air, yet resonant, men speaking in their lower register.

Hippies always fascinated Baer; on his rare childhood trips to Asheville he'd gawk at them like men from Mars. Long hair, big colors, patchouli and B.O. A girl once gave him beads and her stoned man, a book. Heinlein.

From their voices and smells he knew the two men on the rocks came from a similar tribe.

On the dirt path there were no leaves. Baer quickened his pace and stooped as he grew close to the rhododendron barrier between the forest and the rocky outcrop overlooking Gleason, two miles dead ahead south with Swannanoa to the right. The smoke smell was powerful.

Hatchet in hand, Baer stood and stepped around the rhododendron. A man with curly golden hair sat on a rock with his hands propped behind him and a thin cigarette between his lips. From his lap, another man looked up at Baer with glowing eyes. He wiped his mouth while Goldy turned and held out the cigarette, offering Baer a puff. His gaze fell to the hatchet in Baer's hand.

"Hey man, it ain't what it seems."

Baer closed his eyes like when as a boy he walked in on his bare mother pulling a bra from the bureau.

"Honest," came a second voice.

"Yeah, so maybe bug out, right?"

Electricity zapped Baer's arms. He retreated back the trail, grabbed his pack and after a couple hundred yards, threw up into the hollow of a rotted stump.

Vowing to stay on the back side of the mountain, avoiding the trail and outcrop, he descended at a northwestern angle and resumed throwing his hatchet. Instead of imagining splitting Ruth's face, he aimed higher, severing thin branches as if they were gay penises.

He paid little attention to the new territory and before long arrived at a stream and crossed on rocks. Here the trees seemed older, their trunks wider. He turned upslope. The older trees' branches were so high his accuracy failed.

Something else was off.

He stood looking a moment before running the hatchet handle through his belt. Turned a circle and tried to fathom what, beside the size of the trees, had changed.

The air carried a sweet rottenness.

Leaves snapped like a slapped piece of paper and a .22 rifle popped almost beside him. Baer dropped to the dirt, shed his pack and rolled behind a boulder. A gray squirrel landed a foot from his face and Baer comprehended. The tree rat had a bloody head and dead eyes. Baer twisted his neck. Twenty feet away, an ancient man reclined against the wide trunk of an oak.

"You push it to my side. Szank you."

Baer nodded and watched him lower the rifle.

The man's face said he was a hundred years old but he stood without placing the rifle butt to the ground for support. He closed the distance before Baer found his feet and swiped the dead squirrel by its tail.

Baer accepted his offered hand. The man's eyes were watery and kind. His breath smelled mildly of alcohol.

Baer nodded, unable to pull words past the barrier of wanting Ruth dead, surviving a conversation with peter puffers and now, looking into the otherworldly face of an ancient German with Annie Oakley's aim.

He slung his backpack over his shoulder.

"I'll be off," Baer finally said.

"You did not come for ze shine?"

"What shine?"

The old man smiled.

# CHAPTER FIVE

A FEW MINUTES 'TIL SUPPER. TAT'S UNROLLED HER BAG ON A TWICE-folded sheet of cardboard. Be some cushion there, but less so on concrete.

Corazon's set up her bag on the far wall. You got the open bay closest the house. The Mustang with the sloped back—and Jubal out his mind on that. Fastback Mustangs look like puckered asshole and I shoulda said so.

Tat's got her bag in the open bay. Didn't grab me any cardboard.

Been two week since I woke with her on top smacking uglies and since then she's took a bit of domestic ownership. She does little things I'd ordinarily do, 'cept she get there first. Clear some ground of rocks and twigs. Stretch out the tarp, keep the bag from growing damp from the ground. Peel a turnip for my lunch. Haul the wood and start the fire. She do all that. Her years running wild ain't stomped out the part of her that wants to build a home and cage a man in it.

But here after Longhair stutters twenty seconds and fingers the locks out his eyes, Tat's taking care of number one and to hell with number two.

Baer Creighton is number two.

Tat's set up in the open bay and Corazon's on the other side the garage. I check on her.

She say, "You snore."

"So do you."

Piss on this. Piss on all it.

Outside.

Stinky Joe come.

Snow fall thick and steady. Adds up on the ground whether you count or not. Five inch at least, mostly filled in the tire tracks since we got here. I slip to the Jeep and take a long, long, long snurgle from a fifth of Wild Turkey under the seat. Girls bitch and moan if I take nourishment at the wheel. On travel days I don't eat.

One more reason to divide the party.

Fill my belly with heat and meditate on the snow coming down, on the mostly black sky, on being the guest of a cop with a son likes 'em young and got his eye on my girl—and I can't think of a single 'nother thing make me want to keep her so much.

Fold my knees and love on Stinky Joe. Get both hands behind his ears and press like to pop his skull off. Dog love it. He lick my nose and duck to the garage door. Squirts yellow on white metal and snow. Inspires me. Tool in hand I look up. Woman in the window don't look away. I nod. She shake her head no, curt. Friendliness would be a miscalculation.

But truth told, everything I ever figure was wrong, I did it anyhow. The natural order don't give a shit. Just people give shits. I could stick her and they'd be no more rhyme or reason to the consequence than anything else I done, the poisoning, shooting, killing, tricking, running, hiding, deceiving, fornicating and every other sin. I poke that woman. Her man come after me. I kill him.

All I am these days.

They say the fool expects a different result.

I didn't use to be a magnificent shithead. Not so much.

Well I was, then I learned different and lived different. Then I talk myself into the rage, was helped with a couple punches to the face, maybe a knee in the nuts and no more. All that gimme license to be what I was.

Wild Turkey works the magic. Snow come down and stick to my arm and that's how I know the snow ain't real. It sticks to other shit ain't real.

Me.

I thought all along when I was good and the world was rotten at least I was good. I had perfect shine and a dog to swap stories. But all that was ripped away and I become what I didn't want and find they was no reason not to want it. I thought I was slipping down the evil slope.

Well who give a fuck? I'm at the bottom and they's nothing here but mud. They's no sin. No trouble. No pain or death or eternal damnation. Not on this side. Over here on planet Earth it's just more the same. Now I start killing, it seems my preferred solution. Comes easy. Solves problems quick. I was never a killer, never wanted to be and don't feel right about it—yet here I am. It's what I am, through and through, proved over and agin. I am not what I am.

Gobbledygook.

I just wanna see God Almighty come down; have Him say you figured it out. The show is bullshit. Not just that, but it's Designed To Be Bullshit. You's supposed to have no choice. I make these situations so your head says one thing and your heart another. I make it so you never do what you say. I make it impossible for you to both want good and be good. I make it so your brain demand one thing and your nuts another. I make one man's justice another man's crime. On purpose, to fuck with you. Deal with it, you hated little fucker. That's what I want God Almighty to confess. I made you to love what you can't be and hate what you are. That's my purpose, and they's all kind of other shit with it, gravity and magnetics, but that's the central way things work in the Milky Way. Here's the truth, you little Hated Fucker. They's no solution. Throw up your hands and die. Everything in this world, I create so you know the difference 'tween me and you. You ain't shit. And though I love you and all that, you won't make no progress 'til you confess you ain't shit, never will be, and your whole purpose is to be confused to the point you say this can't be right, this makes no sense, either God's fake or I'm fake. The two don't reconcile.

And at the very end of the showdown I'll have a broken hip and God'll say, that's it. You got it! You ain't real! Your thoughts don't cohere from one minute the next. Your love don't match your evil. How could it be anything else? Could you imagine a world with only human truth? Think how fucked up you are and imagine a world limited by human truth. The atheists have it backwards.

*I exist they don't.*

This don't—nothing don't—ever make sense. The sane man laughs like a madman and the madman add it all up with perfect reason. The people with they shit together quit. And the sanest of the sane go nuts 'cause the world ain't sane with 'em.

All I want is an end to the lies, but in a universe built on illusion and hate, wanting truth means wanting nothing. They is no truth.

That little fucker Dwain was looking on Tat wanting a poke. He inside the house setting the table.

I bet that fucker writes poems.

Mebbe I had more Turkey 'n I thought.

Fuck all this nonsense.

# CHAPTER SIX

IN THE CAVE WITH GÜNTER STROH AND HIS DOG, BAER REACHED FOR his pocket but the hatchet haft was in the way. He pulled the weapon from his belt and shoved his hand into his jeans. With a crumpled wad of green in hand, he said, "Two?"

"I don't vant ze two dollars."

"Then why you say you was charging two bucks?"

Günter shook his head. "Zat jar is full of money. Du blöder?"

Sounded like an insult. Baer's fingers tingled. "Blöder?"

"Shdubid."

Baer popped to his feet.

The dog growled.

"Nah, bullshit. That ain't something you get to say to me."

Günter waved his hand. "Money! Vat you need! Come here sniffink und cryink. I'm old, you zee? I'm old! No time!"

"The hell?"

In a single motion Baer swooped to the hatchet, spun and hurled it at a wooden crate sitting deeper in the cave, illuminated by lantern. It jingled on impact and the head stayed stuck.

The old man's jaw clamped. He swiped his Winchester from the wall and levered a round before Baer looked back at him. The dog lowered his head and carried his bristling teeth forward a step.

Baer grinned.

"I can throw that hatchet better'n you can hit a fella five feet away. Better'n that mutt can lick his nuts."

Günter shook his head and closed his eyes. He lowered his rifle and rested the barrel across his lap, pointed at Baer.

"Zat jar is money. Zat's all."

Günter seemed more offended by their lack of communication than Baer's display with the hatchet. Baer looked at the mason jars lined on a weathered barn board stretched across mud-mortared stones. They didn't contain dollars, only clear liquid, some with faint rainbow hues.

The man grabbed a third jar from the barn board shelf. Held it aloft. "Twenty dollars."

"What's it made outta? Gold?"

Günter shook his head. "Twenty dollars is vat I take for it."

"Look mister, I ain't dense so say what you mean."

Standing there, Baer was struck by how pleasant it felt to have an altercation without his advantage causing him pain. The old man held his position without puffing himself up with deception. No prancing around with a swollen chest. Just an old man, truth, and his brush gun.

"You know what? I apologize."

Baer strode to the wood crate and yanked his hatchet. The razor head had found a knot and he had to work it a couple times—again creating the sound of metal on metal. Must be where the old man kept the quarters and nickels he earned from selling his twenty dollar moonshine.

Blade free, Baer shoved the handle in his belt. "Appreciate the hospitality and didn't mean the disrespect. Well that ain't true. I did, but change my mind. I be on my way."

Günter's head tilted forward and he closed his eyes. His face seemed to move back and forth, *no*.

When Baer crossed in front to make his escape, Günter said, "Szit."

Baer stopped.

Money talk didn't make sense. Old man in a cave, selling hooch to nobody... Nothing made sense. Leaving his backpack across from Günter, Baer stepped a few feet to the cave entrance and looked downslope. A stray bolt of setting sun cleared the mountain to the west, penetrated the canopy and cut through a cluster of small trees with mostly dead leaves. Metal glinted. Peering, Baer saw the foliage belonged not to trees, but limbs stuck vertical in the ground to camouflage a metallic contraption as tall as he, next to the stream.

Baer turned and looked past the row of mason jars to Günter.

"You made that likker?"

Günter nodded.

"You sell it to people for twenty dollars a jar?"

Another nod.

"And you live in a cave."

Günter tapped his temple with his index finger.

"You sell homemade hooch for beaucoup dollars and other'n that it's you and the mutt, alone."

The old man's smile projected pure joy. Rommel followed his master's lead and whined.

A bar in a cave nobody could find... Two bucks a swallow... Günter looking like he hadn't changed nor washed his clothes since the summer thaw.

Wonder filled Baer. He approached the dog, got on his knees and came forward with his hand flat, palm down. The dog sniffed. Wagged. Baer stroked his cheek with his thumb.

Günter Stroh extended his arm. "Before you szit, grab two logs from around ze zide. It vill be cold tonight."

Baer exited the cave and to his left discovered a log hut built against the rock wall, again disguised with limbs and protecting at least four cords of split firewood. He returned with his arms full and placed them next to the fire pit while Günter struck flint and steel to a fistful of mouse nest.

He placed a pine cone on the delicate flame and then twigs stored in another wood crate next to the bar. Last he selected the smallest three split logs Baer brought and formed a teepee. It took him thirty seconds.

Baer sat across from Günter Stroh and studied the flickering lines on his face. Günter exhaled and seemed smaller, as if he exhaled vitality with his breath. Baer nodded for no reason.

Günter smiled as if he saw a different scene from far away. After a moment his eyes shot to Baer and he smiled.

"You sleep zere." He nodded to the other side of the fire, next to the cave entrance.

"Zanks," Baer said. He chinned toward the barn board bar. "What's in that third jar?"

# CHAPTER SEVEN

GIRLS IN THE HOUSE TWENTY MINUTE AND I SIT ON A FROZEN ROCK looking the hills. Ass numb and wet. What is it? Snow eight inch? White stuff keep coming down.

Turkey keep going down.

Suspect Tat ain't going down no more.

Turkey...

Gurgle.

How you like being an old fool, Baer? How you like that? Take what you got no right.

Thought occurs I could step in that garage, grab my pack...

Know what?

Hell with it. I'm gone.

Push off the rock. Hold the bottle to the garage floodlight. Two inches in the bottom and for a seal broke an hour ago, I confess a flash of pride.

They's inside for supper and not a soul come to find Baer? Must be at the table by now. See 'em through the glass.

Twist on the cap 'cause the thought of another pull give me a rolly stomach. Lurch a step and it ain't forty feet to the garage entrance, but after two three paces I got it in the back my mind if I make it up the mountain they's a good chance I'll stay there under snow 'til the wolves or coyotes dig me out. Least somebody wants old Baer for dinner.

Ain't got winter boots but my socks is thick. Make perfect sense.

Open the garage and on accident, by huge mistake, walk across Tat's sleeping bag. Muss it up. Get my feet tangled and give the sleep sack a kick. Grab my pack, shoot an arm through the strap and toss it to my shoulder as I turn back to the entrance. The weight concerns my balance. I get 'r steady. Spin.

Door's open. Tat... Jaw open. No words.

"What?"

"Where are you going?"

I point.

"The Mustang?"

"You looked like you were going outside."

I point at the Mustang again. My eyes glow. Whole world goes red, me looking through 'em.

"The food is ready. Everyone's waiting."

Behind her snow falls. Porch light go on and Longhair Dwain stand at the door. Mama shouts inside and he step out and close the door behind. Got a stance like he's liable to come in here and unfold an ass whoopin' on Baer Creighton.

"Your girlfriend wants ya."

Tat shake her head. Close the door on me.

Drop the pack next the Ford. Catch the roof and steady my feet. Maybe afore I climb the mountain I'll fill my belly on the copper's hospitality. Pack them guts full so I can stand a few days without game, 'fore I eat tree bark.

Joe look sad and I leave him in the garage. He'll nest in Tat's bag.

Outside I follow her tracks and at the door stop my fist afore I knock. Inside, heat. Smells. Light and noise. Silver on plates. Chairs on linoleum. Pissed off woman, surprised by company.

Go inside.

The wife look. She got her hands in oven mitts and a bigass square dish of melted cheese. She flash her best fakey and says, "I hope you like lasagna, Mister Boone."

"I... damn...."

Catch the wall afore it falls. That gravity is some shit. Other folk move quick, stop. Jolted by the motion. I could fill that rubber boot by the door with yak. Maybe I will.

Scan faces. Longhair Dwain don't know I'm here. Him 'n Tat sit there quiet, minds tangled like sweaty arms and legs, jockey a single square inch for a good rub.

Beside Tat, Corazon look past me to the great outside. If not for the food... If not for her sister... She'd maybe cut Dwain.

Or not. I ain't seen her do it.

Aside Corazon we got this button nosed boy with rosy cheeks and awestruck eyes. He says you're a killer. I bite my lip and let the heat glow. You're a boy gonna grow up and be a liar and a thief. And nobody won't give a shit neither.

He smile.

"Hey mister," the boy say. "You ever flush when you're sitting down so the air whooshes past your butt?"

"Percival!"

"Son."

Percival smile even bigger.

"Once," I say. "But you gotta be careful. See when you open the pipes so the water goes out, other stuff come in. One time a hand reach up after my—"

"Alden—" Tat say.

Mrs. White's eyes float back and her mouth fall.

Jubal nod. "I had that happen too. But only in public restrooms—you know—at the park."

Percival face ain't so sure.

I grin at the boy and he grin back. Joshin'. Good stuff.

Pat my pockets. Left the Turkey in the garage. No wine on the table. This house appear dry. I work the spit around my tongue and swallow. Meanwhile the smell of melted cheese and tomato sauce says sit at the table.

Jubal rest his arms on the chair back.

"Why don't you sit down, Jubal," his wife say.

"After our guest."

Tat stare at me. Tilt her head and glare.

"Oh. Shit. 'Scuse me. Damn."

I grab a chair and the woman pull out another. "Would you mind sitting here? I sit there so I can get to the stove."

"Ah."

Drop in the seat. Wife short-smiles me and I see she got the makeup heavy on her cheekbone. I bet if I saw her straight-on, they'd be a little puffy there too. Woman don't bruise her face shaving.

Most don't.

"That dog isn't in the garage alone, is it?"

Spin the head. Longhair Dwain, mouth open and stupidity tumbling out.

"What?"

Jubal raise his right hand an inch and cut sideways another. Shut up. We play the long game on these people, Jubal say. Dead Jubal, by the look. Still got the shooter on his hip.

I'll stick his ass in a tree too.

My face been all over the news. All over them computers. The papers. Seen a billboard with yours truly leaving Flag. You seen this cold blooded murderer? This vile detestable wreck of a man, this bonafide cop killer? FBI killer? No way he ain't seen my face two dozen time. Whole family in on it.

"We had a dog once, Alden," Jubal say.

I hold his eye. Grin and nod.

"Back when Dwain wasn't maybe two feet tall. Turn your face, Dwain. Pull back that mop."

Dwain keep his face low and I got the electric all through me. Afraid to touch the silverware. Jubal don't give the juice—he couldn't glow flashlight bulb. But this youngun want to tangle with Tat... his eyes is coals and the zippy on my arms make the hair stand. Dwain glare at Jubal and Jubal glare back... I'm your old man whether you could kick my ass or not. Do as I say in my house.

Dwain toss his hair like a woman and he got a scar below his left eye back to where the hair's a tangled mess. Silvery almost, in the light. Tinge of pink.

"Dog do that, I take it?"

Dwain nod.

"What you do to the dog?"

He shift a half inch.

"Second worst day of my life," Mrs. White say. "Can we please not talk about this?"

"I uh. Yep." Give her a nod.

"I was ten," Dwain say. "I didn't do anything."

"You bet."

He drop his hair back over his face and Tat swivel her head and rests her meanness on me.

"I remember I hit that dog with a skillet," Mrs. White say. "I was pregnant with Percival and running around. Getting that one to the emergency room. I was about the craziest woman on the planet."

"Maybe," I say. "How would you know?"

Mrs. White grab a burger flipper and Jubal's plate. Fill it with stringy mush.

"You know I can't eat a quarter of that."

"But you have to try."

He look at me. "Had a late lunch."

Elbows on the table. Just me. I drop 'em. With the cold from outside and the long day and the whiskey I got a nose fulla snot wants to run. Inhale it back. Grab a cloth napkin. Woman's eyes bulge.

Gulp, wash it with a pull of water from the glass. Her nose flare wide and that little boy smile big. Percival. You want a boy to grow into a pussy, call him Percy five time a day. He clear his throat with less skill and more sound.

Mama points. "No!"

I wink. Jubal close his eyes and Tat look flat.

Fuck Tat. Fuck all y'all. "That sure smell good."

Wife smile but her eyes frown.

"What's yer name?" I say. "We ain't been introduced."

"I'm Mrs. White."

"You ever make that with elk meat? Bet that'd be the shit."

"Mister, uh—"

She want my name. Fuck if I know it.

"Alden," Tat say.

"Mister Alden, please refrain from using profanity around the children."

Little boy in a trance. Won't take his eyes off.

"Let's say grace," Jubal say.

Family drop heads. Tat shoot me a look. Corazon rolls eyes at the injustice of prayer. I sink my head and Mrs. White take my left hand and Jubal my right. Whole group holds hands. And under the table I bet Tat and Longhair press fingers and palms.

"Dear Heavenly Father, we thank you for this meal. Please give us the strength to take one day's blessings at a time. In Jesus' name."

"In Jesus' name," Mrs. White says. "Percival. You didn't say 'in Jesus name.'"

"In Jesus' name," say the boy.

Finger in nose. Silver on plates. Jubal exhale slow, tired, more 'n more gray in the kitchen light. That boy could kick his ass. Not the Longhair. Percy.

"Percival," I say. "What year you in school?"

"This one?"

"What grade?"

Hold up his hand. Five.

"Wow. You driving yet? That yer Mustang out there?"

Mrs. White grab my plate.

"I don't drive!"

Grin at him and marvel. They used to say kids was good and learn evil but I say they start evil and stay. Probe this little shit for evidence.

Mrs. White shovel a six inch rectangle of drippy stretchy lasagna on my plate and set it afore me. Smells I ain't smelled in about forever. Make the mouth drip. Look up and Jubal's sick as death but he holds his long stare on me, the one that sees all and says naught.

PERCIVAL WATCH ME SO MUCH HE MISS HIS MOUTH. I WRINKLE MY brow. The boy's eyes widen and I see something maybe in this dream, maybe the next. His face darkens in the mind, gray as his father. Grayer, 'til the flesh wrinkle and rot and the eyes go black and wormy. Push that image back, back and his body's limp from the shoulder down. Head droop forward on the neck but them black caves of eyes is still on me. Back, back and his arms hang loose and straight. Long for a boy, like they fell from the sockets. Back, back and his legs is straight down. Specks of red in the eyes now, tiny like its four a.m. and you spot a fire cooked down to coals, maybe a hundred yard off. But closer and closer they get redder and redder and all it takes is a puff of wind and some tinder and they blaze. He's in the dream forest. Back and back and Percy's just one more body in the trees. Now they's a couple dozen. A triple dozen. All the men I killed.

The boy.

I shove back. Chair bark. Catch. Tip over and after the crash I look up from my back. All that booze and noodles... Tomato acid boils like a witch's brew. On my back it comes up the throat easy.

"No!"

I won't do it. I won't murder that boy.

Scramble my feet and arms, grab aholt the counter and pull while Mrs. White has her hands on her lap like to keep her gizzy safe from the crazy man. Percival stand. Jubal judge whether to pull his pistol. I spin. Can't face 'em. Can't hold the eyes of the man and woman knowing I'll slay they boy.

I got to go.

Got to flee this house and mountain. This country and life. I can't. I won't abide killing a boy.

Swallow back the lasagna I swallowed once afore and pound feet to the door. Shove it open and stop.

"You don't deserve this, Ma'am."

Horror on her face and Jubal got that right arm folded and his palm press a checkered grip.

I close the door gentle.

I never been so broke in my life 'cept burying Fred, and that's the exact pain and hate that brought me here. I can't do this no more. I can't be me and I can't be nobody else.

Outside the porch light, snow come from every side, walls closing in.

# CHAPTER EIGHT

GÜNTER STROH CARRIED THE LANTERN DEEP INTO THE CAVE. BAER watched the light disappear around a corner, then fade until distance disappeared and blackness walled the depths.

Firelight danced on the rock wall across from him and Baer wondered about life eons before, in tiny tribes united by family lines and the difficulty of survival.

"Woulda been a cluster, puppy dog."

The second Mason jar rested on its side, open mouth against Baer's leg.

He looked into Rommel's eyes and sensed they were far more rational than his. He stroked behind the dog's ears.

The third Mason jar was tinged with peach. The taste was other-worldly. Divine. Baer hardly noticed how his mouth and throat almost vanished before the likker splashed into his stomach.

"That just peachy, puppy dog."

Baer blew fumes into Rommel's face.

"Where your old Kraut go?"

The dog said nothing.

"You a Kraut, too? Nevermind. No accent."

Baer held the Mason jar in the air between his eyes and the fire. The orange magnified the gold-hued liquid.

The dog's ears shot up. His head twisted toward the darkness of the cave behind them. He whined.

"What?" Baer said. He drank.

Rommel jumped from beside Baer and trotted into the blackness, though no sound nor light suggested Günter's return. Baer looked outside where night was a dozen shades brighter than the void to his left. Could the tunnel loop around to another exit, allowing Günter to circle back and surprise him?

Didn't even make sense on peach likker.

Baer drank. Hardly felt anything, except the delightful foreknowledge that deeper intoxication must follow. He rested the back of his head to the rock and rolled until a second pressure point lightened the pressure on the first.

Ruth.

Baer remembered the first time he took her. She wore sweaters tight enough to go without a bra and he had more difficulty getting a hand on her boobs than his sausage in her bun. Oh, and lungs like a Hoover. When he pulled her away from his mess to get on with the real encounter, she started on his neck and left a black mark the size of a walnut. Baer touched under his jawbone. Rolled out his left leg and contorted his hips until his bound up undershorts didn't feel like a tourniquet. He closed his eyes.

Her breathy words entered his ears across the many months and miles. "I love you. Never let me go. Take me now!"

Baer opened his eyes and clamped his molars until they felt ready to shatter. He placed the peach likker on the cave floor and made sure the lid and ring were clean before gulping another swallow and resealing the Mason jar. He grabbed his hatchet and looked for the wood crate full of quarters and nickels; it was barely there in the darkness. Baer reached back and hurled the hatchet and as the haft cleared his hand Rommel bolted forward from the blackness.

Baer opened his mouth; dog and blade crossed before a warning cleared his throat.

Rommel skidded. Stared. He whined and turned halfway to the void. Returned his gaze to Baer and barked twice.

"Wasn't aiming for you."

Baer rested his head on the stone wall and closed his eyes. Summoned Ruth's face back to his lap. He'd take her sixteen ways to Sunday but nothing beat good head.

The revenge was good this way: imagining her doing what she'd done before but no longer would. He owned the memory and could make it do what he wanted. And yet...

No memory was as good as two lips.

Rommel clamped his teeth on Baer's wrist and tugged.

"You want to play, hunh?"

Baer slap boxed and the dog bounded to the wooden crate holding the hatchet. He looked back at Baer. Whined. Barked.

"Hey, puppydog, where's your fuckin' Kraut?"

The dog sat. Stood. Turned a circle. Then he stared into Baer's eyes and moved his mouth.

Baer twisted his head. Blinked and shut his eyes and behind them in his mind he saw a flash like television static. A burst of snow that pulsed and disappeared.

He shook it off. Put his hand on the peach likker and contemplated another heavy gurgle. He thought of Ruth and noticed that between the dog's playfulness and the likker, he'd had at least thirty seconds free of her.

"Whaddaya think a that?"

Rommel charged. Baer crossed his arms before his face and the beast clamped his teeth on the same wrist as before. His head was like a black-smith's anvil and his eyes caught firelight. He shook as if to break bones and Baer heaved him against the cave wall. The dog released, barked six inches from Baer's nose and the sound fried his mind like a burst of static. He shut his eyes and Rommel again pressed jaw to arm. He jerked Baer from the wall. His breath was like old food and Baer caught a glint of the hatchet's poll, the blade still stuck in the wooden box twenty feet away.

If the dog sank those rotten teeth in his neck he'd be dead.

On all fours Baer jumped his feet beneath him only to have the dog topple him forward again. Baer swatted with his free hand and missed. His brain reeled. That peach shit, wow. Amen. The dog spasmed back and Baer fell to his chest.

Rommel released. Turned away and barked into the cavern's depths.

"Yeah, call your old man—"

Baer sat.

"What?"

Rommel's jaw moved. Static, in Baer's brain. The dog spoke and slivers of awareness assembled in Baer's mind, like a picture forming when the antenna tunes just right.

He heard the dog's words.

*Günter needs your help!*

Baer shook his head. Blinked.

*Come on! Hurry!*

Baer crawled toward Rommel. Got on his knees. "Well shit. Why'n't you say so?"

*I been screaming at you! He's down here!*

This's bullshit. Right?

*Help!*

Baer pulled himself erect and kept a hand to the cave wall. He passed the crate that jingled, kept going another ten feet and turned a bend. Ahead in the depths he discerned the indirect glow of Günter Stroh's kerosene lantern. The dog yelped and ran into the intervening darkness, then his muscular shadow penetrated the orange penumbra and cut right as if leaping into the rock wall.

Baer dragged his hand on the wall and focused on maintaining his feet beneath him. His mind swam and he doubted what his senses reported about height, depth, up or down.

Or a talking dog.

As Baer progressed the barking returned. The old man was around the bend. Baer closed with.

He shifted from the left wall to the right and stumbled. Knocked his head on a ledge and dropped. Consciousness slipped but a nub of awareness held Baer upright on his knees and urged him awake.

The old man needed him.

*Hurry!*

Baer felt along the wall and finding a hold, pulled. He knocked his head to the same jutting ledge which he now saw formed a low ceiling.

Baer grunted and felt lighter when the angry sound escaped him.

"Günter?"

At the bend he discovered the cave turned back at a harsh angle. The lantern was ahead on the cave floor, fifteen feet away. The old man lay unmoving beside it, and Rommel said, *too late.*

# CHAPTER NINE

GRAB MY PACK AND STUDY WHAT SUPPLIES LONGHAIR DWAIN LEFT ON the garage floor. They's a nice hatchet. Tat still got the Sig Sauer Nat Cinder give her, so she good for protection. But I know her, she'll be in the woods in no time. What girl don't need a cutting tool?

Leave the hatchet.

Back of my throat burns with stomach acid and the head swims in memories and visions that don't make sense. I was never a killer, but I am a killer. Kept my nose to myself and let people go about they sins as I went about mine. Never said I was better'n nobody and I ain't.

But I won't kill a boy.

Stinky Joe look up from Tat's sleeping bag. I'm at the door. Joe cock his head.

"C'mon."

*You ain't right.*

"Well fuck. I know that. C'mon."

*I ain't going no place with you, 'til you right. Just go up there and die someplace. I'm over that shit.*

"If I planned on dying I wouldn't bring you."

*Pull your head out your ass. Give up the sauce, is what you need.*

"I need shit."

Joe rest his head in the fluff.

Leave the door open and kick snow to the Jeep. Got the Glock in my back but the box of shells is in the center console. Pull the gloves out my pocket and stuff the box there instead. Cut 'tween house and garage and Joe watch at the door. Warm inside, blizzard out.

"Suit yourself."

*Good luck.*

I walk.

Not thirty yards the flat land end and a trail begin. Got a mountain dead afore me and the trail start straight up like to change my mind, but a few paces along it grow tired and cuts left around a boulder musta fallen from the heights. These new yuppie boots is half nylon and if I could meet the fella...

I'd kill him.

Can't escape myself.

All that lasagna cheese swimming in Wild Turkey got my gut about to blow out the side. Heavy sick feel, back my throat. Five minute in, the trail curve hard right along the mountain contours. Moon punch 'tween storm clouds. Maybe seven o'clock. Snow's bright and thick. Toes wet.

After due consideration, I would murder the yuppie dipshit made these boots.

Calf feel damp too. Old punji wound never quite dry out. Heart pound from the cheese in my veins. Stop and take in the land below, now I got a couple feet elevation. Can't see Jubal's house from this side, but off the left the valley's a-glow in yellow. Fat snowflakes float like D-Day parachutes gonna storm Glenwood.

My head don't feel near as good as the days I didn't soak it in likker. But what's a man to do when the heart beat strong but pump poison? A man want justice so he rob the thief. Want truth so he lie to save his ass.

Nah.

I know what I am. Can't lie about it. Most I can do is make it tolerable, and for that Wild Turkey do the trick.

'Til it don't.

Cold begin at the feet but travel fast. Got the nerves up the back wound tight for a shiver even as sweat damps the shirt.

Stop and jiggle the pack on my back. Reseat. Cool air rush up under the coat and that shiver does an encore.

Rolly stomach gurgle up a burp taste like brown radiator fluid and somewhere at the back of my brain a blackness swoop across—wings wide as the sky—and that's all they is.

# CHAPTER TEN

BAER LEANED AGAINST THE CAVE AT THE TURN AND STUDIED GÜNTER Stroh's corpse. The body might be far enough inside the earth's bowels that the pungency of his rotting flesh wouldn't foul the air at the cave mouth. If it did, maybe Baer could get some blankets, roll and drag the body another hundred yards deeper. The cave seemed to go on forever.

Wasn't a comfortable thought, having ten million pounds of rock and dirt above his head. But Günter had left eight or ten jars of shine and they'd last a week. Two? How much more had the old man hidden in the cave? Or outside, as with his firewood? Wouldn't make sense to leave the cave and provisions to marauders with less claim, who didn't even know the old man.

Rommel sat watched.

Baer could hunt with Günter's rifle and ammunition—and why not cut the bullshit here and now? The dead don't take their belongings with them. The cave and everything in it was Baer's to claim.

And his to defend. He always thought those 30-30 Winchesters were righteous.

How many nickels and quarters were in that crate? How many years had the old man sold two-dollar swallows?

How many men knew to find him here, at the cave?

How the hell did Baer not hear about a hundred year old Kraut cooking shine in the woods?

He could almost foretell the scene: in the wild, the cave was sought after real estate. Best keep the rifle close, 'til he understood. And the hatchet.

Rommel rose and stepped to Günter. He licked his master's face and waited for him to rouse.

Rommel looked at Baer.

*You got more advanced techniques?*

"Nah. I dunno shit."

What about Günter's pockets? In a way, leaving his pockets full of whatever was in them seemed an offense against the human spirit. Those accoutrements belonged to Günter while he was here, not for the eons that would follow his departure. They should serve whatever nomad could make them productive.

What if Günter had a nice pocketknife? Or more coin?

Baer winced at the thought of kneeling beside the body and pilfering his pockets. Dead people piss themselves. And shit. That kind of dented the value of a knife right there, if he had to touch another man's waste to make claim.

Wait.

No smell?

Baer wrestled the implications.

How quickly did dead people relieve themselves? Seemed natural it would happen right off, but dead people grew hair and fingernails and that took a while. Maybe the defecate had to wait for gut bloat to build the back pressure. That would explain why the dead Günter didn't smell dead. It was a combination of a mix-up in the chronology of natural things and Baer not knowing as much about dead men as would benefit him.

The still, dog, cave and rifle. Baer was like a boy slipping into his father's boots at the door to see what being the master was all about.

Should have brought that peach Mason jar.

One day long before he killed his mother she told him she loved him and he was such a precocious boy, he could do anything he wanted. But you don't know how to control your temper and someday you'll wind up in prison. No I won't he said—and he remembered exactly what he was thinking, behind his words. I'm too smart. I got the gift.

Too smart.

Didn't turn out too smart. Feeling pain when people lie helped him avoid some traps... But anyone willing to evade humanity at every turn could reap the same result.

Baer stood looking at one of the only two people who hadn't lied to him, dead.

Another gulp of peach likker would likely resolve the thought, but Baer wrestled without.

With Günter dead, that left Ruth as the only person who didn't lie. If Ruth was to somehow push off tonight, the world would be pure. Every single rat bastard in it would be a liar, and Baer could turn his back in good conscience. Wander west like an Old Book prophet. Chew lichens and bugs 'til he hit the plains, then eat grass and worms. Go around telling people the truth: you're liars. Your cities will crumble under the weight of your deception and it won't even require The Almighty to muster a miracle. You'll doubt and then you'll hate—yourself as much as everyone else. You'll look up in the hills where I'm dancing around a fire, laughing curses your way.

And if you charlatans come after the truth teller, I'll call down the bears.

Oh you old man. I might coulda learned something from you.

Baer swallowed. He squatted. His knees quickly tired and he sat. Günter lay on his back, legs and feet directed to an even darker blackness beyond. His head was an arm length from the lantern, as if in his last moments he clung to light. His unblinking eyes stared at—

That fucker blinked.

Baer exhaled.

"How long?"

"What?"

"Until you do it?"

"Hunh?"

"Kill me."

Baer rocked forward. "I didn't kill you."

He crawled closer. The motion tumbled his stomach and he turned his face aside while acid burned his throat. Expecting vomit any moment, Baer waited. None came. He rested on his knees and shuffled on them to Günter. Baer hovered.

"I breathe, blöd," Günter whispered.

Baer clamped his teeth and placed fingers to the old man's neck but no matter how he moved them, he barely felt a pulse.

"You do this much?" he said.

"Die?"

"Uh."

"Effery day. Grab ein cabbage."

Beyond Günter's feet was a series of wooden crates. Baer stood, leaned against the cave wall and lifted the lantern and held it above. The first held dozens of green cabbages. The next, leafy corn ears. A third held apples. The last crate was covered in hide. Baer lifted and the smell was strong.

Salted game.

He turned to the sound of Günter's exhalation; he had lifted himself to an elbow but had fallen flat again.

"Cabbage," he whispered.

"How about I get you back to the fire and come back for this when I don't gotta carry an old man too?"

Günter nodded. His smile was faint.

"You be good." Baer cleared his throat. "You'll be all right."

A moment ago he thought he'd just missed seeing Günter die. Now Günter was alive and the crossover point seemed like a holy place. Something moved in Baer's heart. Immersed in an eternal moment, he sensed danger the way a flailing man who can't swim senses danger. The ugly fear coalesced into a thought: the mystery-force that animated bones and flesh, that pushed a wrinkled face into a smile, was in danger of disappearing into blackness a thousand times colder and emptier than the guts of the cave. The void that had swallowed his mother lingered nearby. Death wasn't even a concept; it was nothing, an arm's length away.

Baer recalled how moments earlier he took mental claim of Günter's belongings... while the old man in that moment stood contemplating a river bank with nothing but void beyond. Baer lowered his head. The germ was there: it was the same as stealing, as lying.

"How about we get you back to the fire?"

Baer released the cave wall and knelt beside Günter. He pulled him into a sitting position, lowered his shoulder and put his arm around the old man's withered back. Baer eased erect, careful, with Günter draped like a half-empty meal sack.

Steadied against the cave wall, Baer squatted and grabbed the lantern. Mindful of not banging Günter's head against rock, Baer walked back towards the fire with his feet wide.

Günter said nothing.

Arriving at the fire, Baer lowered to his knees and placed Günter in his blankets. He stood dizzy with his blood still at his feet and watched Günter like sometimes as a child he'd watch his mother's eyes when she took a nap. Sometimes he could see motion beneath her lids, like a dog twitching after a dream rabbit.

Günter's closed eyes didn't move.

Baer added two parallel logs to the coals, positioned with the flame between and nestled them so they wouldn't roll when a fry pan rested on top. He looked around; surely Günter Stroh had a cooking iron around, somewhere.

He'd find it later.

Peach shine.

The Mason jar sat where he left it. Baer tightened the lid and placed the jar on the shelf.

*Cabbage?*

Baer nodded at Rommel. He grabbed the lantern and returned to the depths. He found a head already lopped in half, took it and a piece of meat a quarter the size.

Baer placed them beside the fire. Looked at Günter. "Can you eat?"

The old man's eyes were open and staring at the heavens beyond the cave roof. He said nothing.

If Günter was dead again the cabbage was more than Baer wanted for himself. Maybe the dog ate vegetables—but his nose was more interested in the venison. Baer held the meat to the lantern and sliced off an end that didn't look quite right, even for salted meat, and picked deer hairs from the fat. Satisfied, he placed the cut on his thigh and used his hatchet like a chisel to slice off a slab of fat, then placed it in an iron skillet resting on the logs he'd placed on the coals.

He squinted. Looked at the dog and the dog looked back.

"You put that there?"

*Me?*

Baer glanced at the old man and the old man's eyes rolled from heaven to earth and he smiled.

"One of these days you'll die and I won't believe it. Like the boy who cried wolf. Then what'll you do? Dead, and no one to believe it."

"You go first," Günter whispered. "Vay you drink."

Baer shrugged. "I do, you can take my hatchet."

# CHAPTER ELEVEN

SHIVER IN MY BACK. BILE IN THE THROAT. SNOW ON MY FACE AND
nose at my ear. Tongue in it.

Stinky Joe whine.

*C'mon dipshit. Wake up. C'mon.*

Neck's twisted and my right arm's pinned—and that's the one I need
to push up. Once I get my head back.

"All right, Stinky Joe. All right. The hell's going on, here? Shitfuck.
C'mon now. Stop lickin'. Aright. Shit, dog? Let up."

So pissed I giggle.

I got a left arm too. Flail and squirm but the backpack don't give.
Roll on my face and my left hand grab snow and earth. Push off and the
right is weak and too useless from sleeping on it.

"Joe, I get what you're sayin'. I think."

*I bet you don't.*

"Well, I'm trying."

*Bullshit.*

"Hunh?"

*You heard me. Bullshit. I said my bit. You drink that stuff, you're an asshole.
No friend to nobody. Give it up, or it's the end of the line.*

"That a threat?"

*Fuckin' right.*

"Can I get up and think on it?"

Stinky Joe look away.

Push up with the legs and get the belly off the snow. Tripod on two knees and my face. Arms, push. Got too damn much practice at this. How come the body grok how to right itself when the brain ain't there yet?

Bile taste is strong. Eyes sting. Means one thing: I yakked and rolled. Snow stink of Wild Turkey, tomato sauce.

Basil.

Splotch the size of a kiddie swimming pool. Maybe got it all out.

Roll to my backside and wiggle out the shoulder straps. Lean the head and take in a black blotch of sky laid siege by storm clouds all 'round. Now I'm awake and the body think maybe it'll survive, the shivering take over. A good quake start at the small of my back and Elvises through, up and down both directions at once. Gimme a guitar I'll make the girls weep. Ha! Fuck I'm cold. Feel alive. Clear.

"How you get out, Joe? I leave the door open?"

*Tat's coming.*

"Shit. Jubal with her?"

*No. That punk that don't like dogs—he's with her.*

"Longhair. Even better. You watch that prick."

*You watch him. What's it gonna be?*

"'Bout what?"

*You giving up the likker...*

"Sure do feel better without all that Turkey in me. Garfadel—then some. Even more'n that."

*What?*

"I dunno. Shit."

*What's it gonna be?*

"Fuck. Dammit dog."

*You was sober all winter. You come out the cave a new man.*

"I was, at that."

*First sign of trouble, glud, glud.*

"That suppose to be a gulpin' sound? Your throat ain't right for it."

*You get the point.*

"Yeah."

*You got to give it up.*

His voice go soft.

*Right? Can you do that for me?*

"What if I need it?"

*Be someone who don't.*

He cock his head.

Throat's raw. Grab a fist of snow and eat. Try to collect reason but she float away and it's me and the dog looking at Glenwood Springs in the blizzard distance. Try to recollect the moments that led to this situation, cold wet feet, frozen yak on my face. Shivering dog.

"You ain't dressed for this, puppydog."

Joe nestle close. I wrap my arm around his shoulder.

"Better?"

*Put your balls in the snow, then talk to me.*

"Least you got em, buddy."

He'd a been better left in the garage. Tat could trail an ant across rock but she need Stinky Joe to follow Baer in ten inches snow? I don't understand sometimes and most times don't want to.

Stinky Joe jump out from under my arm and step downhill a couple paces.

*Ready to go back?*

"Don't think that's the place for me."

Stinky Joe talking on his balls in the snow make me recall something about a hand coming out a toilet.

Ah—Percival. The boy.

Saw him in the trees. Red eyes and stiff limbs. Murdered.

All at once I know the entirety—like unwrapping a present, cut open the box and inside they's a conclusion. No thought required.

I didn't want that fight. I didn't want Stipe and his boys to come after me but I couldn't hardly let 'em murder Fred. A man don't sit life out and not take a stand, then get a say on the fracas he miss. I had to do something. But what I did *is what they did*. They murder for evil and I murder for what?

The thinking's broke.

Now other people was good to begin with is servants of the lazy stupid. The good man want law and virtue so he take orders from the corrupt. Hell—do he know? Not a bit. But he'll sure as shit kill for what he think he know. So I was on the right side but they made it the wrong side, and now it's me agin the whole world that otherwise woulda said hell no, don't fuck with that man's dog. Now they say, string up that killer by his nuts, 'fore he git us too.

Ignorance.

They come after a fella, what choice he got? Give up? Let a bunch of dipshits don't do they own thinking take his life?

One good man woulda broke the chain. Stipe never woulda come after me. The archangels woulda said, you was in the right. The Gleason police woulda said, we's corrupt as fuck—apologies. Get on about your business. The federal dicks in Flagstaff woulda said, it was a good thing you took out those miserable dogfighters. Here, take this medal. Hero of the United States, or some such.

One moral man.

Instead they turn it upside down. Like I got no right to defend myself. No right to my labor. Nor property.

I didn't want this path but got no choice. Don't fight the evil, it's same as joining.

Oh—I got another choice: Die.

More and more hound me. Same time—I got to elevate... what? Me? My soul? My virtue? I can't kill for every transgression. But I got one life. One me. One minute. Can't squander it on kindness to the fool ready to point the gun and pull the trigger on another man's say so, without so much as a guess what made the command.

Any man take a life, he better damn well know the reason.

And if he don't, why it up to Baer Creighton to be civil while the other man's a hired thug? He want me to respect his self, his soul, his being a man—if he want the rights of being a man, he need to use his head for a damn change. A man can't harm another and have the weight of it sit on yet a third man's shoulder. Badge or not.

All that thinking open up out a pretty box with gift wrap. Boom. And the conclusion: I got the right to defend myself. If these people threaten ultimate force agin me, I got the right to ultimate defense.

All pretty in a box.

Stinky Joe look at me.

*You got it figured out?*

"I'm of two minds—and neither cognitates worth a shit. I'm right but that leave me a killer."

*Then you're a killer. Fuckit. Let's get out the cold.*

That punji wound in my leg's been seeping. Back my pantleg is froze solid.

They use shit on punji sticks.

That's like human brains. Caltrops rubbed in shit—no matter how a man lands, he's always got a pointy side out, warning the world not to get close.

Stinky Joe nudge me. Want an answer.

"Nah, puppydog. That place is trouble for ole Baer."

*Yeah, but it's warm.*

"It is that. But I'm in a conundrum, see?"

*What's to think about? Cold outside. Warm inside.*

"Well, see Odiferous Joseph? This is why you ain't evolved into a man. You don't got the moral sense. I can't go back that house. That woman didn't want company but she did right by her husband and suffered for it. So the company—me—show his ass. Terrorize the kid, show off how foul and obtuse his mouth can get without saying a single thing good. Make a spectacle, bust a chair."

*Apologize. Give her the satisfaction of seeing you hate yourself. Then sleep yourself sober where it's warm.*

"You got a point. Fessin' up ain't bad when you're comfortable."

"Who are you talking to?"

Turn the head and look back toward the Jubal White place. Tat's arrived, huffing. She stop climbing the hill ten feet off, and in the half-light her black eyes look slitted and mean. She shake her head, turn back down hill and walk three steps. Look back.

"You coming or what?"

"Where's Longhair?"

"What? He stopped climbing farther down. How did you know?"

"Stinky Joe said so."

Shake her head. Walk.

*Hey, dammit! The booze. I need your word.*

"All right, Joe. You got it. All right. I quit. Done."

Tat turn. Wrinkled brow and set jaw.

"I'm right behind."

*You mean it?*

"Accourse."

*Awe, wow! That's awesome. You can do it. I'll help.*

"Yeah. I'm afraid of that."

All the way down hill I stew on that box of concluded thoughts and it boil down to me being right and the world being wrong, just like always and everything, except now the stakes is so high it ain't just like regular people thinking each other's assholes, but they pretend to get along. Now we think each other's killers need put down.

I got a fight I never wanted and the only thing I can do to keep my mind right is not escalate the situation. Buy some time, somehow. Disappear to Canada or Mexico. Guam, something, so the people I see every day don't jump out the shadows saying give it up or die.

Mind's clear when we get to the Jubal White estate.

Tat enter the garage and look back. Stinky Joe scoot inside too. I turn to the house. Tat close the garage door.

On the porch I rest my pack agin the wall and kick snow off my boots. Try to pick frozen yak out my beard but it pull hair and I quit.

Knock.

Jubal open the door like he was already there.

Start out looking him in the eye but drift.

"I got nothing to say for myself. I ain't that man, but I did and I was. No excuse. And if you let me, I'll apologize to Mrs. White the same."

Jubal's head jiggers side to side but then he nod and the jiggers seem like he just tired and weak.

"She'd appreciate that."

"Afterward I'll grab my stuff and be gone."

"What, and leave your Jeep on my driveway?"

"I—uh."

"Say your piece to the wife and bed down in the garage. We'll talk in the morning. Now step inside so I don't heat the valley."

Jubal steady himself on a counter and make room. I step inside. Mrs. White tramp from another room, look at me and halt. Look at Jubal. Me again.

"Back so soon?"

"Ma'am, that lasagna was pretty special and your hospitality too. Sometimes a fella's humbled by his own stupidity. I apologize for the hubbub and my foul mouth and pretty much alla me. And like I told Jubal here, I be moving on."

Her smile's wore out.

Dip my head and slip out backwards. Jubal follow to the porch, reach back and turn on the light. Close the door.

"I appreciate you doing that for her. Sets a good example for the boys. They were in the other room."

Under the light his face is yellow while inside it was gray.

"I want you to stay in the garage tonight. You wouldn't last very long outside in these conditions and there's something I need to talk to you about tomorrow."

I search but he's stingy with his meaning.

"I'll help you get the Jeep fixed, but I need a small favor."

Grab my pack and throw one strap over my shoulder. Head for the garage. He still on the porch when I go inside, like to make sure I don't angle for the mountain.

Tempting. But if I can walk the line—if I can treat regular people as regular and avoid the ones want to kill me, maybe I'll get through this without taking more life, and taking more of the evil on myself in the name of all that's good and virtuous.

Clear as a bell with a bow on it. Fine as water. And shit. Is all.

Girls must be in the bathroom.

Tat's fixed her sleeping bag and Joe's curled at the bottom.

Drink some water. Think on Jubal White.

Cop ain't fooled by Alden Boone.

Cop's a dying man.

Cop wants a favor.

And I give up the likker forever.

# CHAPTER TWELVE

GÜNTER TOLD BAER HE'D FIND LEEKS AND A COUPLE MORELS IN YET another crate deeper in the cave, this one liberated decades ago from a milk truck.

Baer said, "Why keep it so far back? Animals might be interested in the meat, but leeks?"

Günter shrugged. "Not everyzing ve do has ein szatisfactory reason."

Baer cut the venison in two parts and dropped them in the sizzling melted fat.

"Nein. Take it out."

Baer burned his finger and sat with meat on a wood plate.

"Ze deer is cured vith salt. It is tough. Ze salt extracts ze vater."

"I always wondered. Don't the germs eat salty meat?"

"Ja. But ze zalt extracts vater from zem too."

"How you know?"

"I vas ze chemiker."

"Yeah, but salt ain't a chemical. It's salt."

Günter stared.

"I vould zay everyzing is chemical, but most everyzing is not. Cut ze meat in slices."

Baer sat long enough that taking instruction didn't feel like following orders. He shaved meat edgewise and added it to the cabbage, morels and leeks.

"We need salt. Pepper 'n shit."

"Vu need less alcohol."

"You was a chemist."

"In ze var."

"Dubya dubya..."

"Vun."

"One? Shit. I thought you was a hundred. What you do in the war?"

"I vas ein chemiker."

"What do chemists do in a war?"

"I made fuel for military fehicles."

"What you mean?"

"Ve made ezanol." Günter tilted his head to the Mason jars. "Like zat, from vood."

"From wood? No shit?"

"None. You burn ze cabbage."

Baer moved the pan to where the cabbage wouldn't brown and said, "You got a lotta rules for a cave man."

"Every man make rules. First for himzelf. Zen for ozers. Zen everyone liffe in cages." Günter pointed. "It is done."

Baer grabbed the cast iron handle. Burned his hand again. He used a carved wood spoon to shovel the meal onto two square wood slabs with a groove cut around the edge to contain liquid, and passed one to Günter.


SAUTEED IN FAT ON CAST IRON WITH THIN STRIPS OF SALTY VENISON and half fermented cabbage, the meal made Baer feel like a king.

Günter mostly fed his dinner to the dog. "My bowels no longer agree vith zis vorld."

"You already shittin' in the next?"

Baer met his eye and looked away, wondering why sometimes he said stupid things.

"You don't know it yet but sometimes I say stupid things."

"Youth."

Baer accepted the wisdom. "I don't like it," he said at last.

"Vat?"

"A man has to cross 'tween this world and the next."

"Someday you vill vait for it."

"I'll go when I gotta, but I'll fight every inch."

"You von't fight."

Baer looked up as he spooned a mouthful. He gulped crick water from a dented metal cup.

"I go every day," Günter said.

Baer shot a glance to the shelf of likker.

Günter tapped his temple. "Here."

"Same thing."

"No."

They were silent.

After eating a few bites, color returned to Günter's face and he had Baer bunch his blankets to the cave wall so he could lean against it.

"Cloze your eyes."

Baer's stomach was full and his veins saturated with shine. He'd switched to water for the meal. Now that the Mason jar was back on the shelf, it would take another permission to grab it. Baer's stomach churned like he'd told it to make butter but humoring the old man cost him nothing, and might earn more likker hospitality.

Baer closed his eyes and allowed his hand to slip to the hatchet head on his side.

"Now cloze your smell und taste."

"Close 'em?"

"Cloze 'em. You taste nothing. If you must, imagine you taste nothing."

Baer opened his eyes, gulped the last of his water. Shut his lids.

"Okay. I don't taste nothin' but that dog kinda reek."

"No. You do not smell ze dog."

"Saying I don't smell it ain't the same as not smelling it."

"Whose noze is on your face?"

"Mine."

"Good. It is your responzibility. You do not smell ze dog."

Baer shook his head. "I'm kinda used to it anyway."

"Now cloze your touch. You feel nothing. You float, ja?"

"My ass is on rock."

"You feel nothing. Vait..."

"Let's go with it. I don't feel nothin'."

"Good. You float. My foice—you do not hear my foice. You float in nothing. Zere is nothing. Only vords. Ven I schtop talking zey vill be your vords. New ones vill come. Zere is nothing around but vords. Zere is no earth, only intellect."

Baer drifted in inebriation.

"Vith nothing but vords, und no ozer senzazion, how do you know vich vorld you are in? Could you not leave one und enter ze next vizout knowing?"

Baer opened his eyes and blinked. Squinted. "Sounds like bullshit."

Günter half smiled. "You are ein fool und ein covard but one day you vill be more." He closed his eyes.

No juice, no red.

Baer closed his eyes and watched firelight glow on them.

*You are a fool and a coward but one day you will be more.*

# CHAPTER THIRTEEN

ALL THAT PUKING LAST NIGHT DID ME GOOD. HEAD'S CLEAR AND MIND is sharp. I hear that train a coming. Jailbreak. Time to bust outta Dodge City and step down to the okeydoke corral.

Gunshot! Jump so hard the Mustang rock.

Tat unzip and zoosh her nylon bag. Commotion.

Corazon mumble, groan, other side the garage.

Gunshshot! Agin...

Throw the flap, find my shorts in the footwell, yank 'em up. A man loves freedom sleeps nekkid. Pants. Shirt. Heated garage—I was a sweating fool.

Corner my eye, Tat's legs is out the bag, smooth brown and lean, folded. She spin on her butt and I understand something 'bout women. Corners is nice. Round is nice. Straight places—I see her arms and the morning glory wilt.

Racket outside... pop pop pop pop pop popopopopop!

Whole magazine empty.

Tat's got feet toward the door, arms across knees and Mr. Sig Sauer ready to greet.

She ain't yet run across country folk like to shoot. Now she has. Most likely that's Longhair out there, him and dad shooting a cardboard box.

"No need, Tat. They shootin' targets."

She twist her neck and give me a narrow look.

"You didn't hear a hammer on meat, right? Nor metal on metal. Nobody cryin' out, I'm hit! They target shootin', is all."

Dip my feet in wet nylon boots and wrangle out the vehicle. Grab my coat from the front seat. Though I cleaned last night's yak off my beard it carry the scent.

Hungry.

Door swing inside. Outside is maybe a foot of snow—and it's a rare man knows twelve inch on sight. Why's a woman uncanny bad at guessing a mile? 'Cause she's all her grown life been told five inch is ten.

In a sprightly mood for some reason. Maybe since the past is dead and most of me with it. Feel like I put on a good drunk last night and resolved some things, though I don't recall precisely what. Dunno. But when the good demeanor touches down on my soul I make a spot next the fire and offer up the welcome.

Someone—Longhair likely—shoveled a path from garage to house and it meet up with the driveway already plowed. I dreamed I heard 'em. Glad they was up to work at dawn. Step around the side. Jeep's buried but all around is plowed clean. Sky's blue and the sun ain't even over the mountain. Feel like ten degrees. One more reason to be happy. I'd a froze last night if I was in it.

It's like the snow covered the sin and now all I got to do is remember not to shoot nobody.

Nor drink.

Now was it the whiskey I swore off, or all of it?

Path shoveled to the garage back corner. Voices. Big boot prints with the small. I set mine on top. Linger and watch.

Jubal set up a firing range in the snow. Teach the boys how to be lawmen someday. Decked out like noise and light's the enemy. Yellow shooting glasses cover half they faces and each got on a headset like for flying B-17's, something. Got 'em loose on the neck so they can talk about they fine shooting.

Growing up we plug the ears with cigarette butts, if anything.

Still it kinda baffles. Spend money to complicate a simple and pure joy.

The little one wear a winter parka with the fuzz about the hood hanging on his back.

Longhair wear a hat with dope smoking colors.

Jubal got the balaclava with the flaps about his ears but not crossed in front. Man look half dressed. He got an arm on Longhair's shoulder and lean in for instruction. He point downrange—another thirty feet and the hill curve straight up to a nest of rock looks ready to topple.

"Like this," Jubal say.

He stand with feet spread and knees bent so his ass hangs like he cut a water fart. Both hands on the grip.

Percival stand like a man with a sword ready to duel. Left arm at his side and right pistol finger toward the target. No gun for the little one. Just a gloved hand shaped like a pistol.

I think on the last sixteen times I fired a handgun and none of 'em took more'n a second. No stance or nothing, just pull and shoot. Aim longer'n a second, get tired, bored, confused or outfoxed.

Hell of a day for shooting lessons. My ears is already cold. I sniff back a nose drip.

Longhair change out a magazine and Jubal look at Percival—then me.

He nod.

I nod.

He wave me forward. I look to the house behind to be sure, but Mrs. Jubal White's window is empty.

"I'm willing to bet sight unseen," Jubal say, looking at his boy, "that Alden Boone can put ten in that circle faster than you can give me five push-ups."

Dwain blow a cold breath.

"Oh boy," Percival says. "Whoa."

"Dad—don't."

"How about it, Alden?"

"Shit. You maybe didn't notice—I tied one on last night."

"Tied one what?" Percival say.

"It's an expression," Jubal say. "Dwain, give him that."

Dwain flips the pistol in his hand like a cowboy holsters it backwards and offers the grip.

It's a Glock, same as mine from the FBI fella. No art, shoots like a brick fires bullets.

"It's loaded," Dwain say.

I pull the slide and spot brass. The grip's wide, got room for fifteen or twenty in the magazine. Press the release and look. Lotta bullets. Push it back inside 'til the latch click.

They's two boxes downrange. Ground slope up so the targets is chest-level. Dot in the middle and a circle around.

"Use the one on the right," Jubal say.

"Plug your ears, little man. Gimme room."

Percival step back.

I swing and shoot. Pop 'em off fast as I can pull and though I can't see 'em hit the cardboard, it's all by gut, anyway. Gun holds so damn many bullets it worries my finger. Finally my ears is ringing and the slide locks. Empty chamber.

"Stand back. That hill's 'bout to fall over dead."

I take out the magazine, eyeball the chamber. Flip grip to barrel and hand the Glock back to Longhair.

Percival jump in the snow and try to follow boot tracks made by men with bigger strides.

Corner my eye, Longhair Dwain look me up and down. Can't help but draw a smile. I was his age I was dumb as shit and knew it. He likely do too.

Percival holler back, "You didn't hit any."

I nod.

"You didn't hit any at all. Not even the box."

Jubal sniff like to call bullshit. Holds his tongue. Dwain smiles. That's right, Youngpecker. You win.

"I woulda thought a Southern man would have at least hit the box," Jubal say.

"Well I never was fond of the firearms, per se. And things of that nature. And whatnot. And I'm a Yank... Is all."

"Uh-huh. Well maybe we'll give you some lessons while you're here. We'll talk about that later. I called a friend of mine, owns the transmission shop right off the exit there, first exit."

"I ain't been to Glenwood."

"He said bring the Jeep in. We'll tow it this morning."

"That's mighty white."

Dwain shoot a look.

"What?"

His lips move while he turn away.

"What?"

I don't follow. Ain't my place to push but teenagers is assholes in general and this one's both a smartass and a coward and maybe a kidfucker too... though me pokin' Tat kinda blur that line. Regardless, his bullshit irks.

"Something on your mind, boy?"

He face me.

Jubal inhale.

Dwain glare. "That's racist."

"The hell you say."

"Mighty white is racist."

"I was sayin' yer dad's a decent man."

He roll his eyes. "Like brown people can't be decent?"

"Who said anything about brown people?"

"You did, when you said white is good."

"What?"

"What? You heard me."

Look at Jubal. Can't twist the brain to follow this boy. Five minute of pure sunshine and happy joy, then this.

"Son," Jubal say. "He didn't mean what you took from it. Let it go."

"No. Redneck... *assholes*... say things like that all the time and no one calls them out. How's our society ever going to change?"

I can't noodle any of it, but Jubal seem to get what his boy is saying.

"Jubal. What the hell he talking about?"

"Mighty white—he's studying social justice at the college in town. Colorado Mountain. Mighty white means it's something a white person would do."

"It means..." Dwain say, "it's something GOOD, like a white person would do."

"Social justice?"

"Social justice. You know, racism," Jubal say.

"It's not just racism, Dad. You know that. It's climate change. The environment. Sexism. Wealth inequalities and power structures."

Crazy ass world, bitch about the cut and ignore the saw. Nobody here got the red eyes nor the juice so I smile like to ease up on my part in the nonsense... but a thought occurs and I open my mouth afore I give it a second think.

"If I got problems with brown people why am I driving two across the country and pokin' one? And yeah—the one you want. I seen you look."

Dwain clamp his teeth. Shake his head and his voice come out in a jumble afore he figures the words: "The—are—yer—that's sexist! You're objectifying women!"

"God Almighty put them objects on the women—and trust me, they like 'em much as we do."

"You people."

"Son! Stop. Just shut your mouth. Go inside. Shooting lesson's over."

Dwain whirl on Jubal and more sounds come out his mouth but Jubal open-hands his face. Not hard like to set him on his ass, but light, take the steam out.

For looking half dead, Jubal got speed.

"Inside the house. Now. You made your point. And clean that Glock before you do anything else."

Dwain stomp away on snow and it ain't near as good a look as I bet he wish. So he stop by the garage corner and look back. Point his gloved finger. "If you cared at all about other people, you'd learn how to talk so you don't offend them everywhere you go."

"I said your old man's a decent fella. All I said."

Jubal look at the snow. Percival watch my eyes. I'm torn by the heart-felt stupidity.

Dwain shake his head. Heeds his Bible—why suffer fools? Knock the snow off his feet and goes inside the house.

"Percy, go get those boxes and help your brother clean the pistol."

With Percival outta earshot I face Jubal.

"I'm ready to go. You want to tow the Jeep to town that's good. Or I'll push it down the hill and dump it in the river. Don't matter to me. But it's time I get out your hair."

"Ah, don't mind him. He's at that age. His freshman year he chewed my ass for saying I'd jew down a car dealer."

Jubal silent.

I think on it.

Jubal use his toe to push a clump of snow. Fold his arms. "Dwain hasn't learned yet. He thinks the injustice is out there, in the world."

"Uh huh."

"It isn't. It's in here." Jubal thump his chest.

"Didn't figure you for the philosopher type."

"Well, yeah. I guess that's so. Find out you're down to two months—everything becomes philosophy. Or religion."

"Shit."

"Shit is right. But you enjoy the stupid stuff too. All of it, what you got left."

Percival drag the boxes and stand beside his dad.

"Inside, son."

Percival go.

"What is it? The cancer?"

"Lung. And I never smoked a cigarette in my life."

"That's a kick in the sack."

"Yep."

# CHAPTER FOURTEEN

GÜNTER'S SNORES WERE LIKE THE NOISE A FISH MAKES LAYING ON THE bank after it quits flipping. The dog slept with more enthusiasm. Baer remained sitting where he was when he and Günter had stopped talking, except now with the peach Mason jar between his thighs and his mind sometimes slipping into that senseless space Günter described where there was only void and words. He'd never thought of the afterlife like that, and didn't know if it was better or worse than a heaven made of clouds and angels.

Günter had said, "Zat's vere you came from too. But you don't remember ze vords because you did not speak English yet."

"Is your words in Kraut or English?" Baer had said.

"Both. Zometimes neizer. Zometimes it's only Got's vords."

"Yeah, far out."

While Günter slept, Baer tried to hear anything but the words of his mother, Larry and Ruth; the assholes at the diesel garage, the swinging dicks shooting stick at the bar and the simple manipulators selling life insurance. All regular English words, used entirely for self puffery or deception. What would a divine word even sound like? Would it sound? Or would you just know it?

The moon rose and the terrain outside the cave entrance glowed in melting grays and blacks. The closer Baer looked the harder it was to see anything, yet when he allowed his focus to drift, the scene resolved. Maybe the old man's trips to death were like that.

At last the peach Mason jar lay on its side, empty. A stray thought—I ain't pissed since morning—left him happy. All that likker still worked its delirious magic.

By and by with the dog snoring and the old man off in death land, Baer twisted his head toward the cave mouth and detected a light gray hue on the tree leaves. Time passed then everything glowed. The leaves frosted with reflected light. Baer passed out and roused twice—the second time, his bladder mildly pressing. The moon blasted silver slivers between the trees and as Baer meditated on whether or not he should get up to relieve himself, the glowing orb ascended to a gap in the canopy and fired moonbeams straight at him through the cave mouth. One of his teachers in ninth grade science said the ancients worshiped the moon and gave it a woman's name. He couldn't recall the woman's name and then it arrived: Artemis.

She had a Greek name and a Roman name. Artemis—Ruth.

What were boobs like before bras?

Couldn't have been bad; they were boobs not elbows. But surely they weren't as proud as Ruth's. If he hadn't seen them he'd have suspected they were foam domes. That was the shame and mystery: the most beautiful thing in the world, but nearly always hidden. Granted, the moment of revelation mattered. They wouldn't be near as spectacular if chicks walked around with them hanging out all the time... yet it seemed a crime they didn't. Every woman walking around with a Mona Lisa swaddled under wraps.

Girls could be selfish.

Ruth's tits: Baer recalled the bottom curve seen from the side, and registered how it'd be perfect on the front end of a car, only upside down and with headlights. Probably work for the ass end too. You'd have to leave the bumpers off and when the cops pulled you over they'd say, this car's the tits but I gotta cite ya. Baer nodded. Saw what he did there. Grinned.

Maybe he ought to slip out, take a leak, then find a tree to lean against...

Maybe he ought to take a leak and then keep walking. Go find the real thing.

One time he fell asleep with his face against Ruth's boobs and woke up that way too. He may as well be buried six feet under: the distance between that moment and this was the same.

Günter snorted in his sleep. What was to say his spirit wasn't floating around right now, keeping an eye on his guest? Listening in on his God thoughts. Or devil thoughts. Which was which?

Fucking Krauts.

Maybe Larry was still at night school. When Baer scouted their rented duplex a couple nights in a row, Larry didn't come home 'til late. Ruth had the baby asleep and she sat like a moron with the wall behind her flickering in television light. Leaned forward into the lies. The woman was a miracle, submersed in untruth and wicked cruelty, but she never gave off the red or the juice.

What to do?

If the old man waded into the river and Baer dispatched Ruth, it'd just be him and the liars.

She actually chose Larry.

Chose him.

Set Baer and Larry side by side and said, I want the football geek with prospects.

Baer closed his eyes and saw her press her mouth to Larry's neck.

"I love you. Never let me go. Take me now!"

Baer stood and squeezed his eyelids. Short-punched his head eleven times but the image remained when he quit.

An idea formed.

He left his pack and looked backward from the cave mouth. Rommel's head was up but he didn't say anything. Baer set off downslope. The stream trickled to his right but the sound disappeared as his feet struck leaves. He pissed in the stream and realized the air was chilly.

Should he grab another shirt from his pack?

Nah.

The moon's brightness swelled his confidence and he stumble-walked without a hand protecting his eyes. Before the slope leveled he followed the contour of the mountain, knowing at some point he would cross the trail that led to the lookout. Following the other way toward the trailhead, he'd arrive in Montreat and only three miles would remain to Gleason.

The hatchet slapped Baer's thigh.

After Baer stole Ruth, Larry stole her back. Though it didn't seem precisely against the rules for Larry to take her—and it did seem against the rules for Baer to have another poke, now that she'd had his brother's kid—the backed-up feeling in Baer's loins didn't care.

He'd have her again.

He'd claim those moans and whispers.

# CHAPTER FIFTEEN

JUBAL AND ME TALK OUT FRONT THE GARAGE THEN I STAND WITH MY thumb in my ass thinking on escape, while Jubal back the truck to the Jeep. I hook the metal loop.

Jubal say, "You want to start the engine for some heat, and put on the four ways? We'll sneak up the interstate a mile. Got no choice but the highway."

"That legal?"

He show me dimples. "No, but I have friends. We'll be all right."

He walk toward the house and I get in the Jeep. Jubal grates. Lawman oughtta be all law or all man. Not this fuzzy nonsense, get away with what he can. I got friends. Nah. Hell. You supposed to be upright. Got the gall to hold another man to account, hold your own damn self first. Is all. My mouth is moving and sound steam the glass. Start the engine and look out the window. Tat.

Roll it down. "Mornin', Love."

She smirk. "Why you argue with Dwain?"

"I'm sure he'll tell you."

"Where are you going?"

"Transmission shop."

She look back and forth. Fix on me. Elbows on the window and close enough I smell Colgate.

"We must leave quickly. I don't trust these people," she say.

I nod—without a lick of insight for this girl.

"Tat, tell me true—you and that Longhair—"

"'Bout ready?"

Jubal come around the back and stand beside Tat. Where the hell? Somehow he circled. Press my back to the seat, glad for Glock.

"Yep. Lessgo."

Jubal tromp by Tat to the truck and open the door.

Tat hold my look and give me a squinty love smile—make me want to shave my head and bust a wall. I know how to operate a woman. What to do with the knobs and holes. But lift the hood... not a damn clue.

"Well?"

"Dwain? He talks *a lot*. We need to go."

She poke her head through the window and kiss my cheek 'cause I'm too slow to twist my face and get her lips.

Tat wince. "You smell."

She back away. I roll the window. Jubal rev the Ford.

Straps go tight and we ease forward. Left turn, half a country mile and hop on the highway. I think on Longhair Dwain and Tat—and if her play with him was trolling for information, what's that play mean when she turn it on me every day the last six seven month? Same damn look. Same one. Except maybe add a handful a tittie and it might could mean something new.

I'll ask Longhair since he know how to communicate better'n me.

Prick.

Ain't right driving with no engine sound. The roads is slop and Jubal go slow. Still, it ain't four minute to the exit and another to the transmission shop. Fella with a green cap and brown coveralls open the bay door on one side and then the other so Jubal tow me all the way in. Man loose the strap and Jubal pull forward out the back side. Genius.

He take my place in the Jeep, put it in first, release the clutch and they's no grab. Nothin'.

Second. Third.

He chuckle.

Fourth.

"Yep," he say. "Two days. No choice but a new transmission."

"That settle it."

"Likely run you three grand. Maybe."

Jeep was free. I'll take it. "Two day? You got a new transmission layin' in back?"

"Half the vehicles in Colorado is Jeep."

"Ah."

We shake.

"I'll need a deposit."

I keep his eye. Reach in back, lift my coat. His face is steady and not squirrelly like some. No red. I slip a coin out my belt and drop it in his hand.

He search my face like we's forgotten kin.

"One ounce gold," I say. "Ain't seen spot in a few week, but that'll be eight hundred plus."

He toss it. Feel the weight.

"That a good deposit?"

"Hell yeah."

I got a new friend.

"Tell me," he say. "You with the movement?"

"I need a movement." I slap his arm and git before he says gubmint.

Jubal's circled and parked in front. He push open the passenger door and I hop inside.

"Come back tomorrow, close of business," Green Cap say.

I wave. Close the door.

Jubal turn right and grab the lane to go left.

"We only have a minute before we get back to the house."

"I'll be out your hair tomorrow night. Appreciate you, I do. But it's best for all if me and the girls keep movin' on."

"That's why I wanted a minute."

"Uh-huh."

"I mentioned I got the cancer."

"Uh-huh."

"Don't go silly on me."

"No guarantee."

"Your name is Baer Creighton. I don't know who the girls are but I know your name and some of the story."

Jubal's truck is comfortable as all get out and with the heater on my feet they's about warm the first time in thirty minute. But I want to bounce off his seat and take my chances rolling down the highway.

After a two-count I figure if Jubal wanted me arrested he coulda called ahead and drove to the station. Nah, he got something ten times worse up his sleeve.

Jubal want a favor.

"Well I feel for you, I do. I knew a fella had the cancer in his lungs."

"Yeah. Well it's like I told the missus. We live, we die. It's the process. You know."

Jubal shift in his seat. Gimme a long glance. Put his left elbow on the sill and turn down the fan.

"Reward on your head's only a hundred grand."

"Dead or alive?"

"For information leading to your arrest. They don't do dead or alive anymore."

Road go by.

Fucking say it. Must be a big ask.

"Who did that?"

"Did what?"

"Bounty."

"FBI. They don't take killing their men lightly."

"Hundred grand for three? Seem kinda light."

"I thought so too. So I uh... I got a job for you."

"No you don't."

"You need to hear me out."

Jubal got no red and has both hands on the wheel so I may as well listen 'til we get back. Then gather the girls and scoot on foot. Steal a car and stomp the pedal. Shave and a haircut. Or leave the girls. They's merit each way.

Me and Joe eating dumpster cheeseburgers one day, jerked roadkill the next. Won't never be free 'til I find a big enough wood to disappear in. That's the truth.

"Turning you in for a hundred grand when half the people you dealt with were corrupt... that isn't justice for anybody."

"Well they's *all* corrupt. I didn't kill 'em for shits and giggles."

"You killed police. FBI. Men doing their jobs."

"If the job's corrupt, then so's the man that does it."

"Let's agree to disagree."

Fill my lower lip with tongue. Got an empty belly I'll need to fill 'fore we skedaddle.

"I took a second mortgage on the house, you know?"

"Uh. No I didn't know. You didn't say."

"Yeah. A couple years ago they were giving money away and with the boys at that age, I wanted to have meaningful time with them. You spend time with your dad? Quality time?"

"Just when I chucked rocks at his car."

"So you know what it means. The other way. You know what it could've meant if you'd had a real man about. You follow?"

"Uh."

"You'd been a different man. Different life."

"Not with my father."

"Well a different one. A good one."

"So what's this favor?"

"I need you to watch a movie with me and the boys, tonight."

"Fuck. What?"

"A movie."

"At the theater?"

"Nah, on the television. DVD."

Jubal's kinda lit up and got some color.

"What's this movie?"

"It's a good one. About surfers."

"Jubal, y'out your head."

"You got my word. I'm not setting you up for trouble. Hell, it's with my boys. No trick. I want you to watch the movie and after we'll talk."

"And after you'll ask some favor—and I'll tell you no. Then you call your police buddies."

"Word of honor. I won't do you like that."

"You're a cop. On sick leave, whatever. A cop."

He look straight ahead.

"You boys is different from regular people. Lock arms, right or wrong. I know what you want."

Jubal hold my eye long enough I want to take the wheel.

"No you don't," he say. "And even if you do, just hear me out. Watch the movie and hear me out."

"Scout's honor. You ask your favor. I say no. You let me leave and don't do shit."

"Scout's honor."

No red nor juice.

Don't know whether to trust the curse or common sense.

"How long since you had popcorn?" Jubal say. "Butter—and we got this powdered cheddar from the Amish down in San Luis Valley."

"Ahhhh. Fuck."

# CHAPTER SIXTEEN

After his long walk to Gleason, Baer stood looking towards the street with his shoulder to his brother's duplex wall. Behind him a wooded strip divided the wrong side of town from a development of cookie cutter houses sitting at an elevation of general superiority. The hill glowed pink with dreamy deception. The woods between were black and this side where the single-income, less educated folk lived in older houses glowed the same shade of pink, punctuated by red hot spots near the churches. The red lit houses used to puzzle Baer, so he paid attention when folks invoked the Lord in every sentence. A man named Koop, who was especially verbose about the Lord, had placed a hand-painted warning on his lawn:

*THE WAGES OF SIN IS DEATH.*

At length Baer estimated the religious people were no bigger liars than anyone else. So how to account for their homes being red as the hell they feared? Baer's only guess was that living in constant proximity to a house of God imposed a subtle but constant awareness of their rottenness. Maintaining sanity required them to lie to themselves, not just other people, so they exuded twice as much deception.

It was a working theory.

Leaning on Larry's duplex wall, the proximity to so many people caused Baer's skin to tingle with ambient electricity.

Immediately before him a window revealed Ruth and Larry's tiny living room. The duplex had a barred front door as well as all the windows, even the narrow one in back, where Baer presumed the bathroom was located. Twisted black metal protected every opening just like the bars they used below the handrails at the parlor where Baer's mother spent her last nights above ground.

Before he killed her.

He'd never heard of any murders in Gleason but there were a few stabbings the summer of 1965 when it stayed cool as spring until August and then became a scorcher. They found the degenerate—a man who'd arrived in town on the new Interstate 40 and decided to cut some girls. As justice sometimes happens, he hung himself from his jail cell bunk bed with a noosed rope, after suffering a fall that broke both his legs and knocked several teeth into his throat.

His suicide made the paper.

After the freeway came through, barred windows became common. Some folks felt better living behind them. Shortly after the drifter killed the girls, Larry told their mother they should get some bars installed. Larry was fifteen, an avowed peacenik feeling his sauce. Nerd. His mother glanced at Baer and then addressed Larry.

"You be better off learnin' how to kill a man with a knife. You won't always have someplace to hide, nor someone stronger to protect you. That's what being a man is. Or's supposed to be."

"You can't win every fight. Violence isn't the answer."

"Two things. One—don't backsass. Two—don't be a dumbass, neither."

"Yeah Larry, don't be a dumbass."

"You're like all of them. Get yourself killed for The Man. What for?"

"You and your bullshit," Mother said.

Baer's mother was beautiful in most ways, particularly beautiful in the rest.

Leaning on Larry's duplex wall, Baer placed his hand on the cold steel butt of his hatchet and slid his fingers along the edge, lubricated by deer fat. He pushed out his hip a little and lowered his shoulder, allowing his temple to rest against the rough red brick.

The walk had taken hours and during them his anger weakened. But now as he stood in the center of the civilized world, resentment accumulated. Being in the proximity of so many people brought the feeling of being under attack, but by nonmaterial forces that moved between shadows and never struck from where he looked. Sometimes he felt an impulse to cover his head and strike at the air knowing something dark moved within it.

The curse was getting worse.

He wouldn't be able to linger but a few minutes before the atmospheric electricity drove him away.

Baer leaned out and peered through the glass at an angle that made the interior wavy like a circus mirror. Reds and yellows flickered on the wall. Ruth loved her television.

Intoxicated, tingling, Baer closed his eyes.

As a boy he watched snowy images on a junker with an oval screen, a gift from one of his mother's friends from the restaurant where she picked up shifts. Baer remembered when the woman's husband—he never saw the woman—delivered the television in his truck. Baer's mother knew a lot of generous married women whose husbands liked to drop off things. They got the sofa that way too.

The black and white still worked in the late 50's... a miracle. But the screen no longer lit up in the summer of 1963, when Baer was almost eight. Mother bet Larry and him they couldn't drag it into the woods. She went to her waitressing shift and after easily negotiating the television into the woods the brothers farted around with slingshots trying to demolish it. Acorns were abundant but this job required crick pebbles. Baer made a bucket with his shirt bottom and transported enough ammunition to last him and Larry a few minutes. The rocks shattered the glass and dented the wood but hardly brought the destructive force Baer had hoped. He walked to the stream and this time returned with five larger stones, each big enough that hurling them strained his arm.

Rubbing his elbow, Baer suffered a moment of genius.

"Thermonuclear," he said.

Larry's jaw fell. "What?"

Baer returned to the house and even though his mother wasn't there, tiptoed into her bedroom, a forbidden space his curiosity and affection sometimes forced him to violate. He grabbed a shotgun stowed on the left side of his mother's closet.

While Larry plugged his ears, Baer rested the stock to his elbow like Shotgun Slade in a hurry, pulled back the hammer and fired into the very television where Slade taught him how to point and shoot.

The shotgun leapt from his hands and Baer couldn't fold his already-sore elbow for fifteen minutes but the blast provided the desired destruction to the television cabinet. The boys took turns hurling splintered wood at each other. They danced like shamans until Larry said, "Do it again."

Baer retrieved the shotgun from where he'd leaned it against a tree. Larry, still many years from becoming a peacenik, said, "Hold it like Audie Murphy, dipshit."

He tapped his shoulder.

Baer adjusted but it didn't feel right. He squeezed the stock hard to his body, closed his eyes and pulled the trigger.

Nothing.

"Did you reload it?"

"How?"

Larry shrugged. "I didn't even know she had a gun. Where'd you find it?"

Baer pushed the only thing that moved other than the trigger and the shotgun broke open, ejecting the spent shell.

"Just put another one in," Larry said. "Where'd she have it hid? How'd you know?"

"Where are they?"

"What?"

"The bullets?"

"Shotguns take shells not bullets, asshole. Besides, you're the one always sneaking in her room."

"Am not."

"Are too, faggot."

Baer closed the shotgun. It flopped open. He closed it with force and it snapped shut. Baer pointed the empty shotgun at Larry.

"Call me that again."

"You're not supposed to do that."

Baer left Larry standing there.

Replacing the shotgun in his mother's bedroom, he wondered if she would smell the burnt powder from the tube. Shotgun Slade never cleaned his gun on screen, that Baer had seen. He could take the shotgun outside and blast the water hose through it, along with some dish soap. Or he could do like his mother when the cast iron needed re-seasoned, take it to the crick and scrub it with sand. One way or another, he could get the weapon clean.

But a larger problem remained.

He sat on the corner of his mother's bouncy bed with the closet open, thinking, if one day she needs that shotgun and it isn't loaded...

What Larry said about him sneaking into her room all the time wasn't true, not exactly. It wasn't like he went through her things. Other than the closet—and he only knew what was in there because most of the time she never closed the door. It didn't fit right in the humid summer.

Of course he saw what he saw, lacy items that went over her curvy parts, but that didn't mean he went sniffing through her bureau like Larry implied. Why would anybody want to smell underwear anyway? Detergent made him sneeze. Sometimes Larry repeated stuff the older boys said. None of it made sense. Sitting there didn't cause any harm and shouldn't be a punishable offense, not like moving things around and looking underneath.

Those extra shells had to be somewhere... but this seemed a matter of breaking his mother's intimate privacy and some kind of animal spirit reared up and froze him. Baer was powerless. He sat on the edge of his mother's bed, unable to contemplate that sort of depravity and lawlessness.

Eventually his mother's car backfired and died in the driveway.

The time to flee her room was now... But Baer sat.

The screen door screeched then rattled as his mother preempted the spring to close it. Baer winced. Holy shit, confessing this sin was gonna suck. Her feet struck the linoleum hallway. She could already see him— the line of sight from the bed corner was clear. She said nothing but her pace slowed as she neared.

Tears streamed down Baer's seven year old face.

Mother always changed out of her waitress uniform right away because she didn't like how it fit her ass—the body's got to breathe, she'd said once—and it struck Baer as funny that a butt needed to breathe because that meant the stinker hole was like a throat for poop. That always stuck with him, and he thought of it while looking at the floor and feeling her stare on his salty face.

"Baer? What'd you do?"

# CHAPTER SEVENTEEN

BOOTS SIT UNDER THE HEAT RADIATOR. NAP MOST THE DAY IN THE Mustang bucket seat while Tat braids Corazon's hair and they chatter in gibberish. Sound like girls.

Are girls.

Half my mind says the crick water's high... stay back. Other half says jump in, see what's around the sandy bend.

If they didn't talk so damn much. Even with the door closed. Got no plugs so I stick a 9mm shell in my ear and push it agin the window. Too big. Wish I had a hammer.

"Tat!"

Yammer yammer.

"Tat!"

She perk up. Look at me through the glass.

"Ease up on the bullshit."

She make a face. Jibber yammer.

They was a day I pined on Ruth. Wish I could go back to them days I wrote letters and enjoy the quiet.

Likely time for that movie Jubal want me to see. I ain't watch a movie since Clint Eastwood give up cowboying so he could be the law in San Francisco.

Now I gotta take a leak. Can't sleep for nothing anyway. Pop open the door and the chatter stop. Wish I knew that's all it'd take.

"Don't mind me."

Stinky Joe see me heading outside and follow.

"Where you going?" Tat say.

"Not sure. Jubal say he want me to watch a movie."

Tat pop to her feet. "A movie?"

Any time she move her hand go to her gun. Her stance say she might pull her Sig and shoot me from curiosity.

"All he told me."

"You need to think about what I said."

"And like I said when I come back from the garage. Jeep's fixed tomorrow. Better wheels 'n feet."

"I don't trust these people."

"I don't neither. But I'm a play along and not ruffle any feathers. We scoot tomorrow night."

"Promise?"

"'Less I change my mind."

Close the door. Stinky Joe's by the porch and Longhair Dwain's turned sideways holding out something look like jerky. He don't see me. Joe jump for the treat and Dwain pull back his hand. Joe growl. Dwain lower the jerky in front his face agin.

Stinky Joe jump and Dwain pull it away.

A man can move quiet on snow.

Swipe the meat from Dwain's hand. He turn. Two handed shove set him back and slipping.

"Taunt that dog again I'll beat the puss out you."

I hunker to Stinky Joe. Give him the meat and scruff his neck. "Don't mind this fucktart, Stinky Joe."

*If I ripped out his throat, would that be wrong?*

"Maybe. Depends."

He gimme a kiss.

*Remember your promise. You're done with the likker.*

"Yeah. Hard to forget."

I stand and turn. Dwain's got a wide stance and arms out. Face snarled back and his hands went to fist—but hell. He never punched nothing but his pillow. It's his mouth that has the guts.

"We know who you are," Dwain say.

"Me too."

House door swing open. Jubal.

"You two goin' at it again? Get in here, both of you."

"He pushed me."

"If you knew your ass from a hole in the ground... Get in here. You coming, Alden? We got the movie ready to go."

"The girls?"

Head shake. "Man thing."

"Oh." Give Jubal my best smile. Look at Dwain stepping in the house, walk narrow like he's squeezing a pecker in his ass.

This whole shebang don't feel right. Copper not being a cop 'cause he dying. Any lawman I ever met was like any other man. Rotten through and through, or straight up law abiding assholes, the good ones. I'll respect a trustworthy asshole. Other hand, nobody wants a likable lawman as it only means he's a two face liar. Upholding rules nobody wants ain't supposed to be likable, so the best a good cop can hope for is people call him fair. He hold his territory—and I can keep outside. Easy to avoid and just as easy to find. That's a good lawman.

But Jubal's got me squiggly on him. Man don't know or speak his mind. Or if he know, he hide it. He put out the salt lick and I'm the deer come along sniffing. Safe one day and shot the next.

Other hand, popcorn and cheddar...

I stop at the step. Come out the garage without my pistol and still ain't took a leak.

"I gotta piss. I be back in a couple."

"Use the bathroom in the house."

His look says he insist. I insist more.

"I be back in a minute."

Find my FBI Glock in under the Mustang driver seat. Use the bathroom and check the magazine and chamber. I don't like this setup at all. He showed me the boy can shoot. If he told the boy who I am, that mean I'm the only one don't know exactly what's going on. The plan. If I ain't one of the squeezers, I'm getting squeezed.

How? I dunno.

I'm back to where I started. Jubal ain't playing a trick. No red nor juice.

Jubal want a favor.

He likely won't want me wearing a holster for the movie so I slip the Glock in my cargo pocket so it bang my leg when I walk. I'll go in ready to yank, and wait for the red to tell me when.

Back at the front door I knock and Jubal open. He point to the other room across the kitchen. Got a television like that one in the cement cave back in Flagstaff. Big and flat. He point me to a sofa and shit I'd rather sit on the floor.

"You mind if I grab that rocker?"

"Make yourself at home."

It ain't but mid afternoon but my belly been thinking on popcorn and cheese all day. Sit in the wood rocker and wiggle the hip. Pistol clunk but no one look. Percival come in and sit injun on the carpet. Dwain come in, look at me. Look at his dad on the sofa. Sit on the other side. I must be in the big man seat.

Jubal nod at the big screen. "Turn that on."

Dwain huffs.

Glad I don't got a son. Cuff his face half way 'round his head.

Screen go on and the movie start.


Surfers rob banks. Wear masks like dead presidents. Can't understand half they words.

Oh—and prettyboy want to poke a skinnygirl. So they surf. Meanwhile he a cop. Jubal want me to understand something but aside a couple good fights the movie's nonsense.

Jubal, a cop, know he got a cop-killer on the rocking chair. Got his family all about. Watch a movie about bank robbers. Just as weird as bodies in trees.

All in all I like a good bank robber. Banks is thieves and someone with the stones to rob 'em back—shit. Give me a woody. They got that fiat money—this is money since I say so, not since it has any value. They got the fractional reserve. Money piled up on money and only thing give it worth is the honesty of the liars that print it. The politicians.

I always wait for the bank robber in the court room scene to turn the tables. Make 'em prove those printed bills is worth anything at all.

Oh hell yeah. Günter Stroh schooled me on the Weimar Germany and I never play the bank game. But just 'cause I never had any use for the bank don't make me apt to rob one.

So... Jubal want to rob a bank... But he got the cancer. Dwain ain't but a college dipshit. Percival barely fit to load a gun let alone point one.

Jubal out his mind.

But Baer Creighton come along with his girls and Jubal see the solution.

Now they surf again. All these people do is rob banks, surf and poke pretty girls. Maybe after I see Denver, turn around. California.

Jubal keep looking at me like I can't see.

Dwain spin his hair 'round his finger like a high school princess.

Percival says *whoa* one more time I'll kick him.

'Bout an hour in Jubal say, "Pause that, son."

Dwain press the remote.

"You fittin' to rob a bank?" I say.

Jubal sniffs. "You got any appetite? Popcorn?"

"I could finish a bowl of wood slugs."

"Gross!" Percival say.

"Little butter, salt and pepper. Sear 'em in cast iron—"

"Yeah. Let's do the popcorn. Dwain. Get your mother from the back room."

He huff. Climb out his seat. Leave the room.

"He's skinny, ain't he?"

"He's thin, but see him with his shirt off he looks totally different."

"Me too."

"Yeah, well—" Jubal nods, laugh. "Okay, sure. Me too. But what I was saying is Dwain's a wrestler. In high school he went undefeated three years. He had two full rides offered, and passed on Colorado State so he could stay close to home the next couple years, at Glenwood Springs. I know you didn't see it from the shit he was giving you yesterday, but the boy's got character."

"Yeah. No shit."

"Speaking of butter—Percival—go help your mother make popcorn. She likes it when you help with the butter."

Percival leave.

Why I get the sense this on purpose? Look to look with Jubal.

"You didn't say you ain't fittin' to rob a bank."

He shrug. "Money's insured."

"Sheeeeeeeeit. You ain't real."

"No. But you see what they're doing, right? The way these guys go in. Control the crowd, in and out. Got it all mapped out, down to the time of day. Escape route. Nothing left to chance. See, when the criminals do their jobs right, they use the threat of violence in place of violence. They control the situation and no one gets hurt."

"What happens when the fella they don't expect has a gun?"

Jubal says, "That's why you never start something you aren't willing to finish."

"How's a man with lung cancer going to finish anydamnthing? When they kick you in the teeth. Or chase your ass?"

"Oh, no. I'm talking purely hypothetical, here. Purely hypothetical."

"Your boy—Longhair. He know your plan?"

"Not yet. And I don't have plans. Just formulating things. Thinking stuff through."

Red. Juice. I knew it.

"And you got it in your head I'm somehow helpful to those plans you's formulatin'?"

"If you was amenable."

"Never been my favorite word."

"Well it isn't fun to ask, either. But a man down to a handful of weeks, or a couple months at best… Over-extended on the bills." He look at the wall like it done him wrong. Face crinkle 'round the eyes. "Man has to do what he can, while he can."

"Assuredly true. Maybe that lawyer from Denver could help."

"What?"

"Nothin'."

"What the hell are you talking about?"

"It is what it is. Rarely what it ain't. You spend the money on the lawyer—and money only spend once. 'Less you get it back. Maybe rob the lawyer. I dunno."

Jubal square his jaw. Lips a flat line. "What lawyer?"

"Just a story I heard from a web log, is all. Wasn't in the newspaper so it wasn't true."

Jubal probe his upper lip with his tongue.

Pissed off woman sounds in the kitchen. Silverware. Feet half drug on linoleum. Slam-banging nonsense. Dwain come around the corner.

Figgers.

"Help your mother with the popcorn while I talk to Alden, right?"

Jubal breathes hard alla sudden like the words is more effort 'n he can muster.

"You all right?" Dwain say.

"Get me a glass of water and my medicine. On the hutch."

Dwain disappear. He ain't a total dipshit. Just near me.

Cupboard. Sink. Rattle. Dwain come back with gifts. Jubal take a pill and toss back his head. Drink water. Give the glass to Dwain. "Thank you, son. Now give me a minute."

More sounds in the kitchen—this time, popcorn in a pan.

"So what you was saying..." Drop my voice. Elbows to knees. "You ain't right in the head, you want a life like that for your boys. I ain't slept right in six month. You got it all wrong. Live what days you got left and they'll live theirs. Ain't a favor, make 'em criminals."

Jubal loose a huff and his belly go down. "A little cash is all I mean. You buy groceries and gas with cash, right? So they got cash to last until they get my Social Security. That's all I'm thinking."

"Bank cash."

"No. Not a bank. Listen. Haven't you been paying attention? I don't have but two times my salary for life insurance. The long term disability doesn't meet the obligations. We're going backward every month. I'll die soon enough, but it won't be in the line of duty, so no bump there."

He wait for a answer I don't got.

Jubal say, "Life insurance buys the wife and kids two years." He look down. Look up. Look hot. "I can't leave them like that."

"It ain't easy—for nobody. But your boy can work. Your wife."

"Dwain's in college and the wife grew up on a farm. I married her after high school. She hasn't had a single paycheck her whole life. So what kind of work is she likely to find? Waiting tables?"

Think on my mother, what she did to feed me.

"It's work."

"Not enough—and I'm not against them working. That's a good thing. No matter what I do, she's going to have to work somewhere. But in this economy? Fast food jobs don't pay the first mortgage, let alone the second."

"Just who the holy fuck forced you to build a garage and stuff it with cars? Your trouble ain't my business."

"It could be. If you felt like you had some redeeming to do."

"Fuck."

"What? That doesn't make sense? Or redemption isn't your concern?"

"Get redeemed... rob a bank."

"That's what I keep saying. I'm not talking about a bank. But if it was, they're insured—that's what the FDIC is all about. It isn't like taking money from real people. It's like walking up to the ocean and dipping your glass. They print a hundred trillion dollars a month. Why should my kids suffer?"

"All good points."

"I'm just trying to figure out a way to fill in the gaps a little."

Popcorn popping in the kitchen.

Can't hardly get my brain 'round this dying cop think he'll fix things right as rain for the wife and kids... gonna rob a bank.

"I ain't in this. I'll eat your popcorn, but I ain't in this *none*."

He lean close and keep the voice under the popcorn racket. Wife ain't in on the secret.

"This isn't how I wanted the conversation to run. I thought we'd talk after the movie. Take a ride in the truck and I could show you what I had in mind. It isn't a bank."

Close my eyes. I got a nine in the pocket and this whole clan's so pitiful I could beat 'em to death with a wood spoon. And he want to rob a bank. Or not a bank. What? A fucking gas station? Stupidity on a plane so high it piss a man off.

Popcorn jitter clangs and time the noise is done the smell make it to the living room.

I saw that boy of his, Percival, dead in the trees. Said I won't kill a boy. I don't know how the whole thing's bound up. I saw archangels afore and now maybe demons. I ain't in this.

Let my hand ease to my side since this is the moment he don't want.

"I'll watch your movie. I'll eat your popcorn. But no way in hell I'm part of what else you got cooking. No way in hell."

# CHAPTER EIGHTEEN

"Baer? What you do?"

Baer sat on the bed looking down at his mother's feet as she approached. Her tennis shoe laces were white but the ends were dirty like they'd been dipped in oil. She didn't wear socks in the summer and her ankles didn't seem as narrow as he remembered from summers before. Her legs had tiny hair nubs he'd never noticed before and she had yellow bruises on her knees and one on her shin that was purple.

"Baer!"

He looked up, read alarm on her face and diverted his gaze into the closet. He opened his mouth and attempted to issue his voice but he still hadn't thought of a way to profess his guilt without summoning the justice he deserved. She explained one time while switching his ass that she grew up getting a switch on hers. You think it's total horse shit but this hurts me more than it hurts you—and she was right. It was total horse shit. But when she jerked his arm and lifted his heels from the ground there wasn't much he could do but steel his mind. No matter how long he remained silent, she lashed 'til he bleated. Over many lashings Baer learned the noise was the signal. One time he schemed to halt the punishment early by squawking on the first strike, but she dealt a glancing blow and his howl must have struck her as counterfeit. Instead of dealing out pure justice, the ass whoopin' that followed seemed partly fueled by her anger at his intended manipulation.

There was no gaming Barbie Creighton.

That switch was surely coming.

Worst of all, she'd make him go cut it and bring it to her. She preferred birch and always told him to fetch two because she usually broke the first.

At last Baer brought his eyes to his mother's face. He folded his hands together and unfolded them and swung his legs.

"I'll get two switches."

"What are you talking about? Are you hurt? What did you do?"

Without lifting his arm, Baer pointed to the closet. Mother stepped into the room and turned left.

"You shoot somebody?"

Head shake.

"You shoot something?"

Nod.

"Baer! You're scaring me! Say something!"

"Yes."

"Is anybody hurt?"

"No."

She exhaled so hard she seemed to collapse as she sat beside him. Mother took his hand and opened the rest of his fingers straight to match his pointer and pressed his hand between hers.

"Nobody's hurt? You didn't kill your brother?"

"No. But I shot the gun."

"How'd you know how to use it?"

"Shotgun Slade."

She shook her head. "That stupid television! Did you shoot the gun in the house?"

"I'm not that dumb."

"No, but you're a born rebel and your temper's gonna land you in prison one day."

Baer swallowed.

"I shouldn't-a said that. You give me a scare. Show me what you shot and I'll figure what trouble you're in."

Baer led her out the back door and across the short lawn to the patch of black elderberry planted by the folks who lived there first. He took her on the path Larry and he cut through the blackberry brambles to the hemlock tree strangled in grapevine where, in the cool shade, he and Larry once carved pipes out of corncob and elderberry stem and tested smoking everything from corn silk to shoe leather.

There under the tree sat the disemboweled television, glass shattered and wire yanked out like entrails.

"Oh. Wow," she said. "That's not how you fix a broken TV."

Baer snorted.

She laughed. His mother never laughed that way, with relief.

"Look at that." She ran her hand along the top. "I'd find some more rocks but there's no more work to be done."

He studied her.

"You're not mad?"

"I'm not really mad."

"Not really, but sorta?"

"No. Not even sorta." She reached to his head and tousled his hair. "It's my fault."

Baer tried to think how it was her fault that he was a rebel and rotten to the core..

A distant sound snagged his attention. Baer looked back toward the house to the percussion of metal on metal, brought by a change in the wind.

His mother tilted her head.

Tink... tink... tink... the sound seemed like it started with hard edges that rounded with distance.

"It's time," his mother said. She took his hand. "C'mon with me."

"Time for what?"

He walked but her arms swung different from his and she released his hand.

"Keep up."

"Time for what?"

Baer followed inside the house and back down the hallway and stopped outside her bedroom door. From inside she waved him forward.

"I want you to see this."

Baer stood beside her.

"Grab that shotgun and put it on the bed."

He did.

"Now drag those dresses on the right side all the way to the left."

Baer pushed them all at once.

"Whoa."

He stood transfixed. The closet opened on the left side, but whoever made it was clever. Inside it expanded two feet to the right, behind the wall. It was like a trick closet and in the deceptive depths of the right side his mother had hidden guns and guns and guns.

"How'd you get these?"

"Oh, let's just say they were presents. Sometimes I help out the girls at work, or whatever, and they want to do something nice for me so I tell them I like guns. You know."

Baer looked from the weapons to his mother.

"Girls gave you guns?"

"Why is that funny?"

"Girls don't like guns. You don't like guns."

"No, I never did. You're right. But I knew someday you and your brother would need to learn and I wanted to make sure to have something to teach you with."

"You know how to shoot 'em?"

"No, grab one. They're all empty. I only keep the shotgun loaded."

"Why?"

"To protect the house."

"Larry says we should get a dog."

"Feeding a dog costs money. Go ahead and grab another one."

Baer looked at the rifles. Each barrel was a different length. One had a rectangular slot cut through the stock. Another looked like someone used it to send a bucket of rocks over the fence. One rifle gleamed like new—but it had a skinny barrel.

What caught Baer's eye lay on the floor. He picked it up and read the words imprinted in the stainless steel.

"Smith and... Holy shit, Ma! You got a Smith'n Wesson?"

"Baer!" She cuffed the back of his head, light. "We don't use foul language."

"I'm sorry."

"It's awful big for your hands, isn't it?"

Baer's smile grew and grew.

"It's huge!"

"See that shoe box?"

"Uh-huh."

"Put it on the bed."

Baer placed the Smith and Wesson on the bed then lifted the box and placed it beside the shotgun. He pulled off the cardboard lid. Inside were smaller boxes on one side and the other was filled with stray shotgun shells of various colors.

Mother took Baer's hands and used her finger to steer his chin so he looked at her. She kissed his forehead.

"Baer, listen to me. Guns are for killing. That's all they're for."

She looked into his eyes and he returned her earnestness.

"I have that shotgun in the closet because it's just us in the house. If something bad ever happens, I need that gun."

His eyes were wide.

"You understand? That shotgun is important."

He nodded.

"So Baer, I'm not angry. But listen... If you shot my shotgun and didn't know where I keep the shells, how'd you reload it for me?"

"I didn't. Honest, I didn't know where—"

"I know. That's what I'm sayin'. I keep that shotgun for protection. You shouldn't-a used it without my permission."

"I'm sorry."

"You understand?"

He nodded.

"Okay. Take one of those green shells and load it into the shotgun."

Baer grabbed a shell. He looked at her.

"Didn't Shotgun Slade teach you?"

He shook his head.

"You know how to open it?"

"You push this," Baer said.

"Go ahead, then put the shell in the hole and close it."

# CHAPTER NINETEEN

NOON. AFTER YESTERDAY'S BANK ROBBER MOVIE JUBAL TRY TO BEND my ear agin and I said they's no way. He put the hand on my shoulder and I twist off. If they's one way a feller can make sure to piss me off, put his fuckin' hand on my shoulder.

Jubal clamp his teeth but still no juice nor red. Suspect afore he got the cancer he was one of them uptight asshole good cops. Write himself a ticket if he broke thirty-six. Downhill. But maybe looking at the casket he start thinking morals was a pain in the ass and he'd a lived better and had more money if he broke more rules. So he tow the Jeep on the interstate with a nylon strap.

I dunno, but he ain't crooked in the heart. Not enough to do the crookin' he ponder. If he try he'll fuck it up and anyone near him'll pay.

After a mean look his eye got icy and far off. He nod slow like a new idea hit him and until he give it a think, he leave me off the hook.

Well I wasn't never on that hook.

Not that one.

All morning I kept in the garage. He got a grinder on the workbench so I put an edge on anything that'd take one. Test the hatchet on arm hair and for shits and giggles shave my face. Clean off the blood and look fine.

"Hmmm." Tat say, so we bopped squiddles in the Mustang while Corazon took over the bathroom. Now my mind is frayed like rope.

Come out the Mustang with my drawers about the knees and Corazon's at the grinder holding a knife I put an edge on. She look up and smile.


LAST NIGHT TAT SIT ON THE PORCH WITH DWAIN AND I COULDN'T keep an eye out with the garage light on and me in the window. They didn't last twenty minute in the cold. After she come in the garage I let her stew, but if Dwain's part of Jubal's dumbass plan—he the oldest boy and oughtta be—and the way he runs his mouth, he maybe say something to Tat. 'Specially if they ever guess she was part of the body count in Utah last fall.

When she come back in the garage I give her space 'til she find me.

"His father is dying of cancer."

"Uh-huh."

"They won't have any money."

"Yep."

"He says they need our help."

"Wages help. Less bills. Less Mustangs. What everybody else does when they need the money."

"Yeah," Tat say. She wait... ... ...

"He say anything about that fourteen year old girl? Mention that?"

"I asked. Her name is Amber and he said he kissed her. He said she came onto him hard at a party and he was drunk so he let her. He never dated her or anything and then she was screaming at him in town one night, right on the street. Crazy stuff he said never happened."

"His eyes red?"

"What?"

"Never mind."

"Right after that the police arrested him. Jubal was still a cop—they didn't give him any warning. Dwain said the girl's father always had trouble with the police, so he pressed charges. The girl said they had sex when they never did and no one could prove it. If it wasn't for his father hiring a lawyer from Denver, Dwain's life would have been ruined."

"Newspaper said that about the lawyer. Big city. Corazon said that."

She was quiet.

"You think... uh."

She study me.

"Corazon? You know. How she like to..."

Look around.

Tat shake her head. "I don't think so."

"All I know is, don't wake me at a quarter past the squinty hairs and say we gotta run. Don't let her be stupid."

Tat nod.

"Longhair say anything else? Or can I bed down?"

So that was last night.

Jubal's a decent man turned dipshit and his oldest boy's bound to be one of those fellas you wish died young. That leave Percival. Anybody gonna save Percival? Maybe best thing is for his dad and brother to rob a bank and go to jail. A boy like Percival got enough stupidity in his genes, don't need to see it modeled.

First light this morning I dump out the sleep sack ready to run. Roll the bag and stuff the backpack. Made coffee on the propane burner and drink it black for breakfast. Tat chew an apple from a gas station in Grand Junction. Corazon spent two hour in the bathroom. I used a good hour on the grinding wheel putting edges on everything in sight. Shave in the open bay with the Mustang side mirror. Bopped squiddles. Time Corazon see me nuts out, we had everything but her pack next the garage door.

Plan is, I get the Jeep, come back, load and go. Just enough goodbye to be sure they ain't ready to call the cops—and if it look like they is, we got no choice but put 'em down. Don't like it, but Jubal insist we stay. He knew my past and chose his future.

He bank on boxing me in a corner.

Afternoon I open the garage door and dig some packed snow down to gravel for the propane cook stove. Boil water for some noodles and the chemical sauce taste like pork. We each do two pack and eat out the same plastic bowls we use since a gas station outside Moab. Sun's bright and the air ain't bad.

Hear the house door open and Longhair Dwain come out in his dancing leotards, some flappy shorts and a nylon top with racing stripes. He got the red mirror sunglasses and a hat with a tassel. Wave at Tat and press his watch. He run with careful feet on the driveway slope, turn right, away from the interstate and next I see he's past the bend a quarter mile off. Bounce like a deer. Long strides. Almost pretty.

"You oughtta be with a young feller."

Tat still got her eyes where Dwain vanished. She tilt her head.

Corazon get on her feet and go back inside the garage. Always get the feeling she spends her time thinking on killing people.

"I was his age and tangled with a pretty girl like you... I'd last three minute. But we'd scrog forty time in a row."

She huff. Smile. Frown. "It was the right time for us," Tat say.

"Won't always be."

She shake her head. "No."

Nothing like an unexpected honest conversation to discombobulate, 'specially after what I thought was a good poke. Hear the truth I wanted yesterday and don't care for it today. But it's good the words is out there instead of each of us guessing.

"Guess we got it good while we got it."

She take my fingers 'tween her hands. "When it ends, we will know."

Can't argue with that.

We got maybe a couple hour 'til the Jeep'll be ready but I'd just soon wait at the garage, case they finish early. Jubal in the house.

"See if Jubal give me a ride in town. You mind packin' the stove?"

"I'll get it."

In a minute I knock and the house door open. Percival.

"Where your old man?"

"My father?"

"That one."

"In here."

Voice from the living room. Television ain't on.

"Thinking it'd be nice to head into town so maybe when the Jeep done, I get out with some light left."

"Give me a minute. I'll be out."

"Can I go?" Percival say.

"No, son."

"Aw."

Close the door. If Percival came along maybe Jubal'd avoid one more try at the bank robber recruitment program, but it ain't my place to invite the boy. Tat's already moved the propane burner inside and she sit in the sunlight on the cardboard she use like a sleep mat. She lean on her backpack, a lazy minute under the spring sun. The roof drips water. Ain't as cold as it seem a short while back.

Jubal come out the house walking stiff. Looking weak. Jumpy, maybe. He stop half way to the truck, put hands on knees and cough.

Expect a lung on the driveway.

Door opens. Percival come out, then Mrs. White. "Jubal. What are you doing? Have Dwain drive him."

"He's running," Percival say.

She shake her head.

Woman at the door like a ghost I once saw—the neighbor, Mrs. Brown. She die from drinking antifreeze—that and a shotgun—but this woman got a different situation, maybe. A man whose pigheadedness is steered to take care of her.

Get old and time echoes everywhere. Got to wipe the past off the glass to see the present.

Jubal walk his hands up his legs. Clear his throat and spit. He finish to the truck and after the door's open, wait for the ambition to climb inside.

At the window I say, "Maybe we wait on your boy? That good?"

"He'll be gone two hours."

"You good?"

"I'm good."

"Okay, Jubal. Okay."

I cross 'round and get inside. He drive without the seatbelt and that make me put on mine. No words 'til we at the exit and he say, "I'll respect what I said before."

"Then I'll be on my way tonight."

He nod slow. Open his mouth but no words. Close it. Every man alive could bitch about something. Every woman too.

# CHAPTER TWENTY

MOTHER POINTED TOWARD HER BED. "GRAB A BUNCH OF THOSE shotgun shells and put 'em in your pocket."

"What about the Smith'n Wesson?"

"You like saying that name, don't you?"

"Smith'n Wesson?"

"I think the bullets for that one are in the green box. With the orange. See?"

"Can I take some?"

She nodded.

Baer opened the box. Six cartridges.

"They's only five."

"Six."

"What?"

"Count 'em again."

"Oh. How'd you know?"

"Because I was going to sell the — Smith'n Wesson — last winter."

"But you didn't?"

"No, Baer, I didn't. I knew that's the one you'd want. Enough talk for now. I got a headache comin' on." Mother grabbed the shotgun. "Take that pistol."

"It's mine?"

"Be quiet. Where's Larry?"

"Didn't you see him hiding down by the stream?"

"Where?"

"The Ice Age boulders."

"Who said that?"

"He was there."

"No, about the Ice Age?"

"Mrs. Craig."

"She's a Yank. Ice Age didn't come down this far. Those are just boulders."

"Maybe they came from a volcano."

"Maybe they's just boulders. Follow me. Careful with that gun."

"The Smith'n—"

"Okay Baer, yes—enough. The Smith'n Wesson." She led out of the room.

"Where we goin'?"

"Shush."

She exited out the front door—which was strange because nothing was out the front door but the civilized world. The car. Driveway, road, and across, the Brown farm. They walked.

Mother halted at the dirt at the edge of the road. Baer stopped behind.

"For real. Where we going?"

Mother made a show of looking left and right then forced Baer to do the same.

"Why? You already looked."

She exhaled. Crossed the road at an angle and Baer followed onto Brown's driveway. The sound of metal on metal that they'd heard in the woods began again, each concussion sharper. Brown hammered in the shed off to the right of the house, adjacent the barn.

"Are we allowed to come on his property?"

"It's daylight."

That made no sense. Baer followed, now holding the Smith and Wesson in both hands.

"You always said we wasn't allowed over here."

"Baer."

"What?"

"If you're somewhere for the right reason then it's okay to be there. If you're there to do something bad, you're like to get shot. It's up to you to know the difference."

"Are we going to shoot Mister Brown?"

Mother spun and looked at Baer. Dust floated. She clamped her teeth and shook her head.

"We don't shoot people, Baer. What's in your head?"

"You're walkin' mad, is all."

"Well I asked you nice and you won't stop talkin'."

Mother turned and walked.

Baer wondered what was in his head and why he talked so much until they stood at the open sliding door to the shed, large enough to pull a tractor through. He winced at the piercing sound of hammer on steel.

Mother cleared her throat.

Brown kept working.

"Excuse me!"

He turned, unhurried, while his hammer fell to a bracket held in the mouth of table-mounted vise. One last *ding* and the hammer bounced slow to his side like a leaf released from a gust. Brown's forearms were veiny. His farm stood in the middle of fields and with no trees for shade but the orchard behind the barn, heat accumulated in the work shed. Sweat stood on his brow. His arms were dark brown but his face below the brim of his hat was pale. His eyes shifted from Baer's mother to her shotgun and then to Baer, across the road where they lived and finally he studied the size of her heart.

Mother cleared her throat, again.

He smiled. "Miss?"

"We live across the road. We're your neighbors. This is Baer. We never came over to say hello since you bought the place and that's my fault."

"Missus is in the house."

Mr. Brown appeared to be the same age as Baer's mother. His face was weathered and stubbly. He could have picked up a steel pot and carbine and walked into a John Wayne movie. Any time Baer or Larry saw him working his fields, he never let on like he saw them back.

"I'll say hello to her. But let me be precise since I'm interrupting your work. I don't have a fella around the house and this little man took it upon himself to learn how to fire a shotgun today."

Brown nodded. Turned away and pressed his finger to his nose. Blew.

Baer wondered how he could get a runny nose without a cold when he wanted one.

Brown wiped his nose with his forearm.

"Heard him shoot couple hour ago."

"That's why I thought of you. I don't want to be an imposition, but I have guns. Could I trouble you to teach Baer how to use them?"

Brown looked at Baer and smiled so big the answer had to be no. He pulled his head to the side like to shake it.... but didn't.

"He's no trouble, and he's willing to work to pay for it."

"That right? What you say the little man's name is?"

"Baer."

"Like the boxer?"

"Like his grandfather. Who he never knew."

"His grandfather was Max Baer?"

"That's not what I'm saying."

"Look like him. Bet you're a scrappy son of a bitch."

"Mister Brown. We don't use that language."

"I do."

"I don't want to work."

"But you will, so Mister Brown isn't out on the proposition. You want something you got to pay for it. You got to leave people whole, Baer. That's the way of business. And you want that Smith and Wesson don't you?"

Baer shifted the pistol behind his back.

"What's that? .357? Let me see."

Baer looked at his mother.

"Do as he says."

Baer held out the gun.

Brown pushed away Baer's hand.

"Shit, kid. That's rule number one. Don't point that thing at people—least of all me."

"Uh-sorry."

"Uh-huh. And don't never point it at a house, any house, no matter how far. Don't shoot at the sky—bullets come down. And if you ever aim at the livestock I'll beat your ass so you can't sit for a week."

"Mister Brown."

Brown looked at Baer's mother. "Fine, you can beat him but no pointin' at the livestock."

She nodded. "Yes. That's right. No pointing at the livestock."

"You hear that, boy?"

"What?"

"The rules."

"Okay."

"Say, yes sir. It's the polite way, Baer."

"Yes sir."

"You mind lettin' me take a look?"

Careful not to point the gun at the sky, Mother, Brown, the house or the animals out back, Baer surrendered the pistol in case refusing also warranted an ass beating.

".357 Magnum. These come out in '34. No, '35. And from the look this was one of the first. Got one like it in the house."

"Will you teach him to shoot?"

From behind them a screen door thwacked closed. Baer looked and a plump woman stood on the porch wiping her hands on a dishrag. She went back inside the house and the screen door banged again.

"I could use a hand cleanin' stalls and once those apples fall we'll need 'em in buckets."

"Baer, are you willing to work for gun lessons? Otherwise you'll never see that Smith and Wesson again."

"Uh."

Brown broke open the cylinder. "You bring any ammunition?"

Baer emptied his pocket and placed the shells in Brown's hand. Brown took two and returned the rest to Baer. He broke open the cylinder and placed them inside, taking care to close it so the first cartridge occupied twelve o'clock.

Brown stepped out of the shed and stood facing the pasture behind the house. With his boot heel he loosened a rock from the mud next to the foundation and toed it toward Baer.

"Take that down to the fence post on the corner. Sit it on top."

Baer glanced at his mother.

"Boy, when a man tells you something, don't take permission from a woman. Now run that rock down the post like I said."

"You won't shoot?"

"I won't shoot."

Baer ran with the rock, rested it on the post and rushed back.

Mother finished saying something as he slid on dirt and stopped with his hands on his knees, breathing hard. Baer looked at her face and she was looking hard at Brown's.

"Stand back a couple feet and ma'am, you'll want to plug your ears. This one's got a bark."

Brown elevated his pistol arm and held it steady, single handed. He looked back. Baer stared. Brown's eye twitched but Baer didn't know if he winked or had dust in it. He returned his gaze forward and squeezed the trigger. The pistol banged and the rock exploded from the fencepost.

"WHOA!"

Brown flipped the pistol in his hand so the grip stuck out. He offered it to Baer's mother and she twisted toward Baer and nodded. Brown held the pistol toward him.

"That's loaded. If you pull the trigger, it'll treat your foot like that rock on the post. That means don't pull the trigger. You understand?"

Baer hesitated.

"It won't fire itself."

Baer accepted the .357. "Where can I point it?"

"Normally the only place you point it is the ground. But don't you want to see if you can hit that post?

Baer looked at his mother. Brown's hand jarred the back of his head.

"'Member what I said."

"Yes sir."

"Okay. So do your own thinking. You want to see if you can hit that post?"

Baer looked at his mother's feet. Closed his eyes. "Yes!"

"Okay, good. Now look at your mother."

Baer did.

She smiled but her jaw muscles flexed too.

"See how that work, boy?"

"Yes sir."

"Come to your own mind first. Otherwise you won't have one."

"Yes sir."

"Okay, now stand like this."

Brown took Baer's shoulders in his hands and turned him toward the fencepost. He kicked apart Baer's feet.

"Stand like you're ready to squat down and take—like you want to lift something heavy. See how far apart my feet are?"

Baer wiggled his butt into the stance.

"I shot with one hand but you'll need two. Leastways 'til I get you throwin' hay bales. Hold up Smith and I'll show you."

Baer wobbled the pistol level.

"Okay, you right handed?"

Baer thought of looking at his mother.

Didn't.

"I don't know."

"Which hand you use to eat supper?"

Both hands on the pistol, Baer elevated his right elbow. "This one."

"Okay, good. Put that one on the grip first. Wrap the other hand around. Welp! Hoa! Don't put your finger next the trigger 'til you want to shoot. That's another rule."

"Mister, was you in the war or something?"

"What?"

"Was you a soldier?"

"'Cause I know about guns?"

Baer nodded.

"Nah. I'm just showing what my daddy showed me."

Baer nodded.

Holding his finger out of the guard, with his right hand on the grip and his left wrapped over and his feet spread wide enough he could squat down and take a dump—that's what Brown wanted to say—Baer was ready to shoot.

"This Smith'n Wesson," Brown said, "has a heck of a wallop. You want to squeeze hard on the grip so the pistol don't pop out. Go ahead."

Baer squeezed.

Brown swung his arm up under the barrel and jolted the pistol from Baer's hands.

"What? Hey!"

"What, hey. That's what it'll feel like and you won't know exactly when it's gonna go off. Here, let's do it again."

Baer took the pistol. Squeezed the grip. Brown's hand shot up. Baer held on.

"Nice work, boy. Nice work. All right. Good. Now take your aim. You know how to aim?"

"Yes sir."

"Okay. I want you to shoot at that post."

"Where on the post?"

"Anywhere you want, since you won't hit it."

Baer thought that sounded like when Larry taunted him because Baer wasn't good enough, or smart enough or whatever enough. He was a born rebel going to jail for sure and his mother wondered what was in his head.

Baer would show them.

He lined up the sights; didn't know how he knew. The front post between the two in back. He held the pistol hard, so Brown couldn't rip it from his hands.

"Mister Brown, can I put my finger in the hole?"

"You ready to shoot?"

"Yes sir."

"Then do it. Fire when ready."

Baer squeezed the trigger. It was hard to budge. He squeezed harder and the pistol exploded.

Mother jumped. Giggled.

The fencepost split.

"Cool!"

"Shit."

Brown smiled hard. Looked at Mother's big heart again. Then Baer's face.

"What do you say, Baer?" Mother said. "You willing to work for Mister Brown so he can teach you all about these guns?"

Baer changed the pistol from his right hand to his left and swung out his free hand.

They shook.

Baer met Brown's eye and now that he split the fencepost he saw a hard glint, suggesting there was something unpredictable inside the

rugged farmer who looked like a movie soldier. Brown grinned and Baer
didn't know what to do.

The house screen door banged again. This time Brown looked. He
waved and the woman on the porch came down the steps. No dishrag in
her hands. She walked fast and Baer sensed when Brown said something
to him, he'd better move fast too.

"Lou Mae, this is Baer and his mother—uh—"

"Barbie. Creighton."

The women squeezed fingers. Baer watched Lou Mae. Her face was
red and her eyes watery. She wore an apron with blood on it. Her hair
was back and she wore tiny earrings.

"This little man is Baer," Brown said. "He'll be about the place the
rest of the summer, helping with the chores so we'll be needing lunch for
both of us. And Mrs. Creighton's coming tonight with her two boys for
supper."

Baer's mother allowed her mouth to hang open a long moment
without filling it with words.

"If you insist."

# CHAPTER TWENTY-ONE

JUBAL SEE ME PAY THE MAN IN GOLD AND DON'T WAIT 'TIL I DRIVE OFF.
He figger I know the way back. Think he did me a kindness and I repay
in shit, so why follow with more kindness? I was dying soon as him and
want to see things his way, I might could. But I never had the gall to
treat another man as a friend so I could jaundice him to his own interest.

Jeep drive real good. Fella said it pull hard on the road test so he toss
in an alignment for a brother. Since we gotta stick together, I give him
two more gold coin and he tickled pink to have money worth more
tomorrow 'n today. Most folks never hear of it. I tell him stick it in a
rotted-out tree for safe keeping. He slap my arm—one of those people
like to touch folk.

Turn right and left and get the on-ramp. Expect a cop to pull me over
on the mile back to Jubal place but it's an ambulance blast by, make the
Jeep drift right. Ambulance exit and I follow. Wonder if Jubal made it
home and drop dead in the driveway.

Be a load off. Best thing for everybody.

I tramp the gas.

Ambulance blow by Jubal's place and his truck's in the drive. I slow to
turn but from when I climb the mountain and look thataway, the road
didn't seem to go to town, just deeper in the hills. Wonder what's out
there, need an ambulance.

I keep on and hang back. Transmission real smooth, I say.

Got the nerves. My belly gnaws. Ambulance out of sight but I round a bend and see it ahead, stopped next a garbage truck parked where the pavement go wide. Ambulance on the other side, lights flashing.

I pull over while two women jump out and run to a man on the road, spread like he thought to do a snow angel and quit with his arms straight out. One woman drop to her knees. Hands everywhere. At his neck. Astraddle his arm she put her ear next his face. Hand beside his head, study his eyes. She put her hands together and start the CPR.

Can't see his face nor body from the angle, just his long hair.

And the rainbow tassel hat in the snow twenty feet off.

Beside the trash truck a man in a blue uniform pace back and forth, won't look at Dwain. Put hands to head and turn around. Two step. Turn around. Feel his pockets and quit. Look to the sky and then Dwain.

From the scene I'd say the boy's dead and the garbage man know it.

Second paramedic kneel, rest her arm on the other and the first stop her resuscitation.

I put on the four ways. If cops come I don't want to be here but I got a knot in my stomach. Get out the Jeep and leave the door hang. Ten feet off the paramed on her knees look up.

"Please stay back, sir."

"You know who that is?"

Other paramed says, "Do you?"

I nod.

"Who."

"Dwain White. Jubal boy."

"Oh shit."

I spot blood in his ear. This side his head look mostly normal, but other side is flat and the eyeball is on his cheek. No use to start the CPR, is why she made the other quit.

Dwain's good eye look at the blue sky.

"He uh... he don't look to clear this one."

She turn away. "His injuries are incompatible with life. He was dead when we arrived and we did not attempt to revive him."

Got the juice on my arms. She face me. Eyes like coals.

"Oh shit," say the truck driver. "Oh shit."

"You hit him?"

"No. Not me. It was a Chevy S-10. Black. With a camper top."

Paramedic that did the not-CPR go to the ambulance and talk on the radio.

"I was just going to see Jubal," I say.

Woman in command shake her head, slow. Close her eyes. "If ever a family didn't need more bad news."

I study the ground.

"Look," she say. "What you saw a minute ago..."

"Boy's dead. You didn't do it."

She hold my look. Nod.

Garbage man sniffle. "I didn't hit him. I was turning right and the boy was running this way, down the hill. You know? He was on the right side too and when he saw me signal left, he ran out on the road, to cross."

I look where he point.

"I saw the S-10 in the sideview and I hit the horn, but all that did was make him slow down. He mighta made it. Christ he mighta made it but I hit the horn."

Garbage man search my face and don't see what he want so he search the paramed lady.

"I didn't hit him."

Static on the radio and the ambulance woman close the door.

I head for the Jeep.

"Hey!"

Turn.

"Where you going?"

Don't feel like telling but don't feel like lyin', neither. "Jubal White." Get in the Jeep and three-point turn.

Drive.

Up ahead off the interstate two cop cars fly with they lights on.

I take Jubal's driveway, chug up the slope in first gear and the transmission purrs pretty. Garage door is open. Sun's close to the mountain. Got a few hours of dusk coming.

I back to the garage for easy loading. One cop car zoom past and the second swerve to the driveway. He park in front the Jeep, blocking me. Got the Glock in my back and I'm Alden fuckin' Boone again. I'm Alden Boone.

Alden Boone.

Get out the vehicle. Tat stand at the hood. I eyeball her back inside the garage. She see the cops beyond me and disappear like that.

"Excuse me," one say.

I turn. "You here for Jubal, he likely in the house."

They give me a study.

"I was up the road and saw the accident. With Dwain and all. Stopped here to tell Jubal."

"You were there? We just got the call to come out and talk to him."

"Maybe let me give it to him firsthand?"

"You saw the accident happen?"

"No. Came by after the ambulance."

Other cop say, "Who are you?"

"Alden Boone. Old family friend, is all. I saw the ambulance and talk to the ladies. So I come here."

"How—uh—?"

"Pretty bad. Officer—?"

"Bowler."

"Pretty bad, Bowler. Dwain's cap was twenty feet down the road and his head was like you'd expect. Likely he was gone the second that truck hit him."

"What truck?"

"Garbage truck operator saw it. He say it was the Black S-10."

Cops look at each other.

"Said he slow down for the left turn—he's a mile ahead and comin' this way—you know the lay up there, right?—and the Chevy swing around from behind and Dwain had no time to get out the way. Knocked his tassel hat twenty feet."

The front door open.

Jubal. Percival behind. Mrs. White framed in the window and she already got the look no woman ever want on her face.

"Peter... Joe..." Jubal nod. Take a step. "What is it? What's going on?"

"It's Dwain," I say. Tromp to the house while Jubal cross the porch and work down the steps. "It's the worst news you'll ever hear."

"No."

"Dwain was hit down the road a mile. He with the Almighty now."

"No."

Door slam—Mrs. White.

"Jubal? What is it? Jubal? What's going on?"

Jubal knees give a little. He grab me with his right and the rail with his left.

Percival followed Jubal down the step and now he look up with a confused face. Pull his daddy's arm but daddy don't know.

Two cops mumble... terrible, horrible, thoughts and prayers.

"Jubal! What's happened?"

He look at me.

"Someone hit your boy, Mrs. White. Dwain was out running and someone hit him with a truck. He's gone."

"Gone?"

"He's passed."

"No."

I wince.

"No!"

I nod.

Her eyes go small and her forehead shake. Mouth pulled back every-whichway showing teeth never seen light. She cough-moans and drop to the step.

"You said a truck hit him," Jubal say.

Percival cries.

"They was a garbage truck turnin'. The driver say Dwain cut out across the road and a black S-10 with the camper top swerve out to pass the garbage truck and hit Dwain."

Mrs. White say, "Did you see him? What did you do?"

"I saw him. The parameds is there. It ain't a mile up the road."

Jubal's say, "A black S-10."

I nod.

The two cops connect stares with Jubal. One say, "Rauch."

"Fucking Rauch."

"Isn't he already in jail? That elk was trophy, wasn't it?"

"No. He's out on bail. Court in four days."

"Rauch?" Mrs. White say. "Billy Rauch?"

"I'll kill him."

"Jubal—"

Mrs. White climb the step and wander across the porch. Percival sit and cry. Jubal still got my arm, but now he stare.

"Maybe see to the missus," I say.

He hold my look. Clamp his jaw like a man want to do murder but first gotta crochet a bonnet. His hand on the rail go white and he nod at Percival. "Look after him a minute, right?"

Jubal climb the step and I sit next the boy. Two cops point they eyes at the ground, one shake his head, other blow his nose.

Tat's in the open garage door, back in the shadows. Corazon next to her. See a glint in Tat's hand—she ready to shoot her way out if need be. Good girl. Not today.

Jubal up by the door hugging his woman. She shouts words that don't come through his shoulder, if they's words at all.

"Percival, this ain't a good day." I don't know shit 'bout making people feel good on an ordinary day, let alone a bad one and let alone a little person. Never was one. "But you just let the time go by and you'll see tomorrow's a little better on the whole. And the day after that even more, and by and by—"

He climb off the step and run to his momma's waist and her arm come down to cover him.

Wander back to the cops.

"Who's this Rauch fella?"

They look at me.

"Ain't from these parts."

"He's a drug dealer, is about all I can say"

"He up on charges?"

"Not for the drugs. Other stuff. That was yesterday—or the day before? Anyway Jubal led the task force until a few weeks ago. Rauch was released on bond and he's going back to court this week. Friday, maybe."

"And the truck? S-10?"

"It's in his family. Don't know—but I think Billy drives the Silverado, not the S-10."

"Fuckin' Chevy people." I smile. Shake my head. Dumb thing to say since I got the Nova but people is awkward in they grief. "Dwain—I sure's hell can't believe it and wouldn't if I didn't see it."

"We're going to go assist."

"All right. Thanks for stoppin' by, officers. Thanks. I'll tell Jubal."

They nod, look stern—but it pains 'em. Climb in the vehicle and drive off.

Jubal steer his woman to the front door. She turn away with her face low and hands up like to make tunnel sight. Percival trails. Jubal close the door and stand looking at me. Though he ain't said it, blame sit on my shoulders. Jiggle but can't cast it off. That's what he want.

He stride across the porch and down the step like he ain't half dead. Meet me at the edge of the driveway.

"If you would've agreed to help—"

"Bullshit."

"My ass. You're in it now. Get in the Jeep. You're gonna see this."

Exhale long. Sun's slipped the mountain and air's already cooler. Wanted to be on the road by now, making distance. But Jubal want to fight while anger got his back stiff.

"Let's go," I say.

At the Jeep I open the driver door and call to Tat. "Be back when I back."

She open her mouth. I climb inside the Jeep, unlock the passenger door and Jubal pull himself in. He don't say nothing and I drive the mile. Now they's two cop cars with the ambulance. Each cop car parked across the road.

"Anything on the other side?"

"One house."

"Rauch?"

Jubal nod.

# CHAPTER TWENTY-TWO

WHILE LARRY STRUGGLED TO BECOME A WEALTHY MAN, HE SOMEHOW found resources for a brand new television. Baer watched the colors illuminate the wall and when he looked away from the window they flashed against the pine a few feet away in the yard. For Baer, the pulsing colors added a level of torment. He wondered what all that dazzling light did to people without the curse. Ruth seemed hypnotized.

Baer couldn't escape the belief that all those swirling lies were an entity. A person. His overwhelmed senses struggled to focus, but if he tried harder or learned new things about his gift, he might someday resolve the juice into an image. If he could, he knew he'd see the face of evil. His skin was hot and even when he closed his eyes the pink seeped through, almost like he didn't see it with his eyes but his mind. Everywhere.

Baer squinted through the window at Ruth as she rubbed an itch under her breast, forcing her t-shirt to conform to the shape.

Baer grated his teeth. The television had her hot. Her nipple came to a point.

He couldn't leave yet.

Stomping from the old man's cave to Gleason, he'd kaleidoscoped through different pictures in his mind, mixing ideas of taking her on the bed, couch, wherever he caught her and leaving her in a pool of blood for

Larry to find. He thought of the shotgun and his mother. Shooting the shotgun, shooting his load. Double load. Intoxicated, the syllables became a mantra that he repeated: double load, double load doubleload until the sounds meshed, meaning vanished and Baer stood alone with a terrible vision.

He realized the horror he'd ushered from abstract thought to the cusp of accomplished deed, and revulsed, wanted to leave.

Still, Baer couldn't allow enemy territory to drive him away without even grabbing her arm and getting a good look in her eyes. He always held in the back of his mind that if he could get her alone one more time she'd be honest. He'd hear the truth—she loved him still—and after that what could she do but follow the truth?

What person could choose a lie, knowing?

Baer watched her, bathed in light from the idiot box. And her baby was inside soaking it up too.

He shifted closer to the glass. Unless she turned her head she wouldn't see him. The angle was wrong and her peripherals weren't good. Besides, the window didn't cast a spell like the television.

Electricity tingled on his forearms, giving a burning sensation stronger than any he'd ever felt. He pushed back his sleeve and little blue arcs popped from hair to hair. His heart beat out of rhythm.

Baer saw Larry as if from a dream. Larry looked at him with cold eyes while Baer lay blasted from the electrical outlet, his body on shattered glass and a broken coffee table. That was when Larry shaved the lamp wire. Mother took them both to the hospital since Larry's nuts had swollen like a grapefruit after Baer had kicked him. After they released him, Larry walked from the hospital with his legs arched out like he was astride a horse. Baer tried to give Larry the same cold eyed stare that Larry had given him but couldn't muster the hatred.

Baer clamped his teeth but the juice didn't relent. Thoughts floated like feathers but hit like iron. Ruth sat watching the lies, with her legs way off the cushion, elbows on knees, arms continually rotating and flashing and her fingers wide, like she would shriek a warning if not for the baby.

The juice came from all the houses but it also came from the screen and that taught Baer long ago he didn't source the juice from the liars. He wasn't some kind of antenna pulling it in. A lightning rod. A lie rod.

The electricity came from Baer. He generated it and whatever fuel he used, his generator was getting more proficient with age and yet it taxed him. Ordinarily if he was only around a couple of people he'd hardly recognize the drain. But surround him with untruth and it was like hitching him to a house and telling him to drag it.

Try as he might, he couldn't fathom the red eyes. Maybe when the juice was flowing in him it changed his perception of the frequencies of light. Science could explain it, but heaven forbid a scientist ever learned of his curse.

They'd stick him to a board like a butterfly.

# CHAPTER TWENTY-THREE

WE ROLL DOWNHILL. AMBULANCE AHEAD, DWAIN'S BODY TO THE SIDE. Garbage truck ain't moved and the driver man half sit on the front bumper, hands on his knees. Cop cars on each side the accident, block the road. No traffic and only two houses but they do what the rulebook say.

Look at Jubal and his eyes is bloodshot and wet. Face gray and red like old meat under shrink wrap. Most alive he looked since I knowed him.

I stop the Jeep back a little.

"Pull closer. Roll down your window."

I ease out the clutch and drop the glass. Roll.

"That other house you said..."

"Uh-huh. Rauch."

Tires crunch on snow been plowed but barely drove. "How come the road's maintained if it ain't but you and the fella up ahead? He somebody?"

"There's a dump to the right. They plow for that and since they're here anyway they go out the next half mile. Slow down. Pull in there, around the rear end—there's room. You in four wheel drive?"

I look at the shifter. Steer half in the snowy ditch then cut left back on the road when I'm around the cop car.

"Slow down here so I can—sit back, would you? Hey, Pete!—we're going up the hill a little ways."

Officer Pete nod and call to another. "Mike, you want to move your car back a couple feet? Let Jubal through?"

"You guys send anyone back to Rauch's yet?"

"Naw. We got an APB on the S-10. State boys are keeping a lookout on the highway. Got a bird going up in Aspen and another at Grand Junction. We'll get him. So don't go to Rauch's house. You hear?"

"I hear. Thanks, Pete."

Pete nod.

If I was ever a cop I'd be no bullshit like Pete.

If I was ever a dragon, I'd fart Campbell's soup.

Mike climb inside his vehicle. I weave by Dwain and the garbage truck.

Jubal turn his head away, then back forward.

"No skid marks I can see," he say. "But how can you tell on snow?"

"I ain't see 'em either."

Mike back his cruiser like Pete said. Stop with the bumper agin the bank and I don't got to climb the other with the left wheels to clear him. Jubal drop his window.

"Thanks, Mike, I just want to see the situation from up the hill a ways."

Everything Jubal say, it's like he looking through fog and ain't sure.

Mike study Jubal like any sane man'd be back with the wife and young boy. But Jubal lost something so big, he got no way to live in the world he left with. Can't get drug down without a fight. So a man got to do something, even if he just turn circles. A man got to move so he don't find rest —'cause when he lay down he won't get up. Lost in the new world and no way back to the one with his boy in it.

Fred.

I keep the Jeep in first and as the hill rolls over Jubal say, "Slow down. Okay. Stop here."

Brake.

"Now look out there. You see that smoke? That house set back in the draw?"

"Uh-huh."

"That's your bank."

"Don't ken your meaning."

"That house is the bank you wouldn't hit. And that's why my boy's dead on the road. Back up twenty feet."

Reverse.

"Stop here."

I stop.

Jubal open the door and get out. I meet him at the back bumper. Hill seem taller standing outside the vehicle. I take it in, miles of snow and hills that ain't quite mountains, but got the makin's.

Jubal point. "You see where the garbage truck is?"

I look across the whole layout. Garbage truck, wide lane, left turn back to the— "That the dump, back that left?"

"Uh huh."

"You're sayin' the fella in that S-10 saw everything. The truck, Dwain, all of it."

"They murdered him. It wasn't an accident. That house back there, Rauch—he's a drug dealer. His daughter's a liar. He put her up to it."

"Hunh?"

"Amber Rauch. I thought you knew all about that, since you knew all about my lawyer. She tricked Dwain into going down on her and then tried to ruin his life because her father told her to."

"Tricked. Shit."

He eyeball me.

"Other day I trick Stinky Joe into eatin' ribeye."

"She set him up from the beginning. Billy Rauch knew I was onto him. That's what I mean. Now one of them has killed him."

"How many Rauch? How big the family?"

"Turn back around."

We walk to the front of the Jeep and look down on a valley. To the right is the house, set in a bowl. The back end is a draw, disappears into the ridge that follow right from where we stand.

"Billy's the father. He's in his forties. His father—granddad of the clan—is William. He lives in that trailer set behind the house on the side hill. He's part of the operation too. He hasn't left their twenty acres in thirty years—not even when his wife died. When Billy married Molly they took the house and William moved to the trailer. She's trash from God knows where, Golden, maybe. Their daughter, Amber, you know what she is. In fact, she moves their drugs through the high school—some of it at least. But the decision was made—"

"Meaning you didn't make it."

"—the decision was made to focus on Billy and with any luck the kids would grab the chance at a normal life once he was out of the picture. So you have Amber, the daughter, and Billy's oldest boy, Junior—"

"Wait a minute—William, Billy, and Junior."

"You heard me; they're ignorant and proud of it. William and Bill are two completely different names to them. Whatever. Amber and Junior are part of the family business too."

"And you said this was the bank you want to hit?"

"This is the bank. And now that my son's out, you're in."

"Nah."

"Listen. This road goes a couple miles and stops. The only way out is past those two cruisers. So I need you to listen to my reasoning."

"I listen."

"I went to school with Billy. We ran together. Boy Scouts and sleep-overs. We poached deer together once, just for the stupidity of it—or so I thought. Growing up at the house we heard gunshots here and there, every so often. It's normal, right? Colorado. And poaching didn't use to be that big of a deal."

"I don't understand a thing you're saying."

"William eventually got caught poaching. Anyhow, after graduation Billy joined the service and disappeared. When he came back ten years ago, he'd already picked up Molly and had the kids. He worked mostly as a fry cook at any place that would have him. I visited the house once and it was like talking to a stranger. He was already in the drug business, and me stopping by to shoot the bull probably scared the hell out of him. Anyway, about two years ago the school started finding weed all over the place and kids were getting sick. We had some samples tested and they were laced with embalming fluid."

"Formaldehyde?"

Give me chills. Arm hair stand.

"That's right, and we found the shit all over. Kids in the hospital, that sort of thing. I've been on the force twenty years and officially, we uphold the law. Every law. But weed? We never busted kids because we didn't want to ruin their lives. I'm not saying that was the official line, right? But no one went after the kids. Then Billy's shit comes along and gives them brain damage."

Just soon as I get to feeling the rage, how a man can poison a bunch a kids, Jubal give me a look and see I'm angry enough to suit him, so he go on.

"Something wrong?" he say. "You look pekid."

I'm getting played.

"Piss a feller off, is all."

"So the department asked me to track down where the weed was coming from, and that turned into a task force because about as soon as I figured out it was Billy Rauch farming pot in that plastic grow house— you see that, right? Deeper in the draw? Hard to see with the snow."

"I see it."

"Rauch wasn't just growing weed and spraying it with embalming fluid. He started moving crystal."

"Crystal. You don't say. What's crystal?"

"Methamphetamine."

"Oh, right. He grow that too?"

Jubal shake his head. "You don't grow crystal meth. You cook it. It's chemicals."

"So he cook it?"

"No. We don't know where he gets it. We've tracked the weed back to him through a couple pushers—not his daughter or son, they only move a little—but we didn't make any arrests. We needed to find out where the supply was coming from."

"So he grow the weed and buys the other stuff."

"Right."

"And you fellas let him keep selling the formaldehyde dope so you can find out where the other stuff is coming from."

"That's right. Uh-huh."

"And the whole story'll come together when you tell me he got a lot of money down there. Bad-man money, drug money. And since he break the law, and your family need money more'n his, we oughtta go steal it. Or am I getting ahead?"

"Listen, you fuck. My boy's dead on the road back there." Jubal's mouth is full of snot and his eyes is wet. He clear his throat. Spit. "We both know who you are and what you've done. I could've turned you in. I could've had them surround the garage or hunt you down when you were so drunk you couldn't walk. But I didn't."

"'Cause you wanted something."

"You're damn right I wanted something. A way out for both of us. You help me and my family. I got a wife and son and unless I do something, when I'm dead they'll have three times as much debt as the life insurance. You can make that go away."

"I suppose if you was to get out some handcuffs and I leave you dead in the snow, they could say it was line of duty. Would that help?"

He put his tongue in his cheek like a girl faking a blowjob. Don't give near the look he want.

"Remember the two police cruisers on the road back there? Four officers saw you take me up here. No way out but right past them. You wait, they'll come looking. And try to drive past them without me in the vehicle, see how far you get."

When a man got no choice 'cause another man make it so...

Gotta think on that.

# CHAPTER TWENTY-FOUR

BAER CREIGHTON SAT WITH HIS BACK TO HIS BROTHER'S DUPLEX WALL, his arms wrapped around his shins, face lowered to his knees. The tears had stopped but electricity still dazzled the hair on his arms. Pins pricked his mind from a hundred dancing angles. Demons flitted behind, where he couldn't see. He stared at grass flickering pink between his feet. Clamped shut his eyes against swirling thought-fragments. They cohered, but with mismatched forms. Random thoughts gelled with strangers. They writhed without the sense to self-abort. The frayed power cord made it night. His curse arrived when he saw his mother sprawled on her bedroom floor, shotgun barrel in hand. The bruise on her temple came from the iceberg lettuce in the mixing bowl.

Without a shotgun shell, how the royal fuck do you make a salad?

Baer watched, afraid his disintegrating mind would float into nothingness yet still be hounded by untruth.

He felt his voice in his throat and was unsure if it was now with his back to the bricks or a few years before when he was dripped tears on his mother's bruised face.

A door opened. The screen stretched a spring and rattled chains.

"Let's go pee-pee," Ruth said. "Okay? Let's go pee-pee."

Baer blinked open his eyes, lifted his face and wiped away the wetness. He lowered his hand to the hatchet at his hip.

Metal clinking, faint.

Yellow light flashed across the tiny back lawn.

Baer sat. Though his mother no longer occupied his sight she was with him somewhere in the yellow pink lawn. Baer tried to understand the salad. He hated salad. Ruth's voice came in whispers and exasperated sighs. The screen door sounded again, this time as it closed.

He could leave without being discovered if he rallied his body.

A black form eased around the corner of the duplex and bumbled forward. A puppy on big paws, as prone to tumble as walk. It faced Baer and stood, then bounded toward him yipping. It halted.

"Baer?" Ruth's voice came around the corner. "What you see, Baer?"

Ruth's head came around the corner, then vanished. The door slammed. Stomps inside the duplex. Baby screaming. Door slamming again.

Ruth stood at the corner far enough back that the yellow porch light showed her shorts and t-shirt. She clutched a Louisville Slugger. The puppy wagged its back half and came to Baer and sniffed his pants where Günter Stroh's dog Rommel must have left his scent.

She choked up on the bat and readied her swing. "Get away from my house or I'll brain you!"

"Ruth."

"Who are you?"

"You name your dog after me?"

"Baer?"

Everything he wanted to confront her with left him. He lowered his head.

"You can't be here, Baer."

"I guess I'll get on then."

Baer rolled to his side and clawed the wall to his feet. "You take care, Ruth."

She stood there.

"I'm going that way, to the woods."

"Little Baer hasn't peed yet."

"I'll go around then."

"Baer?"

He stopped.

"I didn't name the dog. Larry did."

"Okay."


THE MOON HAD LONG SET AGAINST THE MOUNTAIN BEFORE BAER returned to Günter Stroh's cave. His intoxication largely burned off by the miles, he stood at the mouth with a headache, an empty stomach and a hollow heart. He stared knowing inside was a dog and an old man who knew him no better than a random tree he pissed on.

Why come here, instead of some other place?

"Zat you, boy?"

Rommel growled. Baer smiled at that. The old man's senses were keener.

"Yeah, me."

"Grab ein piece of vood for ze coals. Zaffe me ze trouble."

He'd been tramping for hours through the woods and the farther from pink Gleason he walked, the clearer became his thoughts. The electricity dissipated and he felt more himself, albeit gutted by sentiment.

Standing in the cave entrance his eyes had little capacity to further adjust to the dark, so he stepped into the blackness based on memory, the old man's voice, the dog's growl and the barely visible coals of the fire. He lowered to his knees and blew, exciting a few cherries. Blew again and the fire bed was ready for fuel.

Reaching, he found the wood stack he'd carried from the lean-to that Günter had constructed against the rock wall of the mountain. He probed for the most ragged piece and tore off the large splinters. He placed them on the coals first, then the smallest log he could locate. The splinters flared.

With flames flickering, he shivered and realized he'd been cold for hours and only the constant walking had staved off deep chills.

He knelt before the fire and held out his hands while the flames multiplied. The old man snored. Or was it the dog?

It was both, and this cave was as lonely as any campsite he could have chosen. The only sounds the crackle of fire digesting wood and the throat-rattle of an old man and an old dog. Perfect company that left Baer perfectly alone.

Almost—almost without conscious thought, he reached for the walnut board and the row of Mason jars and took the next in line. He drank, sat with his back and head against the rock, his legs on either side of the fire, and dozed.

# CHAPTER TWENTY-FIVE

JUBAL CONVINCED THEY'S NO WAY OUT FOR OLD ALDEN BOONE. NO way out. Got the land thisaway and that, forever. Bare. One man half dead, body like wrapped meat. Cancer clogged all through him, tells me they's no way out.

What he mean is they's no way out I want.

We square on that.

I club him on the head and skedaddle, what'll that do? I can't drive out, so I guess I got to walk through snow wearing granola boots. Or maybe I hole up with the family he want to persecute?

Right now, only choice I got is the one he gimme.

"Uh-huh. And you said they's a way out for both of us."

"Help me provide for my family—I let you walk. You're good to go."

"Just like you said before we picked up the Jeep... you recall I said no. Just like that?"

His face go gray like a storm already dumped its rain and got nothing left but sorry mood. Then lightning flash and a whole new kinda black crawl in.

And just now I get a jolt of juice.

Jubal put his hand on his pistol grip.

"You're in this now whether you want or not."

"Hell, I am."

"You got a choice. You help my family in its time of need and enjoy our eternal gratitude. Or I'll put you in cuffs and you'll die in the custody of whoever Colorado turns you over to."

Jubal jerk the Glock out and point it belly high.

Fucking Glocks.

"Maybe you better think again and put that away."

He keep the pistol on my belly.

"You thinking to hold that on me 'til we raid the house? How that gonna work? If I say I'll do it, you got to ease up. So we either find accord or not. But I tell you one thing, longer you keep that out, more I'm liable to decide agin."

He hold my eye.

"You look tired, Jubal. You look like beat meat and you ain't thinkin' worth shit. At some point it's my word. Can't take it now, how you take it later?"

He clamp his teeth and shove the Glock in his hip.

"I got to have your help. It's drug money. After all the murder you're accused of doing, why is taking drug money a big deal?"

"I maybe coulda got my head around robbin' a bank. They's assholes. But the drug man work for his money. And I imagine they's a bit of skill."

"Help my family survive when I'm gone. That ought to appeal to your guilty conscience, if a man like you has one."

I dunno what to say.

"I ain't a killer. I done it but I ain't only what I done."

"Well, that's the beauty. It's like I said during the movie last night, if you'd have listened. There's no need for killing. Listen to the situation. Both Billy and his father are due in court in three days, that'll leave his wife and Junior at home."

"So if you arrested him for drugs, didn't y'all search the house? Take all the drugs and money and whatnot?"

"You don't see anything, do you? We didn't arrest him for drugs. Remember dinner the first night? Me getting a phone call?"

"Okay."

"That was a game warden. You see over there—that ridge?"

He point left.

"I do. Yessir."

"You sit on that ridge with a rifle and it isn't a two hundred yard shot over there—look to your right. See that draw?"

"It's there."

"That's where the elk come down when there's a storm. They like the hollow because of the trees. With the trees it's easier for them to find grass to eat."

"So what you saying?"

"You saw Dwain shoot a pistol. He's world class with a rifle. So a two hundred yard shot with a hollow point into the neck of the biggest bull elk you ever saw, just standing there... no wind... no hurry. Easiest shot in the world."

"Why would he do that?"

"Because that family has a history of poaching. And because these days, poaching is a felony. Best of all, when they arrest a poacher, they don't go looking for drug money—especially when they know it'll interfere with another investigation."

"But they take the guns."

"You're damn right they take the guns."

"And that phone call was the game warden saying he picked up Billy and William."

"You're getting faster and faster. They were dumb enough to be standing beside the elk when the warden drove up the road."

"Tricky. Do a man for felony."

"Not just any man. A filthy drug dealer. So anyway, there won't be any guns in the house and he'll be in court."

"Pretty slick."

"I'm surprised they gave bail. My original thought was to hit the house the next day with Dwain, but you dropped by like a gift from God and I thought, this could make things better."

I grin like buddy that's some killer shit you talkin'.

"Don't shoot."

I open the Jeep and find binoculars behind the passenger seat. Take 'em out the box and focus on the Rauch house, the trailer, the plastic greenhouse. It's a long driveway winds up to 'em with the road cut into a hill. Banked on the left and a drop to the right. No rocks nor trees and straight like an arrow at least a hundred yards in the middle. Anyone with a rifle—wife or son—would have an easy time of it. Suspect a fella like Rauch, government take his guns, he get more.

Lower the glasses and study Jubal. "What about the daughter?"

"She'll be in jail. She has to be the one in the S-10."

"Coulda been Billy, right? Or William."

"Could have been, but wasn't. William doesn't leave the property, ever. Billy isn't the kind to get carried away; he's more of a tactical thinker."

"I ain't buyin' some little girl ran down your son."

"A little girl who accused him of rape."

"Why'd she want to run him down if he didn't do it?"

Jubal clench. Look to the snow.

"Got me. But she's the only one left."

I look through the field glasses. Spot motion inside the house, but just a shadow, maybe. It don't look like a drug man's house, but shit if I know. Maybe the drug people live in regular houses. This one's got the normal layout. Two story, garage off the side, set back where the land happen to be flat. Trailer up the hill, and deeper in the draw so you can barely see it, a long ass rectangle the color of city snow.

"They grow them drugs in the winter?"

"Year 'round."

About to quit the glasses I spot a tricycle next the house, mostly covered in snow. Got a red seat and shiny chrome handlebars.

If it was ten-fifteen year old them bars'd be rusty.

And they's a blue plastic boat sled next the house.

"How old you say Junior was?"

"I didn't."

"You said he was part of the drug operation."

"Not yet. He'll grow into it."

Got the juice on my arms and I bet if I caught Jubal in these field glasses up close he'd fry my eyes.

"Now it's a good chance Billy's wife and Junior will be in the court-house for the arraignment. You know—try to show him as a family man. They'll have to drive past the house to get to the highway, so all we do is sit out and wait and see who's inside the car. While they're away, we go right in. I'll stand guard and you go through the house. I'd do it but they probably have money packed in the walls and everyplace else. I won't have the stamina."

"What if the wife and Junior don't go?"

"Then it's just as easy. We go to the door. I show the badge and we go inside."

"You got a super plan, Jubal. A super plan."

"You in?"

Tilt the head like one ear weighs more'n the other and I don't know which.

"What's the split?"

# CHAPTER TWENTY-SIX

AFTER BAER SPLIT MR. BROWN'S FENCEPOST WITH HIS SMITH 'N Wesson .357 Magnum, Brown told the missus they'd have guests for supper.

Baer's mother summoned a smile and Mrs. Brown did too but Baer thought of when his science teacher showed the class how magnets work. One side they love each other and the other they hate. Farmer Brown was a third magnet and the two women were flipped so if it was just the two of them, they'd be fine. The metal look in Mr. Brown's eye said he didn't mind. Baer saw his mother's face out of the corner of his eye and all the softness was gone. She looked like she might tell Brown to go cut two switches.

Adults were all the time having unknowable faces. When they returned to the house, Mother mumbling to herself the whole way and not even stopping to look both ways, Baer went to the bathroom and studied his face in both mirrors.

Mother once said being a waitress was half about making sure her ass looked right each day, so she had a man whose wife she worked with install a second bathroom mirror, mounted on the wall opposite the one over the sink. She could look in the first and make sure her butt looked right in the second.

Baer grabbed the six inch footstool beside the toilet, stood on it and stared into his silver reflection. He tried to give himself the same hard, unknowable look as Mister Brown, his mother and Mrs. Brown. He squinted. Glared. Wrinkled his nose like a cornered animal. None of it worked. Finally he clamped his jaw and looked through to the mirror on the other side and behind his second image saw a hundred more, smaller and smaller. Studying the last face with discernible features, he saw the look. The secret was to be as distant as possible. Someday maybe he'd do it without mirrors.

Larry returned from his hiding place in the woods and Baer was whittling a stick on the back step.

"What happened? She mad? She tan your ass?"

Baer kept whittling.

"She gonna tan mine?"

Baer thought of the distant mirror look. He lifted his face and imagined he saw through Larry to hundred deeper selves. Let his focus slip and his jaw close.

Larry's head pulled back. "Fuckin' asshole."

It worked.

"We're going to Farmer Brown's for supper. Ma says get your ass cleaned up."

In all their years neither Baer nor Larry had eaten food in another person's house. They ate at home or school. The thought of sitting at another person's table perplexed Baer. What were the rules? Mother said he'd better be on his best behavior.

Or else.

She had that metal look when she said it.

She gathered the boys and marched them, remembering to look both ways but demanding the same of neither Baer nor Larry. "I should have made something up," she said. "Oh, shit my head hurts."

Baer followed in third place, allowing his mother and Larry to walk faster. For not wanting to go there she sure seemed in a hurry. Wouldn't it be grand if he had a leather holster for the Smith'n Wesson? He could take it everywhere without hurting his arm. The look on Brown's face seeing his post splinter. He probably never saw a boy like Baer, with an aim so good...

Mother climbed the steps. She wore a dress that went down almost to the ground and made her butt dance with each step. It was funny, but not the kind of funny she would want Baer to tell her about. Larry hesitated at the steps. The front door swung open but nobody was there in the opening, almost like it was on a string.

Some kind of trap.

Baer smelled chicken and vegetables. He passed Larry on the steps and entered after his mother. Inside to the right was the kitchen. The table was no bigger than the one they had at home but looked completely different. At home the table was like a floor, with shiny metal around the edges. Brown's table was made of wood that looked like it was shaped with an axe nobody bothered to put an edge on. The shine was old and weak, like the saddle Baer had seen on the wall of Brown's shed.

"Everything's ready," Mrs. Brown said. "Why don't we all sit?"

She sounded different from before.

"What happened to your eye?" Mother said.

"Oh, silly me. I keep the skillet in the bottom drawer there and coming up I caught my face on the butcher block." Mrs. Brown smiled and spun to the stove. "Go ahead. Caleb, you want to show our guests where to sit?"

Mr. Brown—Caleb—sat in a chair that looked like living room furniture, but was at the edge of the kitchen in the corner between two windows. He was behind a newspaper. "Go ahead," he said. "That sonofabitch Kennedy. This country—I swear."

"Please, not in front of the children," Baer's mother said.

"He's soft on communism."

"With so many opinions," Mother said, "don't you get tired?"

From where Baer stood he saw behind the newspaper but his mother couldn't.

Mister Brown's face had that look Baer practiced, but as he lowered the paper his countenance changed. He nodded. Winked. Lifted the paper and clamped his teeth.

Mother grabbed Baer's shoulder and steered him. "Mister Brown sits at the head of the table, Baer. Let's go to this side."

Baer looked at the table.

"It means the end, dumbass."

Baer punched Larry.

"You two behave," Mother said. "You, over here. You, other side. Now."

With the boys seated and staring at their plates, Mother said, "I'm sorry for their rudeness."

"That's what boys are," Mrs. Brown said. "Snips and snails and puppydog tails."

Mr. Brown stood from his reading chair and it seemed in three steps he was at the far end of the table—the head. Mother sat beside Baer, opposite the only place left for Mrs. Brown.

Instead of sitting, she filled plates.

Mr. Brown leaned back and Mrs. Brown placed his plate before him. He ate.

Baer's mother waited for Mrs. Brown to complete her task, so Baer waited too. Larry took his cue from Mr. Brown, and dug in. When Mrs. Brown finally sat and lowered her head, Baer felt his mother's hand squeezing his. Larry shoveled food. Mr. Brown watched his wife. Baer looked back and forth, wondering if the rules had changed. Mother's head was down like Mrs. Brown's and they both lifted at the same time. Mother released his hand and he waited a few seconds before reaching for his fork—like his mother. Finally Mrs. Brown shoved her fork in a roasted carrot and Baer's mother—at last—lifted hers.

"Smells delicious," Baer's mother said.

"You know I pulled these this morning and have more than we can use. Same with the onions. I'll give you a basket."

The women traded smiles.

Though he'd seen it all, Baer wondered what he missed.

# CHAPTER TWENTY-SEVEN

PARK IN FRONT THE DOOR AT JUBAL HOUSE. THREE-MINUTE DRIVE gimme time to think things through.

Jubal get out the vehicle. Dark closing fast.

"This the way it's gotta work."

Jubal give a half snort. "You're telling me how this is going to work?"

"Hear me out. I won't say nothin' ain't reasonable."

He nod.

"No matter how things break when we go in, I got to plan on all Colorado knowin' Baer Creighton's been by. And drive a Jeep."

"You want a contingency plan."

"Nope. No such thing. Plans fall to shit every one. What I want is time to set up for the getaway after things go the way you don't want."

"I gave you my word. You help me, no one knows you've been here."

"And like I said, no plan work the way you think. You don't know the situation. Who's where. You don't know what he want or what he'll do to get it. You think Billy won't be in the house, but what if he got a brother come by to visit—"

"Billy's an only child."

"All I'm sayin' is things never break the way you think. Shit, how many years you been police? You know that."

Jubal lean on the front fender. Look at the house. I look too. Woman in the window. All that woman do is look out the fuckin' window.

"What do you propose?"

"I move the girls out tonight. Get them camped somewhere they's safe."

He frown. Nod his head slow, test the idea.

"Fine."

"Dog go with 'em."

"Uh-huh. And where do you stay?"

"I got to find a new vehicle, case I got to make a switch."

"Hold on. You're going to move the girls out, and the dog, and yourself, and I'm supposed to take your word you'll be back to do a job you didn't want to do to begin with?"

"Perfect. That's it."

"Baer."

"No?"

"Let me ask you something. Why'd you kill all those men, back in North Carolina?"

"They murdered my dog. For sport."

"That's what I read. Pretty good series of newspaper stories, some investigator-reporter dug into it."

"Why you ask?"

"The dog stays here. You get him when we're in the clear."

Old Jubal White just put my nuts in a vice and give the handle a twist.

Maybe he'd keep the girls instead... But I offer that, he know something ain't the way I'm telling it.

Jubal cross his arms on his belly. "I'll give you the benefit of the doubt. You're only alive because you're wily and good at thinking ahead. I often wondered how the master criminals get away with it. You have to plan ahead for everything and see every possibility. I understand. But if you want some leeway to get set up for your getaway, the dog stays here. That's the end of it."

Garage door open.

Tat stand there and Corazon behind. These girls'd do murder right now if they freedom depend on it. Stinky Joe trot out. Come say hello. I scruff his neck and he shoot across the plowed drive to paint a snow bank. Next he go around the corner a bit, but I can see his back curled and butt low. Look away for the courtesy and see Jubal keep looking.

"Never knew a feller like to watch a dog shit."

Jubal gimme a look.

"Me neither. The dog stays here."

"All right. Stinky Joe stay here."

Back of the Jeep I pop the latch and swing the door. Spare tire free, I lift the window. Look at Tat.

"Load up."

She look at Jubal. Corazon look at me.

"You want to give a few minutes, Jubal? So I can give 'em the skinny?"

"Go ahead."

Jubal don't move.

"Tat. Corazon. We load up and I take you to a new camp site. I gotta come back here and help Jubal with something in three days. After that, he let us off the hook and won't tell nobody we was here."

"That's about it," Jubal say.

"What is going on? Why the police here? Where is Dwain?"

"Shit. You ain't talked to Mrs. White?"

Head shake.

"Neighbor up the road hit Dwain with a truck is why the police was here—they stop to let Jubal know. We drove up and he know the folks who did it live over the hill. They drug dealin' sons a bitches and owe Jubal and the family, for what they took."

I wink. Her stare flicker.

"What are you helping him with?" Tat say.

"We're gonna take that drug money and give it to Mrs. White. Only right, what they done."

"But we go to new camp first?"

"Yep."

"Dwain is dead? I want to help."

"Nah."

"Sounds good," Jubal say. "I'm sure we could find a job—"

"Nope. No way. No how. Or we fight it out right here and now. The girls go like we said a minute ago. This is exactly the kind of horseshit you can't plan. Things get whacky. I won't do it."

"Easy," Jubal say. "Fine."

"Grab your gear. Mine too, while I talk to Stinky Joe." Give Jubal a glare says I'm ready to shoot his dumb ass. "Oh, shit. Tat—leave Stinky Joe's food and dish. He stay here 'til we're done."

Tromp across the drive to the corner and Stinky Joe come around looking wary. Get on my knees. Wanted more room so I could shoot him straight but Jubal too close. Get the fur in my mouth and talk next his ear.

"Hang in there, Stink Dog. This ain't like last time. Don't you go nowhere and I'll be right back for you and we'll never deal with this sorry nonsense agin. You and me, puppydog. Y'hear?"

Stinky Joe don't say nothing.

Feel the water, cold in my eyes.

"I swear, Joe. I'll be back if I got to murder half Colorado."

Joe lick my nose. Growls.

*You can murder half Colorado. But don't drink no likker.*

# CHAPTER TWENTY-EIGHT

"WHY'D YOU CALL ME SON?"

"I didn't."

Baer watched Mr. Brown. He'd heard what he heard. Brown called him son. In the two weeks Baer had been working with Brown he had grown accustomed to his mannerisms. He was generally in a decent humor but sometimes flashed the metal look for no reason. The glare always left Baer unsure of his next action. Insisting he'd heard what he'd heard might could fetch Brown's hand to the back of his head. The cuffings he received in front of his mother were almost friendly but every time it happened when they were alone working, the hand was hard as a plank and left him stunned like he'd missed ten seconds.

Still, Baer couldn't bring himself to say he hadn't heard what he'd heard. That was lying—the very thing everyone always told him never to do. After mulling it Baer decided folks didn't care whether he lied or not, so long as he said what they expected him to say. Their truth, not his.

He decided not to push then did anyway.

"You said son. You said, all right son, move those tools from this wall to that."

Brown's face changed, but didn't call up the metal look. It was something altogether new, like Brown lopped off his finger with that two inch chisel hanging on the wall.

"I guess I did say that."

"I'm not your son."

"Do you know whose son you are?"

Baer shook his head.

"I don't either. Maybe your mother does."

"So why you call me son?"

"You're a persistent little shit."

Baer smiled. Thought better. Frowned. His fingers tingled. He kept his eyes on Brown's face but directed part of his attention to his lower right field of vision, where Brown's hand would shoot out, if it had a mind.

"You know what barren means?"

Baer shook his head no.

"Means a woman can't have kids. You know anything about fuckin' yet?"

"Bad word, all I know."

"Nah, hell, it's a great word. You'll see, someday. You'll love it. Everyone does. The whole point of fuckin' is you make babies. Every single thing on this planet loves it."

"Do trees?"

"Sure, long distance. Corn, trees, bugs. Even fish. Now plants use pollen, so it's different. I guess in fairness we ought to keep it to the animals. And that ain't a word you use around your mother."

"I thought you said everyone loves it."

"If anyone—I'd lay money your mother does. But it's so popular they had to make the word bad. You'll see. They do that with everything good."

"So why you call me son?"

Brown huffed. Grinned. "All right, I can appreciate that. You get aholt and don't let go. That's good."

"So why?"

Flinty look.

"Every man wants a boy to carry his name."

"Well if you like to and she likes to..."

"That's where the other word comes in. The missus can't have babies. She's barren."

"Oh."

"Don't you go saying nothing about that. To no one. She'll get to bawling and sooner'n shit I got to correct her. Tiresome. So keep your mouth shut, all right?"

"Yes sir."

"Good."

"So when are you going to teach me to shoot?"

"Suppose after I take down that leather strap and teach you not to be so meddlesome."

"Deal was you was gonna teach me to shoot."

"Damn, you got spunk. Get your Smith."

It was only ten feet, but Baer ran to the corner of the shed where each day he'd placed the .357. Ran back and careful to keep the barrel pointed toward the ground, offered it to Brown.

"No, you hang onto it. Let's go outside."

Brown walked outside of the shed and Baer followed.

"Stand up here beside me. I don't like you waving that thing all around behind me."

Baer galloped so he was adjacent to Brown. His legs bounced to keep up. Brown led past the fencepost Baer split—still not replaced—around the corner and into the cool shade of the orchard where fifteen apple and pear trees sagged under fruit. A thin stream cut a path through, water arriving from the farther hills. One day Baer had followed it back to nothing and found even when the water stopped, the path was deep through the fields, splitting a half dozen times until he stood wondering where the water came from. None of the beds carried any, and yet all summer long a small flow trickled through the orchard, crossed under the road and joined the larger stream behind his house. It was like the water came from nowhere.

"We gonna shoot the trees?"

"Trees are like livestock. I'll beat your ass, you ever shoot my trees."

"Yes sir."

"You see that flat rock over there—near that little waterfall?"

"Yes sir."

"Go stand it up. Put a handful of mud in the middle. Gimme that Smith to hold onto."

Baer stared.

"Go on, gimme that pistol."

Baer held it out.

"Okay, 'nother lesson. Don't give a gun to somebody so they have to grab the barrel. That's like handing over a knife and makin' them grab the blade. It's the same thing."

Brown took the gun, flipped it and offered Baer the grip.

"See?"

"Yes sir."

"Take it."

Baer took it.

"Now give it to me so you don't lay it down in the mud."

Using both hands, Baer turned the gun in hand and held the grip out to Brown.

"Good, but you'll be better off in the long run if you don't point the barrel at your belly. Always—*always* mind the direction of the barrel."

Brown placed his hands around Baer's and shifted so the tube pointed past Baer's body to the ground behind him.

"Got it?"

"Yes sir."

"Okay."

Brown released Baer's hands and pushed them down so Baer had to do it all over again.

"Give me the gun."

Baer offered the grip while keeping the tube pointed away from him.

Brown accepted.

"Good. Now go stand up that rock like I said."

Baer raced, leapt the stream, landed on mud and slipped. He righted himself and bounded to the rock. He stood it against another and slammed a handful of mud in the middle. It fell away but left a dark area. Baer splashed his hand clean in a small pool, scared away a two inch crawfish and bolted back to Brown.

"Catch your breath a minute."

"I'm fine."

"Tell me, how'd you start shootin' to begin with?"

"The first time?"

Brown nodded.

"Ma keeps the shotgun in her room for protection. I used it on the old television when it gave out."

"In the house?"

"No sir."

"Good. That's all. I was curious."

"Can I have back my Smith'n Wesson?"

Brown flipped it in his hand. "Take it."

Baer took.

"First thing, always the first thing. Check the load. This one's loaded. I already looked."

Baer nodded and lifted to aim.

Brown cuffed the back of his head.

"I said always check the load, every time."

"Then you said—"

Baer shrunk, expecting the hand.

"That's the point, son. Check it every time. Don't trust nobody. Ever. They won't go to jail when you kill somebody on accident. You will. Besides that, most folks is all hat. Like to talk when they don't know dick. So you check every time, right?"

"Yes sir."

Brown nodded at the Smith.

Baer opened the cylinder. Four shells.

"Go ahead."

"You want me to shoot?"

"Go ahead."

"Now?"

"Put one in the middle of that mud spot. You remember. Both hands on the grip. Right hand first. Get yourself a steady hold and squeeze that trigger nice'n easy."

Baer squeezed. The pistol jumped. The rock shattered.

"All right. Back to work."

"But they's three bullets left."

"And they gotta last all fall. Back to work."


MOTHER STOPPED STIRRING A GIANT WAD OF MAYONNAISE INTO yesterday's macaroni salad. She placed the mixing bowl on the counter and turned.

"He said what?"

"He said I don't want to work all summer and only shoot three more times."

"Why would you only shoot three more times?"

"They's only three bullets left."

"He over there right now?"

Baer nodded.

Mother placed the mixing bowl in the refrigerator.

"Put that mayonnaise away for me."

She marched out the kitchen, pushed open the front door and kept on without closing it. Baer tossed the mayo in the fridge. He raced out the house, closed the door—Mother was already half way to the road.

"Look both ways!" Baer said.

"You stay home."

Mother strode across the road with fists swinging and Baer hurried after. She was going to chew Brown's ass!

The sun was late in the sky but had two hours to fall before sunset. Mother pounded toward the house, up the steps with her heels drumming the boards. She swung open the screen and Brown opened the door.

Baer halted his approach half way up the drive, wondering where he would run if mother suddenly turned. No safety close—he'd have to plan on some hard words. They'd be worth it, if she cussed Brown first.

"Help you?"

"What's the meaning? You got Baer over here two weeks and he's shot the pistol one time? What kind of stunt you thinking to pull?"

"You only sent him with four bullets."

"Oh, cut the nonsense. You telling me it's right you take that young man's labor for two weeks and don't live up to your side of the deal?"

"Said your piece?"

"No I ain't said it. They's plenty men with no honor. Didn't take you for one."

"Said your piece?"

"Now I said it."

"Good." He coughed. "Now go ahead and get the hell off my land."

# CHAPTER TWENTY-NINE

Got a hotel room. Resort style. Couldn't get away from Jubal White fast enough.

While Jubal watch with his hand next his hip, I schooled Percival on how much food Stinky Joe eat each day and tell him to give what table scraps they got, long as they ain't cooked bones. Heard that on the television in the cave. Percival cry. Wobbly in a world without his brother Dwain in it. Jubal watch. Grit his teeth. Percival nod and uh-huh, but I ask and he ain't hear a word I say.

Fuck Jubal. Play his games. Pretend—when the whole fam-damily's been in it from the start. If Dwain kill the elk, he knew. And if Mrs. White took comfort when the game warden call that first night, she knew too.

House White been lies from day one.

And Jubal got my dog?

Fuck Jubal, is all.

Wasn't ever gonna put the girls in a camp site. Want something simple and clean. Hide the girls a couple night. Duck outta Colorado.

Fuck Jubal White.

More I think on it more torqued I get. Like any other man I ever met, he want to twist and push 'til he get a fella where he got no choice but work agin his own interest. Can't make a square offer, let a man come to his own mind. Fuckers like Jubal want to steal a man's volition. That's the word.

Fuck Jubal, is all. And his cow face wife.

Girls sit on they beds. Two king sizers, side by side. Got the fireplace on the right, the kitchen on the left. Out the front door, sidewalk ten feet, turn a corner and they got the hot tub. Girls'll go in they undies and t-shirts like they sleep. Same difference. Outside is snowy mountains, but looking out from the resort they's all clean and pure. Windows with yellow lamps. Even the car traffic is pretty. Smiles and giggles from what people you see.

With all that, fuck Jubal White. Man get under my skin and since I swore off the likker I got nothing but cussing to settle me.

We get the bags inside and I split kindling, bunch up some newspaper. Lay the logs and light.

Corazon turn up the heater. Drag the curtain in front the window.

Boys walk by outside, drunk and loud.

"Girls, you wanna sit down a minute?"

Tat on the edge of the bed. Corazon jump on and kick back, lean on the head rest. Look comfy for a woman's skull if she was getting poked.

"Here the situation. All I said in front of Jubal was horse shit. Except that bit about Dwain. He's dead the way I said it. But Jubal want for me to help him rob a man who work for his money same as anyone else. Ain't my place to jail him and it ain't my place to rob him. That other fella got kids too. I'm goin' back for Stinky Joe tonight. So fuck Jubal, is all. Him and Dwain—"

"We don't know anything about this," Tat say.

"Jubal and Dwain shoot an elk on Billy Rauch's land. He's father of the girl accuse Dwain. Then Jubal call the warden and say he saw 'em shoot it. So Billy and his old man is set to go to jail in three day. Jubal did that so the house'd be empty and he could rob his drug money. That man got a little boy with a tricycle and snow boat out on the porch. I won't do it."

Corazon nod. Pull her phone from her pocket. Already got the ideas.

Tat say, "You want me to help you get Stinky Joe?"

"No. You girls enjoy the hot tub. Get a good soak and look at the stars. It ain't every day you can take a bath with snow all about. Might take a dip myself once y'all clear out. Just leave me the soap and a towel."

Corazon look like she swallow porcupine scat.

"Enjoy your time in the resort, girls. Tomorrow we be on the run. That's for sure."

I leave 'em in the room. Close the door. Open it. "Hey, they's a food joint down the road. Hungry?"

Corazon's already half nekkid for the hot tub. She squeal and turn away. I shut the door and Tat arrive smiling big. She pull it back open. "Cheeseburgers. Many. And Coca Cola."

Close the door and pat my money wallet. Got the coin and some bills too. Twist it to the front and unzip. Pull out the bills here where I ain't exposed. Put everything back where it ought to be, adjust my nuts just because I like to, and instead of driving the Jeep I walk like I did before shit hit the fan last October. Mile underfoot is good for the soul.

Find the place I saw driving in. Feet's cold and I wonder how them cheeseburgers'll make it back warm. But we got a kitchen with fry pans so I enjoy the shivers while they go out back and slaughter a cow for my sammiches. Long 'bout two day later the red head boy at the window call me up. I been shivering all the while 'cause they ain't got an inside, just an outside with picnic tables. In snow country. I pay and forget the Coca Cola and after a quarter mile back I remember, so turn around. At least the motion got me warm, and thinking on Tat's big smile and Corazon's screaming giggles make me think all the world ain't so rotten. They's good things too. They's a woman's nose next your ear, her voice husky. They's people like Stinky Joe, loyal and forgiving—moreso than any man got a right to expect. A dog like Stinky Joe give you hard love 'cause he don't know how to lie. Plus they's good people all over working jobs they hate 'cause the city need lights and water. Others pick up the trash.

It ain't the whole world that's rotten—that's what I think—walking up the valley by the highway in Glenwood Springs, Colorado.

It ain't the whole world.

Dodge RAM blast by too close, kids screaming and waving fuck you fingers. Yelling nonsense.

Even these little pud pullers ain't evil, so much as working off steam afore they get sucked up to work at a plant somewhere. Back as a boy I maybe did a stupid thing the once. Maybe. Who know?

Give the hotel room door a knock and Tat pull it open. From the look she was in bed, left the covers tossed. Corazon in the bathroom, where she live. Tat look like I woke her. I grab a cheeseburger out the bag, start chewing, leave the rest.

"I be back with Stinky Joe."

Tat kiss me on the cheek.

No sir, this ain't an entirely rotten world.


DRIVE THE HIGHWAY TO JUBAL PLACE. JEEP CLOCK SAY NINE. I KEEP going past the driveway and other side the hill, pull over where the garbage truck was fitting to turn left. Turn around and kill the headlamp and the motor and sit in the quiet long as the Jeep stay warm. Outside, snow got a soft glow. I got this fuzzy feel from Tat's smile and me twisting out Jubal's grasp.

Grab Stinky Joe and this nonsense'll be miles behind us.

Get out the vehicle and tramp along the road. It's a mile and I don't expect traffic but I ready a word or two that'll let me walk in peace should someone stop. Folks in Colorado seem just the type to offer help and meddle.

No one drive by. As the hill roll over and I come upon Jubal's place I take in the highway a good mile off. The rocks is tall. The land big. Jubal's house got every room lit, top and bottom. I never was downstairs but they got the narrow windows like every other basement I ever see, and they's lit too.

Walk the road downhill and climb the driveway.

As the drive level off I hunker behind a snow bank. Down on my knees and listen. Garage is dark inside—no light from the side door. Listen hard it sound like television in the house but that could be the nonsense in my head.

Comfortable with the stillness and trusting I didn't give Jubal no cue to worry, I scoot across the drive to the garage door and give the knob a twist. Locked.

But the people that put up this garage didn't know shit about hanging a door. It got some give and I slip in a plastic card they give me at the grocery store so I could pay less money. Send it in corner-first, jiggle and jam, work the door back and forth, and in no time I got the latch figured; couple more shakes and a swing of the hip, she pop open.

"Puppydog. Stinky Joe. C'mere puppydog. Let's git!"

Quiet.

"Puppydog."

Nothin'. I step inside and leave the door open. Allow a couple seconds so the eyes adjust. Moonlight come in from the snow and with the weak orange from the heat radiators I see all I need. The quiet and still air... Smell of cars...

Ain't no puppydog in here.

They got Stinky Joe in the house.

Fuck Jubal White, is all.

# CHAPTER THIRTY

BAER FIRST ATE PIZZA WHEN HE WAS SIXTEEN YEARS OLD. HE WAS walking down the street in Gleason when a so-so girl he knew from school, Lucy Kline, crossed the street to walk with him. Lucy wouldn't know an honest thought if it punched her in the nose, but Baer tolerated the constant electric tingle on his arms because her rack was so bodacious, the sight of it made his knees tremble.

A new restaurant on the corner had opened a few months ago and though Baer wasn't brought up to spend money on other people cooking food he could make himself or go without, the aroma lassoed him from a hundred yards and dragged him until he stood at the entrance with his mouth slavering and his soul aching to digest whatever produced the smell.

"You ain't never ate pizza?" Lucy said.

"That's pizza?"

Every fool had heard of pizza. Baer was the only one who hadn't eaten it. They went inside and Baer saw three pies under glass, golden cheese glistening like sweaty backs after throwing hay bales under the sun. Sure smelled better than it looked.

A chalkboard with prices dangled on silver chains from the ceiling. Forty-nine cents for the one with mushrooms, pepperoni and green peppers. Seemed like a decent-enough deal. He tapped the outside of his pocket trying to remember which coins were inside, then felt them for size: quarter, dime, nickel and some pennies. He pulled them out.

Lucy stood close to see his open hand. Her right boob pressed all soft and mushy against his arm. Baer leaned and she leaned.

"That's twenty five, and uh, a dime. That's, uh. Shit."

"Forty-three cents," she said, and pressed closer.

"Yeah."

Lucy unzipped her purse and withdrew an oval piece of plastic with a slit down the middle. Somehow the motion forced her other breast against Baer's chest. She held her arm to the side, folded the plastic and coins fell out in Baer's waiting hand.

Baer inhaled deep. Stepped back and placed the money on the counter. Lucy smiled. Baer pointed at the pizza with pepperoni, mushrooms and green peppers.

A man with black hair on his arms and none on his head lifted a slice and dropped it on a paper plate. He swiped the coins and jingled the register.

Baer looked at the slice of pizza.

One slice.

Lucy took the plate.

Baer read the chalkboard with the prices again. Forty nine cents, mushrooms, pepperoni, green peppers.

Assholes.

They put the whole pizza under the glass but sold it by the slice!

Lucy carried the paper plate to a stool by the window and Baer walked out the open door. Stood there like a dumb country kid, too stupid to know what everyone else did. Knew there was deception all about and still managed to get tricked. In front of Lucy.

He looked to her, holding the pizza point in her mouth, almost giggling at him.

Pizza could go to hell.

Gleason, too.

He walked twenty yards before Lucy shouted from behind. He waved her off without looking back.

Baer drove his mother's car the long way home, looping out around Murdock's place and Brown's back forty. His mother and Brown never got on after their altercation, and Brown coughed more and more and was less willing to chuck bales and shovel pig shit. Baer had grown taller and had filled out—a little. Baer negotiated payment in real dollars and spent his summers saving as much pay as possible toward the future purchase of a Nova, or anything boss with fat wheels and an engine so big they had to cut the hood. Tooling home on the country roads he saw the future—him sitting in the driver seat, pulled over next a sidewalk. Some Rita Hayworth ten, maybe from Asheville, comes up to check him out. She gets a load of the car and looks inside, gets so horny she trips on flat cement and stumbles her boobs right in his face.

Ringneck!

Three darted from the roadside into the woods. Baer stomped the gas. He knew the terrain, knew where they'd go.

The birds were scarce and nothing was worse than stumbling on pheasants some government kook just released. They stood looking at the shotgun barrel, refused to take wing, and if you shot them anyway they tasted like rubber. That's why real sportsmen, like Ned at the barbershop, always said you never shoot ringneck in the spring.

Being fall, these three birds had all summer to get wily, and no matter how good that pizza might have been, it wouldn't compare to pheasant with carrots and sweet potatoes baked in Donald Duck orange juice.

Baer swerved around the last bend with the pedal on the floor. His mother's car struggled. Baer slammed the brake and swooshed into the driveway sending dirt and pebbles flying. He ran into the house and grabbed his mother's shotgun and opened the box with the shells...

Only two left.

Larry.

Asshole.

Baer grabbed both. He broke open the shotgun. One in the breech. Three shots, three birds, it'd be a hell of a story...

Baer bolted from the house and ran with the shotgun held out, floating up and down as he leaped rocks and the streambed twice because cutting a straight line to the pheasants took him that way. The birds loved a brushy area where fifty years ago someone in a house that wasn't even there anymore planted a hundred-yard stretch with pines. Their bottom branches were mostly dead and hung close to the ground. Ringneck hunkered down and anyone without skills would race right by.

But Baer had skills.

He slowed from dead run to careful walk in two steps. Cocked the shotgun and held it ready to swing and fire.

Motion!

Front left.

Baer's eye and the shotgun found the pheasant in the same moment. He fired and broke the chamber open, slammed home another shell and closed the shotgun before the first pheasant knew it was dead. It dropped close to a rotted elm stump. He fixed the location in mind and kept walking.

Ringneck were smart little bastards. They didn't run away. They ran perpendicular and then exploded some unguessable direction. Or that's how it always seemed. Baer adjusted his course, now holding the shotgun in his shoulder and whoosh!

He swung the barrel—two in the air at once!—fired, broke the breech, dropped a shell—couldn't see the third bird.

Baer clamped his teeth.

If he had a double barrel shotgun or a pump...

Damn. Just damn.

Baer found the second bird dead where it landed and tromped back to the stump where the first lay.

Shotgun in his left hand and two birds swinging by their feet in his right, Baer returned to the house, left the birds outside and lay the shotgun on his mother's bed. He opened the closet, pulled out the shoe box that held ammunition and searched for any stray shotgun shells. Larry must have had some fun and like the slimy prick he was, never told anyone he'd used all but two.

Baer replaced the shotgun in his mother's closet and made a mental note to buy more.

He took his hunting knife and outside at the back of the yard by the briars, split the birds' chests and yanked out their breasts. He left them in the refrigerator to surprise his mother.

# CHAPTER THIRTY-ONE

CLOSE THE GARAGE DOOR AND STUDY THE HOUSE. THE TWO AIN'T square. Garage built at an angle with plenty of turnaround. From the door I see 'long back the house. Basement lights draw the eye. Got the path shoveled from door to door and going off that I'll leave tracks... but I'm here to steal Stinky Joe and when I'm done they'll know anyway. Still feel like a long term commitment breaking the snow.

Think on it.

Nah, fuck it. Stinky Joe, I'm coming.

Follow the path close the steps then break 'round the corner to the first window. Hands and knees. Peer slow, case they's someone looking out. Nobody. Food dish and water bowl next the steps. His blanket tossed on the cement. No cardboard in under. Didn't even fold it double thick.

No Stinky Joe in sight.

Next window, light come out but a cardboard box block the view. Must be a shelf.

Around to the back. No windows. On to the side adjacent the road. Check both windows and no Stinky Joe.

Backtrack five feet and stand next the living room window. Ease the right eyeball more right. Jubal sit on the sofa, wife snuggled. Both they faces is streaked and shiny. Percival on the rug with Stinky Joe, pulling his ears slow, like they's cold and need his attention.

Joe lift his head. Spot me.

Duck.

Damn.

If Jubal come out and see tracks, he'll know it's me reneging. If he ain't armed he'll remedy his lack and once he done that, he'll make war. A man don't judge a situation if he can judge a man instead. Me being the stone cold murderer got bent after someone messed with his dog, he'll wager it's him or me—one of us got to die—else I'll leave him and his family dead. Like a switch goes cold to hot, his wits'll scatter and leave fear to do the thinking.

Jubal come out... I gotta put him down.

Slip the FBI Glock off my hip and get it out, arms straight, ready to swing up and blast away. Got the pulse in my neck. Think it through. Jubal come outside to the edge of the porch, I put him down. After that, be faster to take out the wife through the window.

I won't kill the boy.

Have to take him along. Otherwise it's a phone call and he'll have the coppers chasing the Jeep.

But what trouble I sow taking him? Can't leave him on the cold street. Any place I stash him, if he's warm and taken care of, he'll be but a minute from saying that handsome feller in the Jeep's the one y'alls after. He kill my family and kidnap me.

They's no safe place I can leave Percival, 'cept dead.

Didn't want that for him, but if his old man make me, and I got no choice, then I got no choice. When an evil man force an evil decision on another, fuck him and his.

Burp up a little vomit. Cheeseburger.

Percival.

Shit. Damn. Hell.

Think on it.

If I bust the phone line and steal the car keys, he'd have to wait 'til someone come by to say hello. Check on the old man about Dwain or something, likely tomorrow. I'd have a twelve hour lead. Time to switch vehicles and clear Denver, maybe. Or head to California. Have to yank the girls out the rustic resort and it'd be right back to the nonstop yammer. Accourse Corazon'd be happy. She get out her phone and look for Chesters she can slip out and murder as we go. And I ain't made promises to Tat—fact is, last we talked we said it was over, or not. We'd know.

Shit. Damn. Cell phone. If Corazon got one and know how to use it, Percival do. And Dwain had one for sure. And likely Jubal and Mrs. White. So if Percival live, I got to hunt down four cell phones and hope they ain't no more. And figure out if he know how to do the other computer talk.

They ain't no way 'round it.

If Jubal come out—

Say, where the hell's Jubal? Not a sound save the television.

Lower Glock and stand, slow, ease the eyeballs over the sill and Stinky Joe got his head on the carpet. Percival's face glued to the set. Jubal got his head tall and the wife's leaned into him with her eyes closed.

What kind of son of a bitch am I?

Here's a man ready to do another, either me or his neighbor. A man bristling out.

But inside the home... all cuddles and virtue.

A man can't embrace 'em both. I can't love on Jubal and his kin. If he knew I was here he'd come out with a gun. Make me bristle too.

Drive a man to drink. Some other man.

Fucking nylon boots. Feet cold. Stinky Joe warm.

Hunker down agin.

It's clear Stinky Joe's bedding downstairs when the television go off and the family shut down. I'll need inside. House has a front door and a back. Windows all around. Time to figure out how I'm gonna skedoodle outta here with no one the wiser. I'm sick of the killing and if I can just get Stinky Joe I'll never—

Sound go off. Lights dim. I stand. Television off.

Percival pulling Stinky Joe by the collar.

Quick, I scoot to the back of the house. Careful and slow, press the thumb button on the screen door. Ease it open so the shock go slow and neither chain nor spring rattle. Propped with the hip I twist the door-knob right.

Click!

Open!

Fried chicken. Taters. Maybe green beans or something from a can.

Door open to a boot room. Dark inside but a sliver of light shine on the old fashioned coat stand like to dance with Fred Astair. Want to kick the snow off my boots but 'tween leaving water on the floor or the family's blood I bet the Mrs. White prefer water. Slip inside and careful, slow, close the screen and just barely push the door so it seal. Hope the pressure change don't make the curtains move.

Footsteps! Patter and slipping dog claws on wood.

Shift behind the coat stand and get a hand on Glock—

Percival say, "Dog! Stop it! Go downstairs now!"

"What's going on?" Jubal—

"This dog! He's trying to get away!"

"Smack his nose."

"What?"

"Rap his nose. Easy, not too hard. You don't want him to bite."

Percival body hit the wall. Dog feet skitter. Basement door clap shut afore it open.

"He's trying to go to the coat room!"

Stinky Joe smell me.

Close my eyes.

I gotta kill this family. I don't want more bodies in my ledger but if Stinky Joe make the coat room it's over.

Feet scuffle. I lean and see part the hallway. Jubal block the light then open the basement door. Stinky Joe growl and Jubal's feet pound the wood steps like hammers. Joe's feet slide 'til he's on the steps and the thuds rumble down a couple more. Then rumble up. Jubal slam the door.

"Damn dog. Go to bed."

"Yes sir."

"Brush your damn teeth first."

"Okay. I'm sorry."

"Not your fault. Go."

Percival patter off.

Jubal tromp into the coat room. Grumble and whisper. Stop a few inches away and I can smell his supper. Hold my breath so the cheeseburger breath don't freshen his appetite. He stand too long. I breathe slow and squeeze the Glock—it'll take a shift of the wrist to line the barrel with his ribs.

He stop at the door.

"Damn—"

Shuffle his feet. Step in snow water. Must be in socks. He reach out and lock the door. Turn around.

"Percival. I told you to clean the snow off your boots before coming inside. It's why we have the broom on the steps, right?... Percival? Dammit."

He stomp away. That'll teach the boy.

Jubal out the room, I inhale deep and let the air out my lungs long and slow. Let the blood pressure drift while the mind tingles and the skin feels pin-pricky.

Jubal go up the stairs and after another minute the lights go out in the living room and kitchen. Musta been the Mrs.

Second floor is dark save moonlight through the windows. Don't want to wait another second, but I do. Count. At a buck twenty two I say hell with it.

Creep out the coat room. Open the basement door and Stinky Joe right there.

"Said I'd come right back."

*Let's get the hell outta here.*

Three seconds we in the snow and fifteen minute the Jeep.

I put Joe in the front seat and blast the heat since he ain't got but a pit bull's coat and no nylon boots like me.

I think on Jubal and the Mrs. White, loving inward and bristling out and how I was ready to spill they blood. Look at the stars knowing Dwain's out there somewhere, or down below in considerable heat, with Jubal due to follow...

And the Mrs. White alone with Percival, just her, the boy, and Jubal's debt.

Maybe I can do something other'n kill.

Heat blasting I drop the window for some air and put it in first. Crawl until the White house come up on the left.

Maybe they's another card to play.

Or coin.

# CHAPTER THIRTY-TWO

BAER COULDN'T DECIDE WHAT HE WANTED MORE: ANOTHER SHOT AT tasting pizza or another brush against Lucy Kline's ta-tas. She worked at the hardware and a few days before happened to be getting off work when Baer strolled by on the other side of the road.

Baer whiled away the hours in school dreaming of the day he'd be forever free of it. Sometimes teachers said things and they knew they were fulla shit but said it anyway. Baer did his best to only remember the stuff they believed was true, but some teachers like Miss Powers in social studies spewed nonstop nonsense and didn't believe any of it.

Unlike the other women teachers, Miss Powers didn't wear makeup. She didn't have the best hygiene habits either. Any time Baer sharpened his pencil he took the long way around, behind all the other desks, so he didn't have to pass near hers. She talked about how wonderful capitalism was but from behind glowing eyes. The kids called her Flower Powers and once when she overheard, she smiled.

If it wasn't for his mother's constant nagging to pay attention in school so he didn't wind up unemployed and without prospects, Baer would have quit. Instead, he endured. He learned to focus inward best he could to help insulate from the lies. If he didn't hear them the irritation was less.

But as he grew older the curse became more acute.

The best thing he found to think about to lessen the sharpness of the curse—out of all the things in the world—was boobs. A mind trapped in boob-thoughts had little ambition for anything else. Breasts alone had the power to protect him.

He knew them in perfect imagined intimacy long before he ever saw one—not two—in real life. Barbie Bannon lifted her shirt at the boys coming out of the locker room and one flopped out. The boys charged her and she ran screaming in delight before the second could make it free.

After school Baer waited for his bus but instead of boarding, stood last in line. He told Miss Peggy he was walking instead and she nodded and closed the door. The bus pulled away. Most of the other kids were long gone. Baer walked to town, past the pizza joint with its wonderful smells and shady sales practices to the hardware where Lucy might be starting her shift. Baer walked past slow, saw his reflection and knew anybody inside would think he was self-admiring.

He could go inside—but what if he saw her?

Best to loiter outside looking cool. Play it off. If she came out, she came out.

She'd left school walking that direction with a gaggle of girls, but Baer didn't track her long enough to know if she'd gone to the hardware.

She didn't come out.

The longer he stood on the step with his back to the window thinking about the size of her rack, the less sure he became.

Brown had settled his hours the night before and Baer had a pocket full of cash. He remembered he wanted to replace the shotgun shells for his mother, and glad for the excuse, went inside the hardware. Merv stood behind the counter.

"I need a box of Federal sixteen."

Merv nodded. Grinned.

"You stand outside twenty minute gettin' up the nerve to buy shotgun shells?" He winked. "She's in back."

Baer smiled back. Paid for the box and carried it to the storage room door that was open. Lucy looked up from a cardboard box full of smaller boxes of screws.

Screws. Rope. Pipe. Gaskets. Lubricants. Baer blinked.

"That was awful rude," Lucy said. "Why'd you leave me there with your pizza? I don't even like pizza."

Baer shook his head. "Dunno."

"You better do better than that."

"It was bullshit. Them putting forty nine cents and showing the whole pizza. You only get a slice."

"You left because of that?"

"Sorry."

"Come here, I want to show you something."

Lucy led out the back door to the alley. Baer followed.

The door closed and Lucy leaned against it. "Come here."

She grabbed his shirt and pulled. Wrapped her arms around him, poked her head out past her chest and planted heavy lips on Baer's. He inhaled hard through his nose and marveled at the feeling in his chest, in his mess, in his heart. He kissed with open eyes and when her tongue probed his mouth he couldn't resist a wide smile and that opened her eyes...

Red.

She pulled back and smiled huge.

She thought she was good but he saw it coming.

"Wait here."

Sparks.

She ducked inside. The lock slid.

Baer waited until his trousers were flat then walked around to the front of the store and saw Lucy inside, back by the rope spools. She smiled big and lifted her hand, rotated it while dropping three fingers, leaving the middle erect.

No red eyes.

Baer walked home with his box of shotgun shells in hand, changing it from one to the other every forty nine steps. The discipline would be his farewell salute, even better than floating the bird back at her because it left her unaware and him stronger. By the time he reached home, he'd forgotten about Lucy Kline's middle finger and her kiss, but retained the memory of her marvelous breasts pressed against his chest. She'd play hell getting that back.

He had money left from his farm work and he'd add it to the growing roll in his sock drawer, the account that would someday fund a hotrod.

Something like a Nova but even more boss.

He pulled open the front door and the silence was strange. He looked at the wall clock. Mother was usually cooking dinner by four thirty. A head of iceberg lettuce was on the counter. Tomatoes cut on the board. She never left food out.

Mother usually had the television on for company—or sometimes the radio.

The car was out front.

With Larry at football practice and Baer late, maybe she'd stolen a few minutes for a nap.

Baer walked back through the hallway and each step increased his unease.

Her door was open. He peered inside.

Mother lay on the floor with her chest down but head twisted to the side and up, like her neck was broken. The shotgun barrel was next to her hand. The stock lay in two pieces, one on her bed and the other on the floor.

Baer gaped.

The side of her face was purplish black but the horror of it all was another layer deep.

She was dead and that was fathomable.

The color of her eyes wasn't.

# CHAPTER THIRTY-THREE

Ain't a mile up the highway to the exit. Zig across the bridge and scoot up the valley. No zag.

Resorts all the way. If not for the mountains and hot tub they'd be twenty dollar motels, proud they got the color TV.

Drive by the cheeseburger stand and shit if those I ate don't feel good in the belly. Tasty going down. Just enough onion in the burps.

I bet Stinky Joe'd love a few.

Cut the wheel. Swing along the window. Order six more and pull around and wait. Love on the stink dog, rest a hand on his shoulder and move the thumb a bit so he don't get bored. Sometimes man and dog get along 'cause the words is few. Stinky Joe's a man of character, as the saying go. Fought the wild and survive. Defend his freedom like a canine George Washington. Got a simple Constitution. He'll look mournful but when trouble come knocking, he got your back. Like with them evil sonsabitches at the fight circle. Stinky Joe saw two killers like to take me down and he claw out the front window and charge the very same pit he fled.

Never a better trooper.

Each time I find trouble it seem the trouble's hell bent on getting us apart.

Boy waves behind the glass. Hold up a paper sack. I leave Stinky Joe in the vehicle and collect my cow grease and ketchup. Hop back in and share a burger with Joe. Strip off the onion slice and eat it myself. Then tear off chunks and trade bites with Stinky Joe. He don't eat so much as choke 'em down and tongue-slap his jowl for clean up.

Cars zing by on the highway. Mountains is tall in front and behind; snow still look mostly fresh and part of me says it's time to haul ass. I paid three days at the motel resort and the girls got they wiles. They got guns and knives. Give 'em a couple gold coin, they be fine.

I never wanted this setup.

But truth told I kinda got used to the chatter and commotion. The skulking and cowgirl-style pokin'.

Tat's like one of those jungle girls from Brazil. Corazon too. Imagine an army made of 'em. Shiver the timbers.

And Tat found a kind spot in her. I ain't had a woman spend as much time thinking on me as she do herself. I never had a nice woman.

Save Tat.

Kinda nice getting worried on.

And her looking at Dwain when he was a stud and not dead—shit—I ain't wanted to kill a man over a woman since me and Larry went nose to nose on Ruth.

All in all, things being what they is and not what they ain't...

Think I'll keep Tat and Corazon around, long as they'll keep me.

But first I got a mission.

Engage first and creep out on the road. Felt like a mile to walk, but driving to the motel resort ain't a minute. I park ass-end to the wall for a hasty getaway, grab the burgers and rap the door.

Tat opens. Chain holds. She undo the chain without peering out.

Stinky Joe crowd my feet and sniff the door crack.

"More cheeseburgers."

She open the door.

"Don't loose the chain 'til you see who's knocking. Didn't they learn you nothing in Mexico?"

We go inside, I close the door but don't lock it. Offer the bag of burgers.

"These is hot."

Tat's brows ride low on her eyeballs, doing stunts.

"What's going on?"

"What you mean."

"Where's your bag?"

"Jeep."

"Uh-huh. We going now?" Tat say.

"Nah. No. Not y'all."

"What?" Corazon say.

"I got a thing I gotta do."

"Did you kill them?" Tat say.

"No. Pretty slick is the truth. Just snuck in and stole Joe."

"So now they know," Corazon say. "We have to go. We're packed."

Tat say, "We can eat on the road. Those burgers were good."

"Tat, now hold on. Both of you, ease up. You stay here a couple day. I got an idea I can maybe stop the bloodshed. Solve this problem by bein' decent, 'stead of the other way."

Tat move her head back like to miss a slap.

"I got to run. I be back in two day. The resort's paid for three. I be right back. Don't go nowhere. I uh—"

Tat cross her arms. Tilt the head.

"Shit woman. I got feelin's for ya, so don't go nowhere. But I don't have time to offer up the skinny. I got to go. Time is short."

"Come on, Stinky Joe. Lessgo."

"Oh, sure. You're coming back."

"What?"

"You take your backpack and the dog. You leave us here in this place with the hot tub. You be right back."

"Well, shit."

"Exactly."

"That ain't what I said."

"Fine. Leave."

"What?"

"Go. Leave."

"Now shit."

"Play your gringo games. I see the truth."

"You—fuck. I got a plan. Jubal's gonna cause a mess of trouble on people don't deserve it. I got a chance to stop it, without nobody gettin' shot. But I have to go right now. Stay here. Don't go nowhere. Right? You understand?"

Her face lose the edge. Corazon still look ready to spit venom but Tat's eyes glow just a little. Warmth, not deceit. Like when she got it in her mind she wanna treat me right.

She curl the shoulders. Lift one leg a little. "You said you got feelings for me."

"Accourse. Shit. That what this about? I got all kinda mixed up feelings. I coulda kept driving if I wanted. You think I stop by to give you some fuckin' cheeseburgers afore I duck out for good?"

"Okay."

"Good. Gimme a kiss and I gotta go."

"But you can't take Stinky Joe."

"What? Nonsense. I gotta—"

Damn.

"If you don't leave him, it's because you aren't coming back. If you aren't coming back, we won't be here either."

# CHAPTER THIRTY-FOUR

THEY STOOD IN THE HOUSE. MOTHER'S BODY WAS STILL IN THE BACK bedroom. Police Chief Lou Smylie kept his gaze on Larry while talking but now and again his eyes darted to Baer.

Smylie's son, Horace, was two grades ahead of Larry. They played football together and were part of the same crowd of make-believe badasses who talked big shit but got straight-A's.

At the sound of commotion down the hallway, Smylie reached to Larry and steered him two paces, forcing Baer back as well, as men wheeled out their mother's body. Another smiling man in a suit followed chewing bubble gum. Baer stared and tried to communicate his inner thinking—I'm 'bout to kick your disrespectful ass—but the man glanced at Smylie and never connected with Baer's gaze.

The screen door slammed. Baer twitched. He looked at Smylie and wondered at how, since coming home and finding his mother murdered, he hadn't felt the juice. Hadn't seen a red eye. Almost as if men in the presence of death were naked.

He stood next to the desk, lamp and wall outlet where Larry tried to kill him, but his mind drifted from the moment he stood in and he barely recalled the past. His mother's body was out of the house—but the body wasn't *her*. He knew because he was still tethered to her. With Mother in the next world forward, that tie was stretched like a rubber band, so thin maybe only a couple atoms were adjacent and the rest pulled longways. He wondered if time would stretch it so thin it would break. For right now he could hold back the tears, but someday the band would snap, and that was the moment to fear.

He would be alone.

Baer blinked his eyes clear. Smylie watched him. Larry stared too—his lips pulled up and back, more disgusted than mean.

"Could have been anybody," Larry said. "Any of ten thousand men."

"You see my point," Smylie said. "They's just no way to even start on this."

Baer's mind fell from the atmosphere and his mouth dropped.

"I can see you got something to say."

Chief Smylie hooked thumbs on belt loops.

"You're not even gonna try to find who done it?"

"Look, son, we been—"

"I ain't your son."

Tight smile. "No disrespect to you or your brother. He's worked his ass off to get above his station and you will too, I'm sure. You're fine boys."

"Nowhere to start," Baer said. "Buncha bullshit. If it was your mother you'd find a place to start."

"Watch your mouth. She don't go in the same sentence."

"I say you're fulla shit and lazy too."

"Okay, force me to be blunt. Your mother was what she was. She did what she did. I could name six men that stuck her since Labor Day—and you know seven more. Every time somebody came by to give you furniture. Every time they brought food. Hell I know for a fact Lou Emerson brought a smoked ham every Christmas. You watch and see if he brings one this year, without your mother to lay for it!"

Spittle flew from Smylie's mouth and he blinked three times.

"Plus we got the new highway construction all the way past Hickory and that means word of mouth travels even farther. There must be fingerprints from a thousand men in that bedroom, all of them from God knows where. You tell me how the hell I'm supposed to know which one she smarted off to."

Larry shook his head. "He's being stupid, Chief Smylie. He knew what she was."

"Your mother, you fuckin' dick."

Baer shouldered past Larry. Pushed aside Chief Smylie's arm and when Smylie gripped his shoulder, swung his elbow around and broke the hold.

Baer strode out the front of the house and watched men close a pickup truck's tailgate.

They hauled off his mother in the bed of an F-100.

# CHAPTER THIRTY-FIVE

TWENTY FOUR HOURS ONE WAY, JUDGING FROM MAP AND MEMORY. I fill the tank at the last station afore hopping on Interstate 70 and leaving Glenwood Springs.

Twenty four hours there and twenty four back. Two days plus the time it take to eat and splash water on my face 'long the way. Can't speed, as I don't care to have nobody look too close at the Alden Boone license and papers.

But if this work, nobody got to die but Jubal White, when the Almighty pull his string.

Vail pretty at night, like they never took down the Christmas lights.

Jeep shoulda put a bigger engine in this damn thing. In four wheel drive, can't keep her in fifth. Roads get slippy and flurries in the air heading up Vail Pass. Tall as Everest. Sip coffee and muse on dumb shit. Life.

Wasn't too bright leaving Joe. If I'd a left him in the Jeep to start, Tat maybe wouldn't a had the thought. But she put me in a corner. If I want both her and Stinky Joe, I got to give up Stinky Joe for two day. Prove it.

All Stinky Joe say was, *don't you forget that promise.*

Drink coffee. Coming down the hill, Denver ahead. I'll pass through in the dark.

I think on Jubal White.

Think on all the killing I done and the killing he's ready to, if his plans go sideways and the drug people decide they want to keep they money—and how I got the gall to say his killing ain't right. He's thinking to put the family first and if he made mistakes with the money and got to die, maybe he can set things aright and take down a drug dealing crook too. If I was a cop and dedicated my life to forcing rules on folk, it'd have to be 'cause I thought they was good rules. Or rules in general was good. Or at least better'n no rules. Jubal got to have some philosophy on it. Got to associate himself with the side he think has the virtue.

How's that different than old Baer Creighton butcher forty people?

Fucking black road. They wasn't no snow past Denver and now the headlamps cut a yellow path through yellow plains tamped down by the season but ready to sprout come rain.

Slow down. Pass a car with the four ways flashing. Nobody there, 'less they's asleep in the back.

Almighty looking down on Jubal and me like to think we both batshit selfish and ornery.

Drink coffee.

Adjust the hips left. Right. Shift the seat an inch and stretch the legs. Nothing like good empty highway.

Something up there on the right, too close the road. Ease off the gas. Flip the high beams.

Woman. Pokable.

She stick her thumb out.

Jeep thermometer say twenty-two. She turn toward the road and her breath shoot out frosty. Her knees is together and her back hunched. Got yellow hose on her legs. Woman like to freeze.

Must be her car, mile back.

Brakes. No one behind. Slow it down and drop the window.

"Going east I take it?"

"Yes. I ran out of gas."

"You look 'bout to freeze to death."

"I feel it too. I stayed in the car until I was too cold. I could use a ride, honestly. I think there's an exit a few miles ahead."

General discomfort and scared I bet—but no red nor juice.

"Well I got the heater on and I'll get you to the next exit. Or whatever."

She pull the door handle. Locked.

"Shit. Pardon."

Unlock the door and while I'm leaned, open the passenger air vent.

She open the door. Dome light on. Study me good. Give her my best look, plain vanilla I won't kill ya, and after a shivered think, she climb in.

"Wow, almost five a.m."

"Yep."

"You awake enough to drive?"

"Is it gonna be like that?"

"Oh, I see."

"We can talk anything you want save my drivin'."

"Do you have any coffee or anything hot?"

"Spare coffee's the one close the dash. Ain't touched it—I been drinking the other. They's cold, though. Bought 'em in Glenwood."

"Does it have cream and sugar?"

"Black."

"Good. I can't have cream or sugar."

"Help yourself."

She take the styrofoam and feel about the roof for the dome light. I hit the switch. She pull off the cap.

"You like Ronald Reagan," says I.

"What do you mean?"

"Trust and verify."

"No. I didn't particularly care for Reagan."

"Ah."

"And not that I don't trust you, but since honest mistakes happen all the time I verified the coffee was black."

Kill the dome light.

"Even better. So according to this sign, next exit's in nine mile. You want off there?"

"Wow, there's nothing out here. Yes. The next exit. If they have a gas station."

She settle in the seat and lean back like to get comfortable. "How far east are you traveling tonight?"

"All of it. North Carolina."

"Oh. I see. That's right."

Cock my ear.

"Where in North Carolina?"

"Gleason."

"I thought so."

"Why you think so?"

"I'm an addict. A news junkie. I've seen your face a hundred times and it would have stuck with one. And there was that newspaper series about you. I think the girl who wrote it is getting a Pulitzer."

Push the clutch. Shift to fourth and take the foot off the gas. Third. Second. Push the clutch and drift, pull to the berm. Wobble the shifter and nod at the door.

"You can get out if you want. I don't want nothing from you and out here I'll trust you to keep your mouth shut long enough I can get a few miles."

"You're serious."

"Maybe you oughtta get out."

"Why? I recognized you before I got in."

I puzzle on that. No red nor juice.

"Then why you get in?"

"Because I don't believe you're a bad man. Misunderstood, certainly. But good inside where it matters."

No red nor juice.

My fucking eyes is wet. Just like that. Alla sudden I got to blink and water roll over my cheek. Chin want to fold up and I try to squint my face straight and I got to look away. Chest start to cave in on itself and I'm so fucking tired—got to be—I can't think. That or the cheeseburgers is working my liver so the feelin's squirt out.

"It's okay," she say.

Now the snot run. I want to choke up like Fred died but not with a damn woman in the next seat. Wipe my eyes clean. Check the sideview. No traffic. Engage first and gun the weak ass six cylinder onto the highway. Lucky we going downhill.

'Fore I get too much speed I suck back the snot and drop the window. Hack it out. Clear my throat.

"You ever seen allergies like that?"

"No," she says. "Not like that."

Drink coffee. Sip taste bold and cold and I gulp half the cup. Splash of caffeine in the blood get my mind right. If she a good woman she'll act like she saw my pecker on accident. Look away and pretend she didn't.

"Have you ever worked with computers?" she say.

"No. Never had a computer."

"Ever use a cell phone?"

"Not even once."

"I see."

Half mile. Road noise pretty good.

"Do you know what a computer program is?"

"Tell the computer what to do."

"Right."

"You headed somewhere with the questions?"

"Where were you born?"

"Asheville."

"Where did you grow up?"

"Gleason. Right next Asheville. Down the road twenty minute. Ever been—"

"What made you choose to be born in Asheville and to grow up in Gleason?"

I look. Her face is plain. Eyebrows high like she want an answer—though it's the dumbest damn question I ever hear. Way up ahead the horizon got a glow. This time of night people get funny and they minds don't work. Make a feller weep for no good reason. One last gulp of coffee. I down it.

"Maybe you oughtta have more of your coffee. You ask me why I choose to be born somewhere."

"It wasn't a facetious question."

"Good. I don't know that word."

"It wasn't a question I didn't mean to ask."

"You mean to ask it."

"Right."

"I didn't choose to be born at all, let alone somewhere."

"Oh—I don't believe that at all. But it in a different way than you think."

"That's real good."

"So let me ask this. Why did you choose to be a white man?"

"Uh."

"Why did you choose to grow up in a rural setting?"

"I—"

"Why did you choose—"

"I didn't choose none of that. It's what God gimme."

"Okay, I'll accept that."

Look at her.

"Did you know that the Bible says—"

"Christamighty."

"That the sins of the father will be passed to four generations?"

"Hunh?"

"It's a famous verse. Don't get me wrong, I'm not a Bible thumper. The verse is important because many of the thoughts you have—the program you're born with, like a computer—came from your parents. Did you know that?"

"Uh. No."

"Do you believe me?"

"I. You... Uh."

"Go ahead."

"Look. You're pretty and all. Got good legs and your smile ain't bad. But your brain's mush."

"Is that your best? Deflect and try to get the other person flustered because you don't have an answer?"

"Shit."

"I'm helping you."

"How that?"

"I'm showing you that you aren't responsible for how you grew up or the first program that ran in your brain—the one that said you're a boy and boys pull pigtails and blow up frogs. You're not responsible for where you were born, your color, religion, nothing. All the stuff that combined to become you—you didn't choose any of it. You didn't choose your starting point."

"Then what the hell's a man responsible for?"

"Where you go after you realize you can't trust any belief you inherited."

"I never trust nobody, and where I went is the fucking problem, lady."

"You're not hearing me. You're a passenger feeling responsible for where the driver took you. Until you discover you are separate from the thoughts you inherited, you are not self actualized. You are not the driver."

"Good fucking God."

"I don't think you understand me. Most people are happy to discover they aren't as bad as they think. I would especially think—"

"You want to talk politics maybe?"

"Let's do religion."

"Shit."

"It's okay. You see, materialists believe there is one life and one reality. Whether they believe in God or not, they live the same. All their cares are the same, their actions, whatever. God exists or He doesn't— and their belief doesn't intrude on their behaviors. They eat Cheerios each morning. Right?"

"You say so."

"And if God doesn't exist, it's the same deal. Cheerios. God doesn't win me the lottery. He doesn't put food in my cupboards. I do that by working twelve hours a day. God or no God, what changes—except if I believe then I go to heaven and if I don't I go to hell? Right? So who does that make a believer out of?"

"I dunno."

"The shallow coward."

"Oh."

"Shit. I almost miss it. Here's your exit."

Brake. Drift right. She put her elbow on the door and lean head to hand.

Think ahead: maybe refill the coffee, help this woman with a gas can. Shit. Then I gotta take her back.

Shit.

Follow the loop and cut left at the T. Half mile, gas station got the lights on. Pull in and the place already bustle with the a.m. crowd. Bet the coffee good.

"You sit here. I get a can."

"Oh, thank you."

Go inside, pay cash for the gas and a can. Start the pump in the Jeep and finish in plastic. Put it in back jammed agin the side with my pack and go inside for my change. Two new cups coffee, black, plus a box of Little Debbie.

Wonder if the lady from the psyche ward'll still be in the Jeep.

She is. Now I got to share.

"Let's get you on the road, right?"

"How much do I owe you for the gasoline?"

"Oh, you paid with wisdom."

She twinkle like she offended but too civilized to show, and under the fluorescent canopy her face glows awful damn pretty. She smile 'cause I look too long and on top of knowing all the philosophy ever writ, she also reads minds.

"Fuck. Let's get going."

"Yeah," she say.

"So you was saying religious people is cowards."

"That's not what I meant. I was using hyperbole."

"Excellent. Best I ever see."

Rub a fist in my eye. Get back on the highway, headed back for where I pick her up. Exercise should only cost a half hour. Her talking the whole time.

"There's one life, yes. But it is eternal, and these days, this life, is only a tiny part of it. There's one reality, of course, but we don't see it. We're not in it. We don't dream up heaven. Heaven dreams us."

"You remind me of an old feller. Died way back. Stark fuckin' mad, but peaceful about it."

She put her hand on my arm 'til I look. Car in the other lane light her face. Bold eyes. "I am the sanest person you'll ever meet—but only because I know how tiny we are. How illusory. Tell me: have you ever experienced anything that didn't seem to fit? Anything that challenged your ideas about reality?"

"Not once."

"I don't believe that. We all do."

No red, no juice. Fuck.

"Yeah, every day."

"How so?"

"Tell you later."

"Fair enough. You ever wonder why you experience what you experience?"

"Go ahead and tell me."

"We see the matter that reflects light.... but the spiritual world doesn't often reflect light. It doesn't compress air into sound waves. It doesn't bust up into tiny particles and become airborne so you can smell it. The true higher reality is all around us but is undetected by our senses. But every so often, something happens that's just too coordinated to be accidental. And sometimes the unseen energies push through."

"Bullshit, you ask me."

"I'm not asking. I'm telling. You're like a blind man with a pole scoffing at the Grand Canyon. Your senses are good for when you stub your toe on a rock. But for the things your senses can't report, they're useless. And the more you protest the sillier you look."

"What if I don't believe in nonsense?"

"You believe in God but not heaven. Am I hearing you right?"

"Not the way you say."

"I'm trying to connect you to a healthier understanding of yourself as a thinking being in a Universe that is actually aware of your existence. You see, if you believe in God but that belief leaves you mired in the physical world, and disbelieving the other, that's because you don't actually believe in God. Your belief is mechanical. You're convinced of the math of it—two plus two is four—because you inherited the thought patterns and never questioned them. But you can't add your way to God. You can kick a rock but you can't point to the number four."

Hold up four fingers.

"Those are fingers. Not *four*. Do you understand? Four is a number. It exists, but it isn't made of the same stuff as the world you can touch. The higher reality is like that. Different stuff."

"God?"

"Sure. Your name, not mine."

"Nah. This's bullshit."

"It's difficult, I know. To someone stuck in materialism, you're locked in. It's difficult to even imagine where you were before you were empodded in your mortal coil."

"Come again?"

"Your earthly troubles."

"Why didn't you say that? You fucking people try to sound smarter'n you are."

"You fucking people cling to foolishness when you find thinking too difficult."

"What?"

She smile. Big. "Anyway—"

"Wait a minute. Empodded?"

"I picture it like this. Your immortal soul—your eternal conscious self —comes to a place like an airport. Strips down at the entrance, like going through security. Except in heaven there's no TSA, right? So your soul goes through this place and then boards a baby. Like going into a pod. You know. A pea pod. Or a cocoon. I should have said cocooned. Inside a baby, as its soul. Before shipping out, they say something to remind you not to worry too much. You're only stuck in the human body for a blip of time. It's like you're going to the most powerful movie ever. Full immersion in the story and every viewer is the hero."

"Lordy. You slipped out the hospital and we gone too far. I can't take you back."

"Isn't it cool? Your whole life, you're the hero of your own movie. And then you die and go back to where you were before, heaven with the Eternal. But you know so much more than you did before. Or maybe it's just a vacation. Who knows. Right?"

"You say my soul was alive before I was."

"How could something that is infinite not stretch as far backward as it stretches forward?"

"You tell me."

"It can't."

"My point has been to help you. How can you convict yourself of doing things *you* didn't do?"

"Uh, I did 'em."

"When you wept, you were upset because I said you are a good man. That caused cognitive dissonance because you've made peace—as best you could—with yourself as an evil man. Or a confused man. Either way, you want to be good, but believe you are not."

I got no words for the woman.

"What? Hey—shit. That's your car, right?"

"Yes. I wonder how far the next exit is."

"Right here."

No cars behind and only a couple headlights way off in the coming lane. Median look flat—mostly. No tall plants in the middle. Put the Jeep in four wheel and ease into the snow going thirty. All wheels spinning and we bounce through the bottom, up the other side without losing traction. Smell gasoline—maybe dump the can sideways—but I stomp the gas and we clear the bank and bounce on the eastbound lane. Shift outta four wheel, pull to the right side and stop. Get out, check the gas can. Never did tip. Back inside and ease along the roadside. Maybe a quarter mile to the car, and get my peace of mind back.

"Wow," she say. "That was interesting. I'm going to buy a Jeep. So we really need to finish this conversation."

"We do. Truly."

"So how can you convict yourself of things you didn't do? All those people in Gleason, dead."

"The ones I killed?"

"You killed? *You?* See, the man who killed them believed different things than you."

"Like what?"

That it was okay to kill human beings."

"I believe that."

"Oh. Well. Maybe think about that. Definitely think about that."

"Only way I found to get rid the evil is kill it."

"So... You becoming evil is somehow reducing it?"

"Thirty to one."

"Joking?" She look ahead. "I want to finish our conversation with one thing. Nothing is an accident. There are theories about why this is the case—entanglement—but I won't go into that. Our meeting was no accident, Baer. This is what I want to say. Most people are not human beings. They are cunning animals. They place their intelligence in the service of their emotions, like any other animal. But a true human uses his intellect to undo his animal nature, not serve it. A true man knows his anger reduces him—so he only uses it when he needs to. You have never learned to be a man, Baer, because you have never studied yourself. You have never eliminated from within you what is most basic. Instead you've embraced it as your essence. That's why you've never felt at home in your own skin. Reject that. Build your knowledge without suspicion and judgment. You will finally own your mind because you will have rejected all else and chosen carefully what you stand for. Do this, and you will not kill again. You won't have it in your capacity because you will see your adversary for what he is—a bundle of possibility, as you once were."

I stop behind her car. Headlamps behind us bright in the mirrors. Car zoom by.

She pull the latch and swing her right leg out.

"Hey."

She look. Smile.

"You uh—you know my name."

"I promise not to give alarm."

"That ain't what I meant. You never said yours."

"Oh. I'm sorry. I'm Margaret Lockyer."

"All right. I swear I never met a woman like you. Let me give a hand with the gasoline."

Get out the vehicle. She climb out. "Ah. I'm in snow!"

She giggle. Entirely different situation when the feet's warm. She bounce out front and the headlights make her look almost, I dunno.

Fun.

"Why don't you climb inside your car and pop the gas. I'll handle it from there."

She wave. Get inside. I grab the gas can and she release the latch. Don't take a couple minute to drain the can. Keep an eye on her mirror and inside through the glass, but never get a good look. Pull away the gas can and her window drop. Arm come out. Paper.

"Hey, come here."

Get beside the window and she hold up the paper, folded like the letters I sent Ruth.

"Thank you for saving me," Margaret say.

Look like a bolt of sunlight coming over the horizon. I get the dizzy feel like I stood up too fast. Somehow I know this woman give me more of herself than any I been with.

"I uh. I got to think on what you say."

"Oh drat. I forgot my coffee."

"I'll get it."

Turn and walk. Think. Another car come by. Don't slow. Open the Jeep and grab the coffee. Couple Little Debbies in case.

"Here," she say. "I wrote you a note."

"Like a school note?"

"Something like that."

I trade coffee for paper.

"I won't eat those," she say.

I keep the Debbies.

"Okay, well. Shit. I'll be seein' ya."

She start the engine and roll up the window.

I place the weird feeling, the instinct says we tied to one another. Same thing I felt when my mother die and they take her away. Like we's connected from this world to the next. Or the one before.

Me and Margaret.

She rev the engine, beep her horn and pull off.

Back in the Jeep I open the note and hold it under the dome light.

*"I ENJOYED OUR TALK. I TEACH QUANTUM PHYSICS AT CHICAGO U IF YOU ever want me to replace your coffee."*

*—Maggy*

HIGHWAY SPEED, I READ HER WORDS ONE MORE TIME. TRY TO RECALL the shit she say.

Empodded.

This woman real?

Shit.

I wouldn't dream yellow leotards.

# CHAPTER THIRTY-SIX

BAER SLEPT IN THE CAVE UNTIL SUNLIGHT PRIED OPEN HIS EYES. HIS side ached and his brain pulsed with hangover. He didn't know if his downward side hurt from laying on dirt and rock or whether the numb ache came from the cold. The dog—Rommel—kept a steady gaze on him. The fire was dead and either Günter left a pile of shit in his blankets or he fed the dog his cabbage.

"You stink."

*Blame it on the dog.*

"Ah!"

Baer jolted. Blinked. Shook his head.

*What?*

Baer remembered the static in his mind the night before... when the dog talked to him. He'd had too much drink. His eyelids were the only body part he felt he could move without pain. He blinked again.

*You heard me.*

Baer closed his eyes and opened them. Without moving his head, he rotated his eyeballs. No old man in sight but from outside the cave he heard a wizened song floating an octave above Günter's speaking voice. Baer looked to the shelf of Mason jars.

The dog growled low, not mean, so much as concerned—how Baer heard it.

"Use your words, smartass."

On the left, three empty jars were placed in the same line as the full ones to the right, arranged as if to play the child's game, which one is not like the other?

Which *three?*

Baer remembered the night before and the electric suffering beside Ruth's duplex.

She said Larry named their dog Baer.

Months had passed since the last time he'd braved the populated area of Gleason. Any time he bought food he went to the twenty-four hour grocery on the lower side of town across the new interstate. The other two businesses in the vicinity closed at night and all the houses were on the upper side of the highway, limiting Baer's exposure to deception.

One of his teachers in school who liked to flirt with the senior girls said he was twenty-six years old, which he said, happened to be the peak year for male virility, stamina and power. Luther—no one called him Mr. —was so hairy he shaved to his eyeballs. He flashed a toothy smile and Marla squirmed. Everyone knew he was poking her and it didn't sit well. She was what the boys called PFC, either pretty fuckin' cute or prime farm cuntry— ready to till and seed. But that line about reaching his masculine prime at twenty-six stuck with Baer. If Luther was right then Baer would get stronger and faster and sharper for another five six years... and so would his curse.

It was already nigh impossible to tolerate the presence of other human beings. The only life Baer could imagine was wandering the woods and sneaking to the outskirts of town when he needed something.

That was no life.

He should have run past the blowjob boys yesterday afternoon and dove off the cliff when he had the chance.

The old man giggled like a girl.

"The hell?"

Baer pushed himself up and waited for the pain flash in his mind to dissipate. His stomach turned like he'd dined on a number two skunk ass. As he climbed to his feet he swallowed back the sting of bile, but knew it was at best a delaying tactic. At the cave mouth he vomited.

"You clean zat, I promise," the old man called.

Hands on knees with yakking pressure forcing tears from his eyes and phlegm from his sinuses, Baer spat. He looked partway up but Günter Stroh was downhill so he didn't have to look very far to see him naked on a flat rock, soap suds making his pubic mess a frothy fig leaf. Günter held out a white soap bar while bending at the knees to a tin bucket half floating in the pool.

"Clean body goot for ze spirit," Günter hollered.

Baer spat. Clutched his stomach and slid against the cave wall to a seated posture.

He waved Günter off. Günter laughed and sang something in Hun.

The curse would worsen. All evidence said so.

But fortified with three quarts of moonshine—maybe two and a half, since he couldn't recall how much was in the first when he took it over—Baer had survived the onslaught of lies.

He'd held his own, roughly.

# CHAPTER THIRTY-SEVEN

EYES GRIMY AND ARMPITS STINKING I GRAB THE GLEASON EXIT OFF Interstate 40 and first thing swing by Mae's old place. See if it still standing.

*FOR RENT*

MOUTH TASTE LIKE OLD COFFEE AND DIRT. TOOTHIN' THE TONGUE don't help. Give the house a good squint. They's no one near. Dark out. Took twenty-five hours damn near nonstop and the mind ain't entirely right. Somehow, burning this shitpile to the ground so that crust-gizzied Smotherman can't rent it to some other Mae seems the best idea I had in years.

Ain't had liquor since the mountain affair, so this must be good judgment.

Though holding a lighter to the siding would do the trick, I don't got the time. Get out the vehicle. Look about. Still nobody. This place ain't exactly secluded, got houses I could hit with a rock but not so close they'd know my face. Not at night under the purple light.

Tramp to the step, try the door.

Smotherman lock it to maybe keep the vandals out.

Stand sideways, lean hard right and throw that heel. Boot rubber hit direct under the knob and the door crash open. Glass rattles. Dark and quiet inside, smell like Mae and the kids. Still.

Kitchen got most the food I bought her. Grab cooking oil and douse the mopey sofa. Always hated it. Splash oil to the carpet and some for the curtains. Shouldn't take much to get this place ablaze.

Find matches in the kitchen drawer next the refrigerator. Open it and that old Smotherman unplugged it to save the juice but didn't have nobody dump the food. Smell like rotted meat. Gag. Now the kitchen stink. Slide the window and that'll help the flame.

Back in the living room I get the crazy notion—what if they's someone upstairs? Some vagabond decided this a good place to stay?

Oil jug in hand, Glock in the other, head upstairs. Recall the sound of little grandbaby feet and Mae. Recall Cory Smylie, piece of shit stuffed in a can. Wonder if his bones is cleaned yet or scattered. Maybe found and buried?

This place is ghosts. The dream world, alive in the moment. Like when I step outside I'll see bodies in trees, them red eyeballs glowing.

They real, like Chicago Mags say? Other world showing in this one?

Stop tramping the steps.

"Y'all up here?" Hit the wall with my palm. "Hey, y'all. I'm a burn this shitpile down. Y'hear?

Listen.

Tramp more. Down the hall. Open doors. Nobody. Dump oil on the beds and backtrack, hold a match to each 'til the flame plants root in the fabric. Time I hit the steps going back down the light splashes from each room to the hallway.

Upstairs already sucking air through the house. Don't got to light the sofa but I do. Ain't had sleep and the mind don't add two and two, and maybe that's why an act of arson feel good. Maggy say four is God and four fingers ain't.

It's the animal, Chicago Mags.

Outside I hop in the Jeep and drive a hundred feet down the road. Kill the lamps and engine; set the parking brake. Watch.

Nobody come out they houses. Nobody nowhere give a shit. Just like when Mae lived there with her babies.

Finally some red and blues on the road headed this way. Power up, cut right, zip along a couple nothing roads and I'm on the drag to the old homestead. Watch for deer. Got it in my head I'll keep driving if anything don't look right. Way I hear it, whole United States look at my face twice a day for shits and giggles. Maybe they got a FBI battalion stationed at the old still site, case I come back.

But the woods is still. House is gone. Burnt. I slow by the road but don't turn in. Give it a second. Drop the window. Let the eyeballs roam.

Cut the wheel, pull on the drive, keep the wheel hard left and three quarter turn and back up to the old Nova on blocks.

Headlamps cast to the wood but the edge of the yellow catches the house foundation. What parts of the frame that jutted proud when I left is collapsed. Twist off the key and the lamps fade. Punch the button. Sit in the dark and look in the trees for red eyeballs.

Cool air.

I feel Fred all over this place. Hear him like he's in the next seat. Six month?

Seven month since they put the bullet in his eye.

Get out the Jeep and wander past the house down the little path I kept. Could walk it with a blindfold but my old camp is wrong altogether. They took down the tarp and everything with it, maybe so they could look for clues where I was headed. Took my old still and the barrels they shot and gouged.

But they didn't take the lump of dirt where I buried Fred.

"Hello, old friend."

Listen.

"By Christ I miss ya."

Hand on the dirt. Feel the cold, the wet. Want to growl from the back of my throat, want to shed tears and find the moon and wail.

How come—tell me this Chicago Mags, professor—how's being good and killing bad not the same thing?

PRESS OFF THE GROUND AND STAND. GET MY BEARINGS AND CUT straight to the Jeep. Time to do my task and scoot back to Colorado.

Keep Jubal from killing if I can and put him down him if I can't. Get my girls and find some place to build a fire and let the heart mend a little.

Past the Jeep to the Nova. Open the door and pop the trunk.

Don't got to feel along. What light they is shows up fine: one last bucket a gold.

When I come back from cutting down them dogfighters with the wood alcohol, Ruth had her ass on the trunk of this Nova and I had my mind on grabbing my gold and getting gone. Forgot I hid a bucket in the trunk. Just grab two out the tree.

Nobody looked since.

Heavy as shit but in thirty second I got it in the Jeep, behind the back seat. Slam the gate. Drop the Nova trunk.

One last look at the place I didn't choose to be born and raised and get the hell outta Gleason.

# CHAPTER THIRTY-EIGHT

BAER'S MOTHER RESTED IN A CASKET THAT SAT ON DEAD GRASS AT THE lower end of a six foot hole. This part of the cemetery hillside had a leopard print of brown on green. The dirt salesman had pushed Larry to buy prime real estate.

"You bury her for eternity, son. Now you think on it. Them plots on the east side of the hill—they's only three four left that catch the sun all morning. Grass like emeralds."

"I want cheap."

"Well, uh, you sure?"

"I'm sure."

"Damn, Son. Uh. Well I guess you could put her on the west side, got the blighted plots."

"Good."

"Maybe you take a minute and think on it."

"My thinking's done."

Baer said, "Spend the money."

The salesman smiled. Nodded and raised his brows. He lifted a pen and hovered the point above a box and looked to Larry for confirmation.

"I want the cheap plot. That's what she gave us." Larry sat back and crossed his arms. "Mark the cheap one."

The salesman frowned. Baer clamped his teeth. Looked away. The salesman checked the box.

"Where do I sign it?" Larry said.

"Bottom. By the X."

Larry scribbled.

Baer held his tongue. Larry was eighteen and as far as the law was concerned, the decision was his. Baer's only recourse was to add this apostasy to the growing list of reasons he'd beat Larry to a puddle of snot if he ever got the chance.

Mother's box had three ropes under and was a straight rectangle, without the angles at the head and feet of the more expensive models. It was plush enough inside but that was because no one sold plain pine boxes like in the TV and movie westerns. The woman who nursed Larry at her breast, who bore humiliation but shed shame like water off a duck's ass to keep him clothed and fed merited the cheap casket and no service or viewing.

Larry said Baer could put a notice in the paper since it was free but when Baer thought on the words he'd like to say, he figured why the hell should he write nice words for people whose minds was already made up? Like he'd convince people who thought they knew something that they didn't...

But when he stewed on it more he came to a superior understanding. That small paragraph they'd print for free was his opportunity to punch Gleason in the face.

He studied several obituaries to gather the format and submitted his lines to the newspaper:

BARBIE CREIGHTON DIED BECAUSE A MAN BEAT HER. SHE IS SURVIVED BY A *son who loves her and another. Service at the Gleason Cemetery at 2pm on Thursday. She was a loyal person you sons a bitches—and not a liar.*

THE CEMETERY SKY WAS BLUE. WIND GUSTS FLAPPED BAER'S LAPELS and tickled the hair on his arms. He was so used to the feeling he didn't notice. They were alone save another burial party in the distance, a man wearing a hat and keeping his head down and two men over by a tree.

The distance reduced the mourner to a shape and though Baer recognized the stance, he couldn't place the man.

Baer and Larry stood at their mother's grave site, neither quite knowing if there was something they were supposed to do.

Larry faced the casket and Baer was slightly behind him, thinking, if he walloped Larry on the knot behind his right ear, he might topple into the grave. Let the diggers pull his ass out.

Baer clenched his fist but the thought seemed empty.

He turned to the sound of wheels on gravel.

Chief Smylie, plus someone else in the vehicle. They both got out. The other was his son, Horace. They approached and Larry turned. Horace punched Larry's shoulder weak and Larry nodded. He wiped a hateful tear from his right eye and said "fucking wind." Horace nodded. Baer looked at Chief Smylie and saw he was watching Baer watching his brother.

"It's a shitty thing, boys," Chief said. "That's all it is."

"I don't know what's supposed to happen," Larry said. "We're just waiting on them to put her in the ground."

"Pastor coming?"

Larry shook his head.

"Then you can go anytime you want. There's people that'll finish up here."

"What's he doing here?" Baer said, looking across the hill to Farmer Brown walking toward them.

"You didn't hear?"

Baer was silent.

"His wife suicided herself. Day before we uh, lost your mother."

"She what?"

Larry turned.

"She shot herself in the stomach."

Baer grimaced. "She did that herself?"

Smylie nodded. "On account she drank antifreeze. Pain likely pissed her off and she took a shotgun to her belly."

"A shotgun." Baer considered the size of her belly and the shortness of her arms.

"I know what you're thinking. She pushed the trigger with a broom handle. It was there in her hand when Caleb found her. I don't see a woman drinking a pint of antifreeze unless she's thirsty for it."

Baer's brows settled. No juice, above the ordinary. He couldn't think from the numbness of the last couple days. He'd murdered his own mother by failing to reload the shotgun—so how the hell could he judge Smylie's lack of curiosity?

Still, it didn't sound right.

"Did the broom handle have a round end?"

"Don't be a dick," Larry said.

"It had a leather strap—for hanging on the nail. She looped it over the trigger."

"While she was chuckin' antifreeze. Damn, is all."

Baer stepped away from Smylie but was boxed in by the grave and Larry so the only direction was toward Caleb Brown, now twenty feet away.

Brown stopped ten feet off and removed his hat and nodded and then approached slow. His face was summer-ruddy with wet streaks that caught the sun. Dark sunglasses hid his eyes.

Baer had read about some strange things that were real as rocks, but strained credulity. There was a mystic somewhere a thousand years ago whose hand melted rock. Thomas Jefferson and John Adams both died on the same day and John Kennedy's secretary was named Lincoln and Lincoln's was named Kennedy. Quirky ass shit, but real as real.

Mrs. Brown died the day before Baer's mother and because he was at school all day, he didn't see the hubub at noon when Brown came to the house from the fields for lunch. With an extra day for Smylie's investigation, Mrs. Brown was buried the same day as Baer's mother.

Brown offered his hand and Baer shook it, though he didn't know why it was right to shake hands and afterward felt like he'd sealed a pact.

"I didn't hear 'til just now," Baer said.

Brown started to pull off his sunglasses but left them in place. "I don't know what I'm gonna do without her."

Baer wondered at that. Brown never did with her, either.

Baer looked across the hill and one of the men by Mrs. Brown's plot elbowed the other and they set off with shovels toward the lump of dirt.

Mrs. Brown always did right by Baer when he worked there. Any lunch he ever ate was good and she was always pleasant. Sometimes she watched him too close but it was never with any dishonesty—Baer always figured she would have given anything to spoil a child of her own, and being barren, she emptied some of that pent up affection on him. Sometimes she made him squirm, how she'd get excited to see him and hug him when he came in from the field. He was a boy and she was a woman and any proximity at all was uncomfortable. But her affection was natural and Baer told himself it was best to let her express her big heart if she wanted.

"You fellas ready to put this thing in the ground?" Larry said.

Chief Smylie frumpled his mouth.

"Well I'd sure like to, but my back—you know. In the seat all day. Doc says I got to take it easy."

"Sure, Chief Smylie," Larry said.

Mr. Brown leveled his old cold-jawed stare at Larry and even with his eyes hid behind the sunglasses, his dimpled jaws made Baer wonder. He studied Larry to see what Brown saw. Larry looked back at Brown but only a second. He nodded and skittered his eyes. Far as Baer knew, his brother hadn't said three words to Brown his entire life. He was always playing football or reading a textbook. Even in summers he put in extra work to get ahead in school, and when not filling his brain with mathematics, one of his townie friend's father got him a job at the plant in Asheville, where he made good enough money to put himself through school.

That look from Mr. Brown to Larry and Larry's look back held no information for anybody else, but it sure as hell spoke a mountain of words between the two that shared it.

Larry swung his arm to the coffin.

Baer swallowed a lump in his throat. The finality stumped him. When the men rolled her body out the house he thought he was tethered to her somehow, so moving the body didn't matter. But putting her under six feet of dirt seemed a different matter. He'd been able to take the moments one by one, but putting his mother in the ground was like having forever without her, all at once.

Baer exhaled hard.

"This is a holy moment," he said, and the words sounded stupid to him.

Baer and Larry shuffled feet to opposite corners of the casket.

Horace Smylie stood opposite Larry and Brown took the rope across from Baer.

Chief Smylie held out his hands like a man in front of cellos and tubas and flutes. "All right boys, just make sure to lift her slow and easy so she don't get out of balance."

The men lifted and by four-inch steps shifted the casket up slope, over the hole.

"Chief, you're standing on my rope."

Smylie scooted.

"Let her down fellas," Baer said. "Easy. That's my mother."

The casket wobbled but never more than an inch or two off level. Larry's side touched the ground first and he tossed his rope in the hole before Baer's side touched.

"Do they keep the rope?" Baer said.

"Yeah, they keep the rope," Chief Smylie said.

Baer pulled and Brown tossed his side to the ground. Brown stooped, like the effort had taxed him. He spat to the base of the dirt pile then drove his boot into the spit.

Horace Smylie pulled his rope and coiled it on his elbow. Held it, looking dumb.

A gust blew Baer's hair in his face and his arms tingled.

Brown stood at the edge of hole looking into it.

"Mighty unfortunate. 'Bout your mother, is all."

"Mrs. Brown, too," Baer said, and wondered if a man's grief could make him give electric that wasn't true.

The men stood around the hole and Baer remembered. He'd been in such a flight over Lucy Kline rubbing her jugs against his arm that he didn't think to reload the shotgun after killing the two ringneck. How the hell could he stand there and judge a man's electric for his misdeeds with his wife? Maybe Brown was thinking, I didn't treat this woman like I should've. Or maybe he thought, this woman was flat murdered and I was off somewhere else instead of there to protect her.

How could Baer judge a man throwing off juice for that kind of dishonesty?

Baer's mother was dead because of him, and not just out of some silly accident. It was because he was taken with the same rotten passions toward women as his mother served ten times a month to keep them fed.

It boggled. She'd held the shotgun like a club because it was empty. Baer tried to remember the details of his sudden pheasant hunt. How he'd rushed inside, found the shotgun loaded and two more shells in the box. He remembered thinking three shells, three birds, awesome bragging rights. But how did he leave the shotgun empty? He couldn't recall firing a third time—but sometimes after a hunt he fired just for the hell of it, for the noise. For the frustration of not getting all the game he wanted and sometimes he shot off extra rounds because firing guns was satisfactory and wholesome in its own right. It was like stomping the gas with a car at idle. Sometimes mechanical action celebrates human invention, elevating all who partake. You don't have to have the words for it to feel it in your soul.

It would've been like him to fire the third round.

One thing was certain. Just as he couldn't recall whether he did or not, neither could he remember checking the load on returning home. He placed the shotgun in his mother's closet and started cleaning the birds. He'd been pissed at Larry, happy for the hunt and still roused by Lucy Kline's chest—a perfect stew of forgetfulness and error.

Baer found himself staring at the sky. He blinked away the thoughts and discovered Chief Smylie watching him.

No matter who his mother tried to club with that shotgun, no matter which man drove his fist into her head and dropped her, Baer knew sure as holy shit it was he that killed her in the service of lust. And now he stood next to the police chief knowing if he dared another word he'd have to confess his rottenness was the root of it all.

In that moment his entire existence was a lie.

Chief Smylie said, "Well, boys."

Smylie shook Larry's hand and patted his shoulder. Horace punched Larry again. Tilted his head and frowned, imitating a man giving solace. Larry swung his hand slow and missed. Rolled his shoulders. Shucks. She's dead but it ain't no big shit. Dig?

Baer clenched his jaw like to crush his teeth.

Smylie turned to Baer and offered his hand. "I know you don't like how things sit, but you got my condolences."

Baer eased up his hand.

Smylie grabbed. Electric arced blue between them. Smylie yanked away.

"Shit," Baer said. "Must be static from the rope."

Smylie rubbed his palm and peered at Baer like he sprouted horns. Checked his hand for injury. Backstepped then walked fast to his car.

"What was that?" Brown said.

"You riding with me?" Chief Smylie said to Horace.

Larry chinned toward Mother's Chevy.

"I'll catch a ride with Larry," Horace said.

Chief Smylie drove forward on the cemetery loop.

"How 'bout I give you a lift?" Brown said.

Baer nodded. They walked behind Larry and Horace, Baer wondering how he'd ever get himself right, now that he was shooting sparks. He took in his reflection in the passenger door glass thinking he'd spot heat in his eyes, but they were black like the leaves that flapped behind.

He slumped in Brown's Dodge truck. Brown turned the ignition and the starter ground. "C'mon. 'Mon now."

The engine caught. Brown followed Larry and Horace.

Baer let his shoulder rest against the door and his head against the glass until the jarring of the road forced him to lift it.

"Ain't life a bucket a piss," Brown said.

Baer got the juice on his arms but he couldn't see Brown's eyes.

Whose juice?

"You sayin' that for me or you?"

"You."

"How come you killed her?"

"What?"

"Cut the shit. I know you. I know her."

"You don't know what you think. And you don't know what you don't. Is all."

At the exit Brown turned left. Baer dropped the window and hung his elbow.

"How you get her to drink antifreeze?"

With his left hand on the wheel, Brown twisted his head toward Baer so long Baer looked at the road to make sure they didn't veer onto the sidewalk.

"Shotgun does a lot of convincing."

"Shit. Holy shit."

"You gonna say anything?"

"Seems I gotta."

"Figured as much."

"You don't seem a man suited for jail," Baer said.

Brown cleared his throat. Placed his cupped hand below his mouth, hacked out the proceeds. He held his hand to Baer. More blood than mucus.

"I won't die in jail, Baer."

He grabbed a rag from under the seat and cleaned his hand.

"Doc tell you how long?"

"Let's just say if I wanted the old lady gone first, it was now or never."

Baer wondered about President Kennedy. Did he think about hiring a Lincoln, like maybe it'd be too juicy a temptation for fate to pass by?

Of course with Kennedy and Lincoln there was a kind of symmetry, and with his mother and Mrs. Brown, they were only two dead neighbors and not even on the same day.

Baer breathed but it didn't seem like the same air as a few days before.

"Well? You gonna say something to Chief Smylie?"

Baer thought on it.

"If you don't die quick, I'll be honor bound."

Brown swallowed. Nodded.

"Just die quick, all right?"

Brown coughed. "Can do. Can fuckin' do." He drove. "Hey. They got any leads on your mother?"

"Smylie. Lazy fuck ain't even interested."

Baer pointed to the side of the street to a newspaper dispenser. "Stop a minute, all right? I want to grab a paper."

Brown swung to the curb and Baer jumped out. Fished coins and dropped them in the machine. Back inside the Dodge he opened to the back and glanced over the obits. There was only one.

*BARBIE CREIGHTON DIED. SHE IS SURVIVED BY TWO SONS, LAWRENCE AND Baer Creighton.*

# CHAPTER THIRTY-NINE

Drive back to Colorado, thoughts tumble like crick water after a storm.

Muddy.

All my working years I profit three buckets a gold in the tree. Two end up with Mae spread out in deposit boxes inside every bank in Flagstaff. If I ever wind up dead broke and can't kill a squirrel, Mae'll square me away with some gold.

Letting go the life's profit wasn't easy but I didn't want to haul specie everywhere. They's a good chance this whole ordeal since Fred'll wind up with me pushing daisies. Was better the gold stay with the progeny.

Accourse, back of my mind I always had another bucket stowed in the Nova, what I collected from Burly Worley and that little pecker sucker Ernie Gadwal after they stole it from the hollow tree. It'd be there waiting in the Nova trunk, unless it wasn't.

Driving back to Colorado, I ruminated on killing Burly and Ernie. I justify it 'cause they try to burn me alive and top of that, was stealing my gold. Now I'm 'bout to give that very same bucket to Jubal White to take care his family. Like Burly didn't have a family. Burly was stealing from me and Jubal was fittin' to steal from someone else. So all that means is I'm about a hypocrite. I'll give Jubal the money though he's the same sort of man as the one I murder for doing the same thing.

Some days I don't think I'm doing it right.

Ate food from the gas station, two day. I'd a shat in the Mountain Dew bigmouth but couldn't hold the bottle.

Hauling ass to get home and be a hypocrite.

Thinking, can I really give up the last profit of my life's work to protect the wife and kids of a man sells drugs? The wife a killer too?

Felt a strange kinship with both 'em. Always knew something was spooky 'bout life on planet earth. Me with the curse. The men in trees— the men I sent forward. They's still there somewhere. Thinking on how I almost sent Jubal to hang with 'em, and how he like to send the drug man Billy—who don't know William's the same fuckin' name—felt like a brotherhood of damned men. Each trying to do right as he see it and only one a lawman without the right to make a mistake.

I played it in my mind like Jubal and me talk through a shootout that didn't happen.

Him saying, "From my perspective, he's lawbreaker went for his gun."

And me saying, "You the lawman. You don't got the right to the wrong perspective."

Didn't make a difference in the imagination.

Slept my last at a rest stop two hour back. Comin' down the mountain at first light, it don't take but two minute to drive the interstate through Glenwood Springs and I swing the Jeep into the White driveway at quarter of ten.

Got a puffy feel in my chest, a regular asshole 'bout to do something more noble than my usual. If I was always this kind and generous it wouldn't be nothing. Smile big. Knock the door.

It open.

"You," Mrs. White say. Face bubble with hate like paint under a heat gun.

"Where Jubal? Got something for him. And you and the little Percival."

"You... traitor. Coward. I'm calling the police."

"Whoa! Don't be like that. I brought you money. I had a two-days' drive to fetch it."

"What money?"

"I brought gold. All my savings from my life before. Brung it so's y'all wouldn't hafta do shit you won't feel good about, on down the road."

She study me. I don't give off the juice and she wouldn't see it anyway.

"Bullshit."

"It's back of the Jeep. Pure gold, 'least fifty pound specie—that's gold coin. I had it stowed in the trunk of my Nova where I lived in Gleason. I been two days there and back. Ain't slept hardly the twice and that's hard sleep with the coffee. But I made it and now Jubal don't have to do what he plan. So where the hell is he? Jubal?"

"I don't believe you and you're too late anyhow."

"How? Go get him."

"Jubal left when Rauch went to court. Had to do everything himself, wait out there in the snow and now he's left."

Fuck.

"Left for where?"

She glare at me.

Hand on the door. "Where?"

"The fucking Rauch's."

"How long ago?"

"Dammit let go my door!"

"How long? I'll bust your fuckin' nose!"

"Ten minutes!"

"You was part of this. And that don't make you feel like shit? Your neighbor like to go hungry 'cause his money'll be with you?"

"If you didn't run away Jubal wouldn't be out there on his own."

"He don't need to be out there at all."

"How will I raise his son if he doesn't provide? How? A man like you doesn't know anything about keeping obligations. Doesn't know anything about honor. And given the opportunity to redeem yourself by helping Jubal in his hour of need—this *family* in its hour of need—you run away. Jubal had no choice. You left him no choice. And I had no choice. Now he's off to meet his end and I don't know if we'll be running the rest of our lives or not."

"You got no choice?"

"I couldn't let him do nothing."

"You told him to go ahead with the plan? Alone?"

"You fool."

Shit if I can make heads or tails of this woman.

She say, "He has to die out there—doesn't do any good to die on the sofa."

"Accidental, you mean?"

She hold my look and I think back on wisdom learned thirty year ago, selling the life insurance. The accidental policies.

"You bought the accidental death. Jubal said he couldn't get the life insurance on account his cancer but you bought the accidental death."

She fucked and don't know it.

"You shoulda read the policy. They won't pay someone killed while he out shootin' and killin' other people. Shit."

Her eyes get like beads and she smile.

"They will if he's a cop."

Air go out my lungs.

"He isn't out robbing someone, Alden Boone. He's a police officer investigating a drug dealer. He's going out to talk to the wife while the drug dealer's away. He's doing his job—and that, specifically, is covered."

"Ain't he on sick leave? Ain't he out the force?"

Shake her head. "He took sick days. That's all."

Step back. Woman make the head swim. First plan was to get Billy and William away. Jubal and Dwain would hit the house and rob it. Then I show up they add me to the plan. Then Dwain die, so the plan's the same, one man down. But I run and Jubal all sudden got the life insurance? And now it ain't the Rauch boys he's trying to kill. It's him he's trying to kill—by makin' them the killers.

I'll murder that fucker myself. But—

"Hold on. Three day ago he told me they's no life insurance. That wasn't a lie. I'd a knowed."

"It wasn't a lie. He was turned down. Agent called the day you ran and said Jubal could still get the accidental death policy, and since we paid with the first application, we got the whatever. The paper—"

"Condition receipt. Is what it's called. He bound the coverage."

"That's right."

I hear a gunshot. Two more.

"That'll be him," Mrs. White say. She set her mouth firm and the tracks is so deep it'd take a half hour with sixty grit to get 'em smooth.

I step back and away. Down the porch.

"Hey! You said you brought money."

Piss on this woman.

She come out the door. Hold up her fist. "Damn you!"

Slip on half-melted snow. Feels warm out this morning like to melt everything off by noon. Sun's bright and I hop in the Jeep, fire the engine and stomp the gas. Cut the wheel and as I spin rubber on road Mrs. Jubal White's at the top of the driveway watching like I took what was hers.

Don't she got a funeral or something for Dwain? Arrangements need made?

Bounce and wiggle side to side. Slip it to four wheel. Road's slushy and I pull over at the hilltop. Look down on Rauch land.

After those first gunshots they been no more. Jubal parked in the driveway, back a bit, so he got no line of sight to the house. Or from house to him. So how it go down? He shoot just to wake 'em up?

Truck face the house, driver side next the mountain. Can't see inside the cab but they's no body in the mud. He either in the cab or shot his way into the house.

Sit a second or two. Think. If this whole mess turn out so I got a chance at getting outta here, time'll be short and since they's no way out but the way I come, I three point turn the Jeep and get it headed toward the exit.

Twist the key and jump out. Grab Glock out my back.

If I go straight in I'm exposed and got no surprise. Jubal left the truck on the driveway with no path around. Plus the folk in the house don't know me from any other thug wants they money.

I got to go in from the back.

Set off across the ridge parallel the drive, but on the back side so nobody can look up and know he got company. Lucky me, the back's about blowed clean of snow. I got the ambition. After two days' coffee the ears ring with caffeine and crazy. Set off at a dead run and keep it up like I ate my Wheaties.

Gunshot! More! One, two, three, four—each different. Maybe. Jumbled up and firing one on top the other.

Can't stand it. I need a view. Turn up hill and see at the ridge I got maybe fifty yard to hit the draw where Jubal say the elk come down. But now Jubal's moved the truck forward. Gunshots come from the house—they's two rifles out the top windows and the third must be a pistol. Plus Jubal shooting back.

That's more'n a wife and boy.

Rauch got company.

Jubal's truck engine race like he miss a gear. Grind and jam. He speed backward, swerve and spin in the mud—backs over the lower side edge and the truck slide on its belly. If he fell it'd only be a few feet and he'd be better for it maybe, put the engine up to block the gunfire. But the truck just sit. Front wheels got no pull.

House keep plinking bullets, keep Jubal nailed down.

He'll get out and they'll kill him and that'll be the end of the Mrs. Rauch and her boy with the snow sled. Cops'll come in here and do what they do.

'Less I stop it.

What duty I got to save the drug man's family when the lawman call his number?

We each stuck in our own blindness and though the world's hazy sometime and the borders is fuzzy, with nothing meaning anything firm, no meaning set in cement, and everything a matter of where a man stand when he view it. Everybody red and all the time giving off the juice 'cause every thing's a lie. Nothing fixed. Any truth a ghost.

Why bother with this woman and her boy? What she got to do with me? And them with guns? It'll be someone dead, maybe me, and none of this my doing.

But fuck it.

One real man coulda made a difference, long time back.

Run down the hill and close to the bottom slide to a boulder. From here they's a good line to Jubal's F-150 and the two pickups parked behint the house.

These other people in the house... What I want to know is who ambush who?

# CHAPTER FORTY

CALEB BROWN UNLOCKED A GUN CABINET MADE OF KNOTTED PINE. From the time he bought it the doors had warped enough to bend the glass. Ten years ago the left pane cracked half way up and the next year the right did too. Now the humidity-bowed stiles held so much spring each door popped eight inches when Brown released the latch.

"What you doing?" Mrs. Brown said.

He ignored her.

Brown hadn't been putting off killing her because he was reluctant. He was a man who ate the spinach first because he hated it, and next the carrots because he hated them a little less. He held the beef for last because it was best and finally putting a hole through Mrs. Brown was the same thing. He took pleasure in what he hated and delayed what he liked and thereby enjoyed life more than ordinary men.

He knew exactly how he was going to do it. Just didn't think today would be the day.

When he woke in the morning with his mouth drooling blood he sensed time was short for the missus. She was already out of bed and he could hear her in the kitchen. He smelled coffee and cow liver in the fry pan. Soon as she heard him open the door, pancakes would hit the griddle and coffee would splash into the cream at the bottom of his mug. She kept the mug in the refrigerator so it would keep the cream fresh but also help cool the coffee fast, so he could avoid too much time in the fog of first waking.

Brown slid his pillow over the blood on the sheets.

While he broke fast on a quarter or a single pancake and refused the liver, Mrs. Brown kept her teeth rattling. At one point Brown opened his mouth to cuss her, but decided instead to let her go on so he could savor her noise like he did spinach.

He thought about the time two years back when he returned from the fields in mid afternoon and she was inside the kitchen bent over the sink getting plowed and planted by one Larry Creighton. She was watching out the window over the sink 'cause that was the direction Brown usually came from and this time, by chance, he'd caught sight of a hawk and had been so taken by its soaring circles he wandered watching the sky until it was closer to reach the house by dropping below the orchard and coming in from the side.

Two years back he stood at the side window watching Larry Creighton crank start his wife, and instinct said if he did things right—if he moved to the other window he could pop up and put one bullet through both of them at the same time—and see their dumbstruck faces to boot. No way he'd get the electric chair. Any jury-man in the world would think that was a fine fuckin' shot.

But he hadn't screwed her in five years himself, and truth was, she did the laundry and cooked pretty good. And though she ate like one of his hogs it was better for him to keep her about the house doing the chores he didn't want to do.

But one day...

Caleb Brown nibbled pancake while his wife chattered in bliss.

That morning he fed the hogs and chickens and since he didn't keep milkers any more, got on the tractor, hitched the mower and started cutting hay.

After an hour he asked himself why he was on the tractor.

Got no one to carry on the name. No one to take over the farm. No one to provide for—and there was more than enough food in the pantry to last whatever days he had left. So what the hell was he beating his guts on a tractor for, when he could spend his remaining time in quiet, maybe sipping lemonade?

Quiet?

Only when he made it.

Brown rode the tractor part way to the barn and sick of the bouncing, took it out of gear, set the brake and stepped down. Let the thing run 'til the gas was gone. Let the ghosts care. He approached the house from the side and looked in the kitchen window like the day he first discovered the old lady with Larry Creighton, just in case she was willing to give him a better setup than the one he had planned. No luck. It was a school day.

Brown went inside.

After a long look with her mouth gaping and her eyes taking in the blood on his shirt, Mrs. Brown said, "You see the doctor about that cough?"

"No I didn't see the doctor."

But he had.

He opened the gun cabinet. Broke the sixteen gauge. The chamber was empty. He pulled open the first drawer in the bottom center of the cabinet then remembered he hadn't replaced the shells since he hunted turkey in the spring.

Brown shook his head. Let his half-full lungs empty.

Thought.

Only the day before he'd heard two blasts across the road and down a ways, in a clump of low-limbed pines. One of the Creighton boys, likely.

That's right—their mother had a sixteen gauge shotgun. She'd brought it the first time she came over with Baer. They didn't exactly get on and it was a shame. Ass like hers.

Brown needed one shell. Only the rarest of suicides required two.

Fact was, if there were three things Brown wanted, such as a man on death row gets a final supper, if there were three things the first would be some peace and quiet about the house, instead of that sullen woe is me horseshit that spewed every waking minute from his old woman's mouth.

The second would be a few hours to actually enjoy the silence. Ass deep in the recliner, feet up, boots off. With a glass or two of whiskeyed lemonade.

The third would be some of Barbie Creighton's pink flesh. Brown doubted he could sustain wood long enough to bring a consequence, but just sliding his finger along the folds would be enough. Then each time he sipped his lemonade he could remember his reckless youth when he didn't get laid but at least had the balls to try.

"You need to see the doctor. We got canning to do. We got the fall hams to cure. They ain't but no end to the work and if you get sick now—"

"Woman!"

Brown snapped the shotgun closed.

"What you doing with that?"

"You'll see soon enough."

"Well, you kill something, you clean it. I told you not to use a shotgun the last time. Time I dig the lead out they's nothing left of the bird."

Brown walked toward the door.

"Ain't nothing in season now anyhow."

"Squirrel."

"Even worse. They make my shoulders hurt. You clean 'em."

"I'll be back in ten minutes. I want lemonade."

"Lemonade? What on earth? You never want lemonade. You don't like lemons. What's going—"

He stared.

She nodded slow at first, then faster.

Brown slammed the door. Thought better of carrying the shotgun across to the Creighton place. No need to raise alarm if he happened to stumble across someone. But that shouldn't happen. The car was gone, meaning Barbie was waiting tables. It was late morning and the boys were at school. House oughtta be empty.

He strode across the road, across the drive, looked backward when he tried the door and found it locked. Thought he saw his old woman in the front window but with the distance and angle it could just as easily be a reflection on the glass. Or nothing but his fancy.

Brown closed the screen and loped around the side of the house. The back door was unlocked. Strange, but he never locked his back door either. And it was so damn easy to walk around.

All these years.

Years of planting fields and harvesting them right across the road. Driving the tractor back and forth, sometimes catching a look but never allowing his eyes to hold, or his head to face that direction longer than the tractor made it. So the best he could do to get a look was make sure when he tilled the land he started at the back and came forward, each turn at the driveway affording a natural gander across, since his head and the tractor pointed that way anyhow.

All these years, knowing what she was. Even when the crops were good and there was surplus... Even when they had extra apples canned and the missus said to carry a case over to Barbie.

He wasn't the sort of man that would pay for a woman. He'd never been the sort that would take one unwilling. But hell, until today he wasn't the sort of man who'd murder one, either—and nothing but a bolt of lightning from the clear blue to the top of his head could stop it.

He'd never been a lot of things... but that was because tomorrow's chains always held him in place today.

Brown opened the back door and stood on the cusp of the deepest insight he'd ever had. He wanted to call out and make sure nobody was home, but doing so might jeopardize losing the most perfect thinking he'd ever done.

It was like reeling in a wisp of smoke.

He rested his head on the jamb. Gulped a clump that slid like blood. Closed his eyes.

The thought...

All his morals, all his upbringing, all the rules he ever upheld was just to hold his place for tomorrow. If he ever let on who he really was, he'd have no place at all.

But when a man's got no tomorrow, he leaves the tractor running in the field.

He tells the wife to make some lemonade.

He takes a last stab at his whore neighbor's quinny.

Caleb Brown saw everything coming together. He'd lived a senseless life, working so he could keep working, upholding the rules because he lived in a zoo and the zoo keeper said so...

Brown at last smiled and knew he could live, now that his life was over.

"Baer?"

Brown rapped his fist on the door jamb.

"Larry? You in here? Need something."

He waited.

Rapped again.

Brown entered and stepped to the left where he could see out the front window to the driveway.

All these years. How many? Eight years back they had their little pissing contest. For a woman Barbie Creighton could piss like a champ. There was never any peace between the houses except between the women.

Brown coughed and blood escaped his mouth. Flipped on a light and saw spatter on the kitchen table. The sink had a rag. He wetted it and wiped the table. Coughed more loose from his throat into the sink and splashed some hot water after it. Cleaned the rag and replaced it where he found it. Spat one more time, ran more water.

Baer said all those years ago his mother kept the shotgun in the closet for protection.

Brown walked back the hallway. Pushed open the door with his fist and half expected to see something. A person.

He smiled.

Along with all the other things he'd never done, he never entered another person's house without invitation. He didn't know the rules from the other side—how to restrain the feeling his brain was about to burst open. How to make his fingers stop twitching.

He'd never been in a woman's bedroom. A mature woman who had men there. He stepped forward and looked at the bed.

Exactly how much screwing happened on that bed?

Couldn't have been much, with the boys around. Unless she was the absolute lowest sort, she must have taken her clients elsewhere. Must have because in all the years he'd known what she was, and paid attention, it was only so often that that a fella called. Not enough to give her a reputation.

Did she meet them in cars?

Motels?

Restrooms? A woman like that was no better than a hog in a stall.

Now take a woman from England or something suitably highbrow. Same flesh as any other woman, but she didn't throw it around. She respected it, demanded anyone near her did too. That made it worth something. Brown would never in this life or the next presume to stick a woman like that. He'd not only lower the woman but taking her would lower fornication, as an institution.

But a whore like Barbie Creighton?

Shit. He'd be doing her a favor and if he ever had the chance, no way in hell he'd reduce the thing to paid sex by giving her money.

Wouldn't be fair to her.

Brown snorted and enjoyed his new way of seeing things. Almost wished he'd died sooner.

He turned a half circle and opened her bedroom closet. The shotgun leaned on the inside wall. He broke it open and slipped the shell into his pocket and replaced the shotgun. Wondered if there was a way he could swipe it, shoot his old lady and pretend it wasn't a suicide but a stranger passing through. One of the fellas at the barbershop just two weeks back said now that the interstate was connected all the way across, folks could blame damn near anything on the riffraff passing through. If a man had a mind...

But why bother? All he wanted was a few days of peace—a couple weeks if he could get it—while the cancer pulverized the rest of him.

He left Barbie Creighton's bedroom and gathered speed until he swung the back door closed behind him. He looked at the blackberry briars and elderberry clumped at edge of the yard and at the pines beyond. Somewhere back there was Mill Creek. Maybe he should follow it around?

Nope.

Shit. More smiles—his tractor was still idling in the field.

That's what a free man did.

Caleb Brown turned the corner and walked around the house, across the driveway, the road and back on his own land. If not for the weakness in his lungs and the upset in his stomach from swallowing blood, his shoulders would have carried a swagger.

At the shed he grabbed a gallon can of Prestone and at the front door loaded the sixteen gauge he'd left there.

Mrs. Brown opened the door.

"What you do over there?"

"I borrowed a shotgun shell."

"One shell?"

"One shell."

"What on earth for? What you need with Prestone. That's antifreeze, ain't it?"

"All the makings of a proper suicide."

"Oh, Caleb!"

"Stand back. Let me in."

She stood aside. Swiveled and hurried into the kitchen.

Brown followed and deposited the antifreeze on the kitchen table.

"That my lemonade?"

She nodded and a tear spilled. "There's nothing I can say to talk you out of it?"

He shook his head. "Mind's pretty well made up. Why don't you be a sweetheart and grab two glasses?"

She stepped to the cupboard. Kept her eyeballs pointed at her husband and missed the knob twice. Shot a quick look and got her hand on the porcelain. Pulled out a glass then another.

She placed them on the kitchen table.

Brown looked at the walls, the windows. Unlikely any BB's would pass through her, but still, it would be a pain in the ass if he had to replace a window at this stage. He dragged out a chair so her back would be to a wood-paneled wall.

"There you go."

She said, "You're going to make me watch?"

He rubbed his chin. "You got it good and sweet?"

She carried the pitcher of lemonade. Stirred and the ice tinkled. "I didn't think you'd like it too sweet."

"Pour a glass of Prestone and another of lemonade."

Mrs. Brown glanced at the shotgun then his face. She poured lemonade. Tried the cap on the Prestone and said, "I can't get that."

He opened it. Pushed it back to her.

"Why you doing this?" She poured a glass of antifreeze. "That's not going to help anything. Your lungs—"

He shook his head.

"Sit."

He pointed the shotgun at her stomach.

"Sit."

She sat.

He stood and rested the barrel on her shoulder so the end pressed her neck. "Go ahead and drink that glass on the left."

"Caleb?"

He shifted forward a bit to see her face. It was red and tearful. Her shoulders shook.

"Is this because I never gave you a child?"

"Drink it."

She placed the glass to her lips. Moved it back to the table.

"Is this because I didn't love on you enough?"

He poked her neck with the barrel.

"Drink it."

She grabbed the glass and gulped. Swallowed. Sputtered. As soon as it went down she gagged it back up.

"There's a good girl," Brown said.

He placed the shotgun on the table with the barrel to her chest. She grabbed it. "That's good," he said, and pulled the trigger. The shotgun blasted into her chest and after rolling her eyes up she fell forward. Brown took the broom from where it hung in the stairwell on a nail and positioned it on the table with the leather loop around the trigger.

After a few minutes looking for the phone book he dialed the oper-ator and asked to be connected to the police chief. He stretched the phone cord to the sink and spat blood.

"Yeah, Chief this is Caleb Brown. I come in from the field and the old woman... (cough) the old woman..."

"What is it, Caleb?"

"She uh, I just came in and see she shot herself. Drank a half gallon of Prestone and shot herself."

"Well shit, Caleb. Don't touch anything. I'll be right over."

Brown replaced the phone to its cradle and lifted the sweaty glass of lemonade from the table. Wiped off the ring of condensation and sat on his favorite chair in the corner beside the window, kicked off his boots and drank.

# CHAPTER FORTY-ONE

From the boulder in the draw I see Jubal's truck and some of Billy Rauch's house. Hunker behind and peel off my coat. Shirt. Clump of snow fall from a tree and hit the shoulder. Shiver and shake. I'm about dumb as a frozen frog. Peel off the nylon boots and my pants. The socks.

Keep the skivvies so no one's too distracted. Feet back in the boots. Hands in the air I angle downslope to the house. As the land go flat and the tree cover thins, I make out giant mudder wheels on the pickup trucks parked back the house that I spotted from the Jeep.

More Chevies. People must be family.

"Howdy, y'all!"

Tramp close. Shiver. Feet numb already. Air's brisk, even with the sun. Adjust the nuts—what ain't shriveled into my ass.

"Hey, y'all! I'm a-comin' this way."

Curtains at the window. Girl face flash and move.

Window up, pistol out.

"Hold it. What the hell? Dude, you're naked."

"Uh-huh. Well almost." This ain't the Mrs. Rauch I expect, this a girl. "I kept my drawers on, little lady. You Amber?"

"Who else would I be?"

"Got some family in there with you?"

Man's voice: "None of your concern. Why are you in your drawers? Just who the hell are you? What you want?"

"You see me unarmed. Thought to buy a minute without getting shot, so I could do you a good turn."

Spin 'round so they see my ass. Wait a damn minute. This girl ain't a woman. Where's her mother? Without but they got a second daughter, this is the girl Jubal said run down Dwain.

"Where's your mother, girl?"

"She ain't here."

"Mister, we have a situation out front. Naked or not you're about to get shot. Why you here?"

"Jubal's bought the life insurance and he's counting on y'all to make it pay. 'Cept you'll be cop killers and won't even make it to jail."

"Amber, you know this man?"

"Hell no."

"So it warn't you, run him over. Your mother did it."

Man say, "Run over who?"

"Jubal's boy. Dwain. The one this girl said raped her."

"The one I said. Ain't that something. The one I said."

"Did he?"

"Why you think my mother run him over?"

"Where is she now?"

"She's just fine. Thanks for askin'."

"Dude—if you was right in the head I'd shoot you. Get the hell outta here. Put some fuckin' clothes on."

Girl brush the hair out her face and she half pretty. Man in back the room—I see him now, got a pistol. So maybe the youngun upstairs is working a rifle—'cept they's two truck parked in back. Another man upstairs maybe.

Whole picture flash in the mind at once, wheels spinning in wheels. Jubal come to rob or get shot and these people saw it coming. Maybe already got the dope money out the house. Maybe Ma took it in the Chevy S-10 when she run down Dwain. Or more'n likely it's in these trucks parked in back.

More gunshots out front, close, shooting at Jubal still in the truck.

Pistol fire far off—Jubal shooting back. Lead hit the house and a window shatter.

"Got one more question and I be out your hair. You ever notice up on the hill a man up there with binoculars?"

"Oh we seen him," Half-Pretty Amber say. "All the time. How you think we knew what was coming? 'Cept you're wrong, naked man."

"How?"

"It was Dwain and he had a rifle with a scope, not binoculars. We watched his dumb ass right back. And we got his stupid assed father on video at the front door, sayin' there won't be no trouble if we give him all the cash in the house."

These folk don't need Baer Creighton.

"All good with you, I'll head out the way I come. We appreciate you."

Connect eyeballs with the girl. She squint a mite and give a short nod. Man behind flick his pistol.

"Shit. I'm sorry. Truly. One more thing."

She look. Grin wild, like she found a man to marry. "Yeah crazy man?"

"It true y'all soak your dope in formaldehyde?"

"Fuck no. That ain't our shit. We're organic."

"What about the crystal gayle? Pardon. The crystal meth? That you?"

"Man, we don't have nothing to do with any of that. Way things're going we'll be legal in five years, you watch. Shit. Now get the hell outta here."

Tip a hat I ain't wearing. Turn and bolt.

Fuck Jubal White, is all.

More gunfire, like the fella and girl join war up front.

I see the whole layout, how things unfold.

I bet back when Jubal drop in on Billy to say hello after all them years, he try to put hisself on the payroll. Billy says fuck off, and Jubal come after him with the law. Then Jubal learn he got the cancer and next thing Billy know, they's a neck-shot elk on his back yard and a game man scooting up the drive. Billy watch the warden haul away his guns and he got all the drugs and cash and no way to defend 'em.

A man sells drugs'd notice that sorta thing. Setup pure as day.

Billy know he been had and does the same as Jubal: protect the family.

Killing Dwain was Billy's counter.

His wife—mother of his kids—drove down the man-boy that raped her girl. She haul ass in the S-10 for back country, not the highway. And these boys with the trucks? Family from some other hill or holler. Maybe got a sister operation, so they can make an organic dope empire once it go legal.

Either way these people got they situation in hand. Time for Baer Creighton to fuck off, as instructed by several folk.

Slide around the boulder and the feet's so numb I ain't sure if I want 'em. Look back. Jubal's out of the truck and charging with two pistols flashing. The booms come late. Distance bigger'n it seem.

He already called for backup, I bet, make his murder official.

Gunfire like the final battle. Just as quick it end. Echoes. Peer out and Jubal's flat on his face and people running out back the house for the trucks.

Kick off the boots; grab my pants and jump in 'em. Shirt. Second shirt. Socks on numb feet. Boots. Coat.

Glock.

Run up hill, over the crest. Got no wind in my lungs but if I don't clear off this mountain afore Jubal's backup I'll be telling lies beyond my skill in no time.

Can't see over the ridge but hear the truck engines gunning. Jubal left his F-150 half over the driveway edge and they'll have to push his truck all the way over to clear him.

Lungs about to bust open and bleed, I stop and plant hands on knees. Heave. Look up and down ahead, not fifty yards is the Jeep.

And Mrs. Jubal White's at the back gate with Percival, stealing gold.

# CHAPTER FORTY-TWO

CALEB BROWN WOKE THE DAY AFTER HIS WIFE'S SUICIDE TO THE uncanny sound of birds. He closed his eyes and savored their music. Rolled out of bed, opened the window and climbed back under the sheet. He'd slept wrong and his neck wasn't right. Bed was finally flat and it threw him off. Brown pushed his pillow to the center and lay on his back, arms and legs spread wide. Neck still wasn't right so he tossed his pillow aside and let his vertebrae shift flat. Curled his pelvis, stretched his neck and rested with his elongated body at peace—except the cancer. It felt like a separate animal inside his chest.

They took her body away and afterward he drank a gallon of lemonade but skipped lunch and supper. His lungs were mostly blood and pulp. All the blood he swallowed kept his appetite tamped down. The acid from the lemonade maybe helped digest it and he thought on that with his eyes closed listening to birdsong. He mused on the beautiful irony that after a life of fruitless and petty labor, his last constructive work was to digest himself.

When he got up to open the window he didn't feel all too bad. Hadn't drooled blood all night, either.

Maybe his body was giving him a reprieve.

When he could no longer avoid a session on the commode he rose.

Went to the kitchen to see if he could get some coffee going but shit if he knew where Mrs. Brown kept the ingredients. It would have to wait.

By the time he stood from the toilet and ran a washcloth over his face, he felt awake enough to enjoy the day. But a half hour on the recliner with his feet out, he was groggy and wishing for coffee. He found the grounds in a bag beside the flour and sugar. The percolator was upside down in the drying rack—the missus hadn't gotten around to putting it away.

With the black splashing in the bulb he poured a cup and let the rest sit. It smelled strong enough to run in his tractor and he wondered how long the machine idled in the field before it died.

How long would he, until likewise?

A triple-knock, out front. Brown looked at the clock. A quarter shy of ten.

He opened the front door.

"Barbie Creighton."

"I, uh—I got a call from LouAnne in town."

Brown stared.

"The mortician's wife, LouAnne."

Brown stepped onto the porch in his bare feet. He hadn't shaved or combed his hair and realized he probably looked about right for a grieving husband, struggling to cope with peace and quiet.

"LouAnne said Mrs. Brown took her own life yesterday. Is that true?"

Brown closed the door and motioned to a pair of chairs that had been stationed on the front porch for almost ten years without ever being sat in. He took one and balanced his scorched coffee on the armrest.

"It's true."

"But why? That wasn't like her. She seemed so—okay. Not happy. Nobody is. But she seemed okay."

"Woman had her secrets."

"I guess we all do. Did she leave anything saying why?"

"You mean a note?"

"Yes."

"No. Didn't think of that."

"This must be so difficult for you. Oh my God, I just can't believe it."

He shrugged and sipped coffee. Coughed from the taste since it was five times stronger than he liked and burnt. He covered his hand with his mouth and swallowed anyway.

"Such terrible news. I don't know what to say."

"A woman's got to say something."

She faced him and though her eyes were steady something in them changed.

"I suppose that's so. Men and women are different. You know that, Mister Brown."

He nodded, frowned, closed his eyes and inhaled. His rotten lungs shuddered and his broken health projected the illusion of a distressed, mournful man.

She placed her hand on his arm and leaned in so her shirt opened a little and her tits swung.

"I don't know how I'm going to get by," he said.

"This is such horrible news. I'll bring your supper tonight, so you don't have to think on it."

He nodded.

"Do you know when you'll be having her service?"

"Tomorrow, most likely."

"I'll be there," Barbie Creighton said.

# CHAPTER FORTY-THREE

At a full-out run my hip pops with each right stride and pain shoot out the punji stake wound so I throttle back and coincidental, reduce the wind speed on my lung fire.

Mrs. White see me and turn to Percival. Bend and shout. Point to the passenger door.

Glock out, point at the hill and fire.

She stop in her tracks and throw up her hands. Look at me and see the gun pointing at the hillside—so she start shoving Percival agin.

Close in. Level the gun at Mrs. White. Back off the trot and walk. Last twenty feet I call out.

"Put the gold back."

"You better leave while you can, Baer Creighton. I called the police."

"You got what you wanted. Jubal's dead. Put that gold back where it come from!"

I reach her car. Trunk open, coins tossed in the back. Green luggage, case after case. Almost full but that's me being the optimist. Guess she thought her and Jubal'd bug out with the drug money and once she see him face down in the mud, she figger to take gold and the life insurance claim instead.

Percival got the open face of a youngun can't work his noodle around a situation. Mrs. White look ready to chew my ass. I never seen a person done so little entitled to so much.

Shove the gun to her belly. Poke. Look mean as I can while I want to take a giant shit and be done with this whole thieving back-stabbing world.

"Move, you fuckin'... fuckin'... Just put the specie back in the bucket!"

She shake awake. Eyes lit.

Jab her agin to leave a mark. She swing to the trunk and scoop coin. Must be fifty; she grab two.

Step to the side and Percival cast his best kid-hex on me.

"You little shit. Get up here and help your mother un-ass my gold. Your old man didn't teach you so I will. Don't be a fuckin' thief. And that's a bigger rule than your mother."

"You said you brought this for me anyway," Mrs. White say.

"And I change my mind when I see you set up this whole shitshow top to bottom."

Step back and make room for Percival. Keep Glock on Mrs. White. They scoop and dump two minute and I keep a lookout across the valley where a stretch of highway shows through. When the coppers come I'll skedaddle, job finished or not.

"Get on with it! I need to hit Kansas City before nightfall. Move!"

Woman look. Grab coin, step four feet, toss to the bucket. Over and agin.

"You can carry more'n one coin at a time! Move, damn you!"

She scrape her hands wide on the trunk and gold jingle. Drop a couple to the mud and maybe five six in the bucket.

Those gold coin in the mud, each one earned after hours and hours gathering fruit, hauling grain, tending mash and years of stilling knowhow. Each gold piece is weeks of noble labor, watching the fire, dealing with liars and cheats to make a square dollar. And this stinking sofa snatch want to grab it and make off.

She tell herself what Jubal said, it's dirty money so stealing ain't wrong.

They'll put it to good use, so stealing ain't wrong.

All it is: liars, cheats, thieves, lawmen, politicians, banks, the whole God-forsaken works. Fuck every one. If a man don't own his labor, he ain't free.

Coppers on the interstate!

Look in the trunk—all but empty, save luggage. Shoulder the woman and grab the last coin myself, toss to the bucket. Five six from the ground—they go in muddy. Slam the gate.

"All right. Both of you—get in the car. Now!"

Swing the gun back to Mrs. White's head. "Move."

She look rattled as I want. She move.

"Percival. Get in the car. Now."

He jump inside.

Gun at Mrs. White's window.

"Pop the hood."

I'll pull the spark plug cables.

"I don't know how!"

Shit. Regardless—I go up there she'll run me over. "Gimme the keys."

She fumbles in her purse.

"Ah, piss."

Fire a shot to the front tire. Jump in the Jeep and scoot downhill. Pass where Dwain died. Up the hill and cresting, them cops is already at the highway exit. With the angle they couldn't see me 'less they was looking back through a sunroof.

Down the hill I jam the brakes and slide on mud. Cut the wheel left —won't go far as I need. Four wheel drive binding on me. Hit the snow bank and bounce straight. All four wheels spinning I shoot up the Jubal White driveway. Turn a wide loop so the Jeep's stopped out of sight from the road below and give me the angle to see when they pass.

One cop car...

Two cop car...

Three cop car...

Four cop car...

Nothing.

Shift outta four wheel drive and hit the road headed for the highway.

Stinky Joe, I'm a comin'!

Brake and turn and shift and stomp the gas!

Giddyup you lazy six! C'mon now!

Home free on the highway and one mile to the exit.

Hey Chicago Mags...

I ain't shot nobody!

# CHAPTER FORTY-FOUR

WITH NO FARM WORK AND NO WIFE WORK CALEB BROWN SAT OUT front with his unfinished mug of coffee beside his foot on the porch.

When Barbie Creighton left after telling him she'd bring his supper her ass jiggled just the way a woman's ass ought to, and if there was maybe five six things that merited a man's dying gaze—mercy—Barbie Creighton's jiggle was two of them.

She took the steps slow and he relished the moment. First off, her blue-jeaned ass was near perfect, as far as size. Maybe a touch more than perfect but he wouldn't kick her out of bed for cracker crumbs. Form was nice, but she excelled with the motion. Each step had the primary movement, cheek going down, the direction of the leg. But with each impact Brown beheld a tight wobble, refined, isolated to the cheek in motion. Then the next. As she walked the jiggles offset, one concluded while the other began. His hungry eyes slopped up the vision until she was forty feet away. He coughed and swallowed blood. Felt like a set of claw hooks dragged his lungs. The key to misery was to mix it with something enjoyable, so the hurt clarified the good.

By and by as he pondered her now-imagined backside, it was a small step to stand behind her and reach to her jeans up front, twist the corner and loose the button. Hold the flap and drag the zipper, tuck his fingers where the denim permitted.

Maybe lift the other forearm upward and nudge the overhang, just enough to feel how soft was the underside. How heavy.

Eyes closed he saw himself step back a foot as she prepared herself and then—as thoughts sometimes skip the mechanical aspects and jump to the outcome—he saw those cheeks naked and once again bouncing, but this time, both at once, over and again.

A lot of men had seen that ass. She sold tickets.

The boys were at school.

Caleb Brown lifted his mug and since it was cool and he was a man so rich with life he could afford to leave his tractor running in the field, he gulped the nasty shit and pulled himself from the wooden chair. He turned toward the door and adjusting his pants found himself half mast.

A little work, such as provided by a skilled woman, might could raise the flag.

With death approaching in weeks at the latest and maybe ten minutes—who knew—one last poke seemed worth the effort.

Inside the house he placed his mug in the sink and ran water. From the hunting cabinet drawer he took his gutting knife, tested the blade on forearm hair and mounted the sheath on his belt.

He filled his mouth with Listerine in case things went easy sweet. No need to be a grumpy bastard. Not when courting a woman whose availability was certain.

Never in his life had he paid for a woman but the truth was it seemed like another man's rule. Pride had kept him from it, but what did a dying man need with pride? Free from the constraints of needing to give a shit about tomorrow, one last lay seemed self-evidently good. Paid or not.

He looked at his rotten face in the mirror, eyes like raisins.

Mud for his turtle. That's what they'd called it, as boys.

He'd pay the woman for her mud.

What did the girls call dick when they were young?

Turtles? Likely not.

Brown grabbed his wallet from the dresser and opened it and found a ten spot. What'd a woman cost?

Ten ought to do.

He dropped his billfold in his back pocket. Stopped at the bedroom door, his heart racing like he was sixteen and planning to steal a kiss. He bent his neck and sniffed his pit.

"Shit."

Caleb Brown unbuttoned his shirt and walked to the bathroom. Soaked a washrag in soapy water and stared at his face in the mirror. Allowed his gaze to fall from his caved cheeks to his pencil neck, then his chest with ribs like a prisoner and nipples that sagged on weak skin. Seemed like a full year since he ate a meal until he was tired; just never had the appetite. He had a pale white chest with brown blotches and little skin tags here and there. He pulled the first one that came, years ago, and it bled like a sonofabitch so he ignored the ones that followed.

He slapped the washcloth to his armpit, unbuckled his pants and dropped his shorts. Grinned at his awkward self.

This indeed is how a man rich in life spends his late morning.

After a scrub with the soapy cloth he rinsed and gave another rub to wipe off the soap residue. Toweled and since the missus finished the laundry the day before she went batshit and took her life, he labored into clean clothes, top to bottom.

Even put on clean socks—though it would be a cold day in hell that he took of his boots to ride a whore.

Clothed, he stood in front of the mirror and compared himself clothed to what he'd seen undressed.

He'd stick her with his duds on.

Brown rested with his hand on the jamb. Blinked himself clear and in the kitchen dipped a tablespoon in the honey jar and ate. Sank it again and the second time held the honey in his mouth without swallowing, in case he never bothered to do it again.

The sugar hit him half way across the road and he rolled square his shoulders and lengthened his step. His half-chub from an hour before returned. It was going to happen. After ten years of watching her. Fifteen.

He knocked.

The door opened. Barbie Creighton stood with most of her body behind the door. Her face seemed undecided between concern and surprise. Perfect.

"You got a minute or two?"

He held his hands at his belly, knuckles stacked and thumbs on top.

"I—uh. I suppose. Yes."

She didn't open the door.

"You know, I never said nothing. I'm dying."

"What?"

"I got the cancer in my lungs and, uh, heck—it's like to be most everyplace, now."

"Oh my word!"

The door opened.

"Doc told me it's days, maybe, though to be honest I felt pretty damn pert this mornin'. Pert enough."

"Come in. Oh this is terrible. When it rains it pours... Come inside."

She stepped back and held the door and Brown entered and looked around like it was his first time.

"You got a pretty setup here. Boys in school?"

"That's right. Sit down."

"Maybe I'll stand."

"Okay. I said I'd bring you supper but I ain't even started."

"I'll confess I never thought I'd be a single man and with the doc saying I got but days or hours, my window's pretty tight."

"Your window?"

"Opportunity. You got the window, you see."

"I guess I'm stupid. I don't see."

"I'm strong enough right now and maybe tomorrow I won't be."

She lifted her head and lowered it. Her brows were flat and her eyes a shade cooler than twenty seconds before.

"I'm sorry to hear of your health. Why did you come here?"

"To the point."

He smiled. Moved his hands to his sides and balled them.

"A rich man speaks plain. I heard stories about you a long time now— but I always wondered how you did it, since you got the boys here. How you been doing it?

"What are you saying?"

"The whoring. Where's it happen?"

"That ain't my favorite word."

"I don't know another."

"I'm sorry I invited you in. You have to leave."

"You got me wrong." Brown plumbed his back pocket and came out with his billfold. "I got the money. I just want—"

"Now."

"What? Hold on. I got the money."

"You don't have a window here. Go on and leave. Don't make this any more difficult. I'm sorry for your wife. I truly liked her. But you and me's been sixes and sevens from the beginning and misfortune don't change that."

Brown stood, dumb.

"Now I said go on."

"Oh. Well pardon. Fuckin' whore. Pardon me."

Brown blinked and shook his head. He opened his billfold and inserted a finger next to the green. He closed his eyes tight like he was working a math problem and opened them to the sound of the door opening. She stood beside it flapping her arm like he was some dirt farmer without the sense to know where outside was. He saw her, face all pretty and delicate, but her eyes were like ice and her skin like frost. Her mouth was shaped like the most disgusting thing in the world stood before her. Pretty as a princess and just as high and fucking mighty.

Brown stepped toward the opening and the thought of crossing that threshold without taking what he came for—he may as well just pluck out his nuts and leave 'em on the floor where she could stomp 'em.

He grabbed the door and threw it. The windows shook. Barbie Creighton jumped and her ice cold face turned hot. She shrieked and darted to the kitchen and slammed into the table. Scattered chairs. She grabbed a knife from the wood and waved it. He let her wave it all she wanted. He kept her steady in his eyes the way he kept deer steady in the rifle sights, awaiting the moment.

She pointed the knife toward him and backed to the hallway.

Brown wondered what she'd do with the knife once she had the shotgun.

He'd been swallowing blood for weeks. He'd bleed if she wanted. Keep his ten and pay in blood, if that was the transaction.

He followed. No rush.

She scampered back, facing him. Slammed the bedroom door. He waited outside two seconds, twisted the knob and pushed it open.

She held a shotgun on him and ratcheted back the hammer.

"I'll use it," she said.

"It don't gotta be this way. I said I got the money."

"One more step I kill you. That's it! And it does gotta be this way! Now get out my house!"

He stepped forward until the barrel pressed his sternum. Almost hoped she'd reloaded since he took the shell the day before.

He lifted his hand and unsnapped the strap over his deer knife.

Her eyes flitted. She snarled and jerked the trigger but no sound issued save an empty click.

For a moment her eyes seemed to float away, but it was her fight. When it was gone he saw panic.

"You know Mrs. Brown shot herself yesterday with a sixteen gauge shotgun like this one?"

Barbie Creighton jabbed with the barrel. She turned the shotgun in her hands, choked up on the barrel like she played softball and swung.

Instead of smashing his skull she drove the stock into the wall by the door. The stock broke, leaving her nothing to swing but the trigger assembly.

In the midst of the fight Brown wanted to understand.

"You'd deny a dyin' man—willing to pay?"

"I ain't a whore!"

Brown stepped forward, swung his shoulder, arm and fist. Drove knuckles like to cave her skull.

Barbie Creighton dropped.

# CHAPTER FORTY-FIVE

On the highway I give it a think.

If Jubal's dead and the Rauch clan flee, that conniving Mrs. White'll collect the insurance money. The company'll see it as line of duty, since he was a cop. Hell, maybe she bought from a company caters to police, so that'll work out. It'll be fraud but she'll have money in the bank.

But other hand, if Half Pretty Amber told the truth and took video of Jubal trying for the money, and if somebody was to get word to her she oughtta send the video to the insurance company, then things wouldn't be so damn ducky for Mrs. White. They'd have all the evidence they need to deny paying out.

It won't be me that tell her. I won't be in Glenwood Springs.

Thinking on it more: the value of that video to the Rauch clan is when Billy's lawyer get to play it in court. Show the whole shebang was a setup from the getgo. I don't know what guns they took from the Rauch place, but none'll match the one shot the elk. That video might convince someone to look for it at the Jubal White place.

And you can be damn tootin' sure the insurance company'll find out the fella they insured is suspected of dying 'cause he framed another man for poaching a trophy elk.

What insurance company wouldn't investigate a death like that, at a shootout?

All in all, good chance Mrs. Jubal White just got the best fuck of her life.

Even the Mrs. Rauch like to get away with murder. If they can't find her nor the S-10 hit Dwain, how they gonna prove she was in it? I bet them boys shot Jubal got an idea how to hide a dinky little Chevy.

Take the exit and cut across, zig no zag, past the cheeseburger joint and up a ways to the motel resort.

Back into the space so I can make the quick getaway.

Out the Jeep I close the door, turn and don't like it.

Drapes is pulled and the light's off inside.

C'mon girls. Don't do me like this.

Knock.

Nothing.

Knock.

Fish the key card out my wallet and open the door.

Bags is gone.

Girls is gone.

Stinky Joe, gone.

Baer Creighton just got the best fuck of his life.

# CHAPTER FORTY-SIX

AFTER REMOVING HIS VOMIT FROM THE FRONT OF GÜNTER STROH'S cave with a flat shovel, Baer tamped a fresh layer of outside dirt over the contaminated area, lowered himself back to the ground and slept.

He woke shivering at dusk. Stretched his neck until it popped and shot sparks of pain to mingle with the dull throb of hangover.

The fire was dead.

Baer pushed himself erect against the rock wall and wrapped his arms around his knees. Shivers crossed his back. He studied the ground between his feet.

What must Günter Stroh think of him?

A punk with a giant thirst and no capacity to hold his liquor.

A wet-eyed coward.

Unfit.

A man as old as Günter had five times the life experience and probably a thousand times Baer's wisdom. The old man saw inside Baer the way Baer saw other people's lies; Günter knew what he was.

Baer rubbed his legs for the friction but that didn't warm him. He put his hand to the rock wall and stood. The pressure in his head increased but after a few seconds of light-headedness the pain subsided to a dull current just beyond the threshold of unease.

He turned.

Günter sat on a rock down by the stream. The day before, Baer had noticed a metal contraption camouflaged in tree branches. Now the branches were gone and the metal looked dull in the shadows of dusk.

Baer looked closer. The boiler sat on a horseshoe shaped foundation of rock and mortar that opened toward the cave. Anyone approaching from downslope would see a shape similar to a tree trunk and—at best—a dull corona from the light projected out the front. With the stream bank and other vegetation, the risk of being spotted seemed low.

Baer imagined the view from above, such as a person might have on the edge of the cliff, peering over. The angle likely wouldn't permit a view of the flame—only the glow out front.

Making and selling moonshine was illegal. Doing so put Günter Stroh at risk—and he minimized the risk with his actions.

Instead of seeking it, cussing it, stomping on it, yelling come get me. Profound.

Maybe when Baer was ninety.

A piece of wood snapped in the fire.

Günter Stroh was distilling more moonshine, likely to make up for what Baer drank the day and night before. The substance lessened the torment of the curse by replacing it with another. The stuff was toxic. The cost, too steep.

Baer looked back into the cave. The dog was with Günter.

A memory flashed of his dream before waking. He'd heard himself groaning. He'd woken himself.

What was the dream?

It wouldn't come.

Dreams was bullshit, anyway.

His empty stomach panged.

Whatever food was inside the cave belonged to Günter and had to keep him through winter. Baer would easily enough find something in town, if he was hungry enough to walk there.

He saw what he dreamed and his stomach turned.

He'd seen his mother, how he found her with half her head blackened from a man's fist, her eyes still glowing a faint red as if whatever chemicals in her body focused on that one spot, dissipating her lies into the waiting universe. Because there wasn't enough untruth out there.

Or maybe it was dust to dust. Built of lies and returning them when done, like taking a book back to the library. Or shitting in a compost field.

Baer watched Günter Stroh down by his still.

Careful to not make a sound, Baer shouldered his pack and drew the straps tight against his shoulders, squaring his back. He stood at the cave mouth looking downslope to maple and walnut and smelled wood smoke. A dying beam of sunlight broke through the trees and as Baer thought he could reach and grab some of the gold the beam failed and the dusk was darker.

He followed the path around the left that led to the firewood, silent.

When he'd gone another ten feet he stopped to the sound of bounding feet on twigs and leaves. The dog.

A shout arrived.

More leaves, until Günter Stroh stood before him, looking him up and down.

Baer studied the ground.

Günter nodded and his face seemed to take in a thousand truths Baer never offered.

"Come back ven you ready."

Günter stepped closer and offered his hand.

Baer took it.

"You ein kood man. Come back vile I sdill here."

Baer nodded.

Günter grinned and placed a claw on Baer's shoulder and shook him. Stared with intensity.

"Vile I am sdill here."

Baer nodded. Günter released his shoulder and Baer walked deeper into the woods.

# CHAPTER FORTY-SEVEN

MOVE THE JEEP TO THE BACK OF THE LOT, AIM AT THE YARD 'TWEEN this parking area and the next. Someone come with flashing lights, I got a shot at freedom. Though I don't mostly care.

Ain't slept but a few hours in two day. Pull the seat lever and ease back. Let the brain settle in the head and the neck go long on the cushion. Close my eyes and wonder how I done it agin. How I let Stinky Joe get lost or stole.

Eyes shut, sun come through the window and I got to shift this way and that, get some shade. At last the bright's off my lids. Thought I'd mope later but I guess I'll get on with it.

Ain't fit to keep a dog.

Ain't fit to have a woman.

Hell, ain't fit to father a child neither.

But I can live in the woods and make shine. Go back to what I'm good at.

Time works like waves in the head. Come and go, dreamy, hear myself snore and don't care nor rouse. After long bit the back hurt and the neck's jammed and I twist in the seat sideways. Don't muster 'til water drip on my hand and after checking the ceiling I see it's drool. Was dreaming on them cheeseburgers. Keep sleeping... wipe the hand on my leg and twist the other way. Sun's behind the mountain so I maybe got seven hours under my belt. Feet's cold.

Think on days long gone. How I come to the path I'm on.

Sit with eyes closed and see those days working on Brown's farm, fixing lessons in my mind about men and women. About giving hurt and learning to fight so others can't give it back.

Other days in the cave with Günter Stroh, hiding from the world. Drink myself stone drunk 'cause hiding from the world don't cut it.

Time works like waves in the head.

Come and go.

Dreamy.

Screeching tires!

Look out the glass—cherry red Mustang convertible slide sideways, ass wheels churning.

They got the top down. Smokin' gorgeous blonde and a red with her. Cram fists in the eyes. Jam the bleary out and look agin.

Tat dye her hair blonde. Corazon red—it suits.

Stinky Joe in the back seat, looking to maybe jump out.

*Save me from these crazyass women!*

Tat waves behind the wheel. Corazon got her arm out, beating the door. They lips is moving but the Jeep glass turn the sound to noise.

Tat look back the way they came—like jackboot thugs is around the bend. She search the dash and press a button. Look back. Look front, up top the windshield. Mash another.

Convertible top start coming up.

I got the gold in back. What the skippy fuck? I dunno.

By shit I don't know.

Unlock the door. Stumble out the Jeep and rub the eyes. The girls is still there.

"Get in!" Corazon say. "We must go *now!*"

"Hurry!" Tat say.

Look at Stinky Joe.

He look back, drop the tongue out the side. Grin.

*Well?*

"I got a bucket in back the Jeep. Pop the trunk!"

Race around, unlock, shit this bucket heavy. Lift it by the edges and heave. Waddle like I swapped nuts with a woolly mammoth. Spring a back muscle throwing gold in the trunk.

"Hurry! They're coming!"

Fetch my pack out the Jeep. Feel for Glock. Good to go. Dump the pack in the trunk and slam the lid.

Mustang's a two-door. Corazon pop out and fold the seat forward...

And I see her legs is wet with blood and her sweater too.

Knife on the floor.

I stop.

"What you doing? Get in!" Corazon say. "We must hurry!"

"Baer, come on!" Tat say.

Stinky Joe cock his head.

*Man, don't leave me alone again. Not with these two...*

Deep breath and dive to the back seat. Throw an arm over Stinky Joe.

Corazon jump in the car and Tat's already spinning wheels.

"I won't, Stinky Joe. No I won't."

# NEXT?

*For two free kindle novel downloads, a behind the scenes peek at the next book in the series (no spoilers), along with all the funky one-of-a-kind items at the Baer Creighton Shop...*

*Enter the following in your browser:*

https://baercreighton.com/product/8-shirley-fn-lyle-one-at-a-time-boys/

# ABOUT THE AUTHOR

Hello! I appreciate you reading my books—more than you can know. If you've read this far, you and I are fellow travelers. I suspect you sense something is not quite right with the world. It's not as good as it's supposed to be. We human beings aren't as good as our ideals. Yet, we prize and want to fight for them.

I do my absolute best to write stories that portray the human situation with brutal transparency, but also I strive to tell stories that are not as bleak as the human condition sometimes seems. There's no limit to the darkness. Light is rare. But it exists, and I hope when you complete one of my novels, you find your values validated.

I'm grateful you're out there. Thank you.

Remember, light wins in the end.

Made in the USA
Middletown, DE
24 April 2024